"You didn't have to bark at Francesca," Carrie retorted, grabbing a towel from the edge of the pool and rubbing herself off. Max watched the way her bikini clung, and he gritted his teeth. Frankly, his tongue couldn't form any words—not when her nipples peaked like that. And certainly not when she licked the drops of water that clung to her lips . . .

"We were just taking a break," she said. "There's no reason to get so worked up."

Max grabbed Carrie's arms and lifted her to her toes. "I couldn't give a damn about the work," he growled. He wanted to know what she wanted. What she was doing here.

Why she was tormenting him like this.

He couldn't ask her, so he did the only thing he could think of. He hauled her up and crushed his mouth to hers.

Carrie melted against him as if it didn't occur to her to fight back. Dropping her towel to the ground, she wrapped her arms around Max's neck and pressed herself to his hard, wide body. He growled again and clasped her closer, his kiss savage. He couldn't get enough of her . . .

———

"A sexy world of kick-ass action! You'll want to immerse yourself in the first in [this] thrilling new series, complete with a smoldering hero and the toughest, sassiest heroine around."

—VERONICA WOLFF, author of
Sword of the Highlands, on *Marked by Passion*

ALSO BY KATE PERRY

Marked by Passion

CHOSEN BY DESIRE

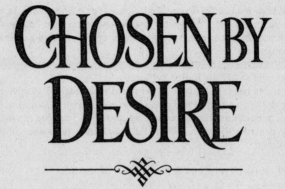

KATE PERRY

FOREVER

NEW YORK   BOSTON

Copyright © 2009 by Kathia Zolfaghari
All rights reserved. Except as permitted under the U.S. Copyright Act of 1976, no part of this publication may be reproduced, distributed, or transmitted in any form or by any means, or stored in a database or retrieval system, without the prior written permission of the publisher.

Book design by Giorgetta Bell McRee
Cover design by Diane Luger
Cover art by Franco Accornero

Forever
Hachette Book Group
237 Park Avenue
New York, NY 10017
Visit our Web site at www.HachetteBookGroup.com.

Forever is an imprint of Grand Central Publishing. The Forever name and logo is a trademark of Hachette Book Group, Inc.

Printed in the United States of America

First Printing: October 2009

10 9 8 7 6 5 4 3 2 1

To Kathia.
I couldn't have done
this without you.

And to Nate.
Yes, love, your swordplay is more
impressive than anyone's.

Special thanks to . . .

The brilliant and steadfast Veronica Wolff. The trophy went to the wrong cp. I'm crossing out my name and etching yours in.

And the crew of On the Corner Café, who kept me amped—with both caffeine and electricity—while I revised this book. I highly recommend their chocolate cake.

CHOSEN BY DESIRE

Chapter One

I can't believe I'm doing this." With a furtive glance behind her, Carrie tiptoed down the dark stone corridor. At the beginning of the monastery tour, they'd explicitly said it was forbidden to wander from the group, and since she'd been on the tour ten times in the past ten days, she couldn't play blond and clueless.

But she hadn't come all the way from San Francisco to China to go home empty-handed. Her best friend, Gabrielle, would have told her that if she wanted something, she should go for it wholeheartedly.

She wondered if Gabe would condone breaking and entering.

Stop thinking. She had only so much time to find the room and look for what she needed before the tour caught up to her. Picking up the pace, she hurried down the hall.

There it was. The innocuous wooden door to the left. The room that held the monastery's archives.

Heart pounding, she scurried to it and slipped inside. Carrie held her breath. She felt like she was being watched.

She tensed, waiting, expecting someone to bang on the door and demand to know what she was doing.

No one.

Just nerves. She exhaled and slumped against the door as it closed. She wasn't used to this kind of strain. Even working as a bartender in San Francisco's Mission district didn't offer this kind of anxiety.

It wasn't her fault. She'd tried to go through proper channels. She'd contacted the monastery and asked for access to their manuscripts. They'd turned her down. Irrevocably.

She was a scholar of chinese history at UC Berkeley, for God's sake—studying manuscripts was her job. The fact that they denied her access was a good indication they had something to hide.

Carrie bet that mysterious something was what she wanted. And since she'd blown her entire savings to fly six thousand miles, she wasn't leaving tomorrow until she got what she came for.

The room looked just like it did the other nine times she'd been in it. A long rectangle, dim but light enough to read. It had that musty smell she always associated with old libraries. She imagined generations of monks sitting at the table at the end of the room, carefully working on their calligraphy. The walls were lined with shelves filled with the fruits of their labor: thousands of rolled parchments and bound tomes.

One of them had to be Wei Lin's journal—proof of the mythic Scrolls of Destiny.

She hadn't been sure what to look for—literally thousands of rolled parchments and old bound texts filled the shelves. Wei Lin's journal could be anywhere. She bit her lip, willing her nerves to calm. She was close. On her sixth visit, she'd noticed one shelf that looked different than the others.

Her eyes zoomed in on it. The one shelf in the room suspiciously free of dust, as if someone cared for it or accessed its contents on a regular basis. The scrolls that lined it were different than the ones on the other shelves: thicker, tightly bound, and a third as wide.

Her fingertips tingled as she headed straight for it. One of those texts had to be it.

She'd tried to get a closer look the last three times she'd taken the tour, but it'd been impossible under the tour guide's hawklike vigilance. Which is why she'd had to take matters into her own hands. She ran her finger along the shelf's smooth wood. Breaking away from the tour had been risky, but giving up wasn't in her makeup. And, truthfully, she felt a rush at her own daring, too. She kind of felt like Indiana Jones.

Carrie slung her bag across her body and kneeled on the floor in front of them. Her blood raced at the thought of her impending discovery.

"Don't get ahead of yourself, girl," she muttered. She was operating on a hunch here. She didn't know for certain that the monastery had a copy of the journal—she'd just overheard Gabe's boyfriend, Rhys, say it did. And she was assuming she had the right Wei Lin. A big assumption, but how many noteworthy Wei Lins could there have been?

She bit her lip, helplessness combining with her nerves to create a cocktail of nausea in her stomach. She had to find it. Her future depended on it. She'd worked her butt off for a position at UC Berkeley, only now her advisor,

Leonora, said her doctoral thesis on the Yongle Emperor wasn't groundbreaking. For Carrie to have a chance to teach at Cal, she needed to provide some new theory regarding this Ming emperor—something to get a rise out of the board. In other words, her thesis wasn't sexy enough.

Sexy enough. Squaring her shoulders, Carrie picked up one of the texts. She'd show them sexy.

Dusting off the cover, she carefully opened it. The scrolls on the shelf shifted, and one caught her gaze. It didn't look as old or brittle as the rest.

Did monks still write on parchment? Oddly drawn to it, she ran a finger over the scroll. It felt as though her fingertip trailed in icy water, and goosebumps rose on her arms.

"Weird," she mumbled. She felt oddly compelled to unfurl it. She reached for it—

Wait—she had a book in hand already. Might as well start there. Shaking her head, she sat back on her heels and flipped to the first page. She read the first line of the tiny but beautiful black script.

My name is Wei Lin, and I have appointed myself Keeper of the Scrolls of Destiny.

"*Yes.*" Relaxing her grip so she wouldn't wrinkle the pages in her excitement, she scanned the text. Her heart beat faster with every word.

Five scrolls, each based on a Chinese element.

To save the scrolls from a greedy warlord, Wei Lin stole them and marked five worthy people as their Guardians.

The Guardianship passes on through each family to the next marked person.

Whoever possesses the scrolls possesses the elements' powers.

Wei Lin was Keeper of the Guardians, but he broke his own rule, despite the danger of reuniting the scrolls.

He brought together all the Guardians to help the Yongle Emperor.

Bingo. All Chinese scholars knew the myth about how a monk named Wei Lin, in giving support to Yongle, brought twenty years of peace to the kingdom through mystical means. *With the aid of the elements,* it was said.

Only it wasn't a myth. It was real.

She'd just found her holy grail.

Instead of jumping up and doing a triumphant dance, Carrie pulled out her digital camera and began methodically photographing the journal. She glanced at the shelf. There had to be a few bound texts there, plus another dozen scrolls. Installments of Wei Lin's journal? Made sense. She checked the time. She needed to hustle.

Even as she thought it, Carrie heard the tour guide's carrying voice. It sounded like the group was down the hall, which meant they were headed for the archives room, because Carrie knew for certain that nothing else in this wing of the monastery was shown on the tour.

Crap. She hadn't even finished copying this book, much less the rest. She took a hasty picture of the end and closed it. Her hands fumbled as she tried to fit it back onto the shelf, not able to make the scrolls scoot back enough to make space.

The tour guide's muffled voice seeped through the walls. "And this is the archives room, containing the writings of centuries of monks as well as recordings of the region's history."

Carrie shoved the other documents aside and pushed the journal back in its spot. But as she retracted her hand, her sleeve caught on the scrolls and a few fell onto her lap.

"Because of the delicacy of the documentation," the tour guide continued, "touching the texts is not allowed. But the library is impressive nonetheless."

The door creaked.

Carrie watched in horror as the door slowly swung open. *No time.* She grabbed the scrolls and tried to shove them back on the shelf, wincing at how brutally she was handling them.

But they just tumbled back down into her lap.

"*Crap,*" she mouthed, panic choking her. She looked over her shoulder to see the tour guide's calves as she backed into the room.

She couldn't get caught. Her mom would *kill* her if she got thrown in jail for stealing from monks, and she could kiss that teaching position goodbye.

No choice. She opened her bag and stuffed the scrolls in. Then, not able to help herself, she grabbed Wei Lin's journal and scuttled to the back of the room to duck under the only table. She could pop up and rejoin the group as they were leaving, no one the wiser. She hoped.

And she'd have the journal to study.

She grimaced. She'd just borrow it. She'd send everything back as soon as she copied their information. She swore it. And she'd treat them very carefully.

Her heart thundered so loudly it was a miracle no one heard her. She couldn't relax even when the tour guide began her spiel. Holding her breath, Carrie waited. Every second stretched like hours.

A white Reebok stepped dangerously close to her hand, and she retreated farther under the desk. God, she hoped no one noticed her stowed away there.

The guide began shepherding the small crowd out. Finally. Carrie peeked from under the table as they shuffled slowly out the door. Seeing her chance, she jumped up and quickly rejoined the group.

No one said anything to her, but that didn't ease her nerves. She ducked her head and slid the elastic band from her hair so the curls bounced forward and covered her face. Huddling her shoulders, she hoped she looked unremarkable and guilt-free, but that seemed a tall order. In China, her blond hair was like a beacon. Fortunately, the tour was almost over. All she had to do was hang in there for the walk through the garden, and then she could rush back to her hotel and lock herself in her room. With her stolen booty.

Oh, God, what was she *doing?*

No one saw, she reassured herself as she trailed behind the group. *No one knows. Just be casual.*

They stepped out into the garden, and she breathed a sigh of relief. Almost home free. Just a few more minutes.

But as she had the thought, she felt an accusing gaze at her back—penetrating and cold. Her shoulders twitched with the need to whirl around to see who stared and why.

Silly, because no one knew what she'd done. It wasn't like the monastery was outfitted with spy cams. At least she didn't think so.

She was *so* not cut out for a life of crime. She even hated keeping library books past their due dates—what made her think she could do *this?* From now on she was walking a straight and narrow path.

The person watching her turned up the intensity.

Maybe she should drop the documents and run.

No—she'd bankrupted herself for this. Her future was on the line, and she was so close. Yeah, she was breaking the law, but she was doing it with pure motives—if that counted for anything. She was going to return them. And if someone had seen what she'd done, she would have been apprehended already.

Stop being a wimp. Whoever was staring was probably only entranced with her blond curls. The past ten days should have taught her how mesmerized the Chinese were by them.

Can't take this. She'd never been good at burying her head and hiding—she had to look. Wiping her clammy palms on her jeans, she turned to face her watcher.

Her heart gave a quick thud.

A man in monk's robes was at the end of the garden. He looked Western, with rough-hewn, carved-in-stone features and blond hair that fell in shaggy layers around his severe face.

No way was he a monk.

She stared, not sure why she was so certain of that. It wasn't as if it was against the rules for a monk to be all intense. Or hot. Or to inspire wicked thoughts instead of peaceful ones.

But a monk wouldn't have such turbulent gray eyes. She met them and shivered. They had none of the gentleness and compassion she'd seen in the other robed men. They glinted, judging and accusing and unforgiving. His gaze seemed to penetrate, stripping aside all her layers to her soul, and found her lacking.

Her arm tightened on her bag. He couldn't know what she'd done. There had been no one in the hallway to see her enter the room, and she'd left with the group. She needed to get a grip and relax, otherwise she was going to give herself away.

She turned around, pretending to be engrossed in the last of the tour guide's speech. She told herself not to look back—he'd go away.

Only she couldn't help herself. As nonchalantly as possible, she glanced over her shoulder again.

Still there.

Why was he staring at her like she was an apple fritter and he was on Atkins? He couldn't know . . . it was impossible. Maybe he had a weakness for corn-fed Midwestern girls? And he'd come to China to work it out of his system, only here she was tempting him. She grinned at the thought, looking him over again. In her dreams.

"This concludes our tour," the guide said in her sing-song voice. Carrie's attention snapped back to the woman, exhaling in relief. "On behalf of the Guanyin monastery, I bid you farewell. Walk in peace."

Carrie sneaked one last glance at the erstwhile Western monk and hightailed it peacefully out of there. The entire way to the bus, she felt his cold gaze on her back, like a sharp knife across her skin.

Chapter Two

Taking care to hide himself, Max watched the tour group emerge from the archives room. In his seven years there he'd grown accustomed to the daily onslaught of tourists, but something about the blonde drew him.

She had the face of a cherub with big brown eyes, creamy skin, and rosy cheeks. Her strawberry blond hair made a stubby ponytail at the nape of her neck. He watched as she undid the ponytail to release a mass of curls that bounced onto her shoulders and into her face. The embodiment of innocence.

Except for her bowed lips. Her lips were pure sin.

But the innocence was a ruse. He stilled, feeling waves of elemental energy emanating from her. The way she clutched her bag to her side like it contained precious treasure confirmed what he already felt.

She'd taken the Book of Water.

He took a step toward her before he stopped himself. This wasn't his concern—he wouldn't get involved.

Let someone else deal with her. Max looked around for another monk but found no one.

Anger flooded him, cold and steely. It was like fate taunted him. He'd be damned if he had to deal with another less-than-angelic woman with light fingers. No way in hell.

He followed the group silently into the garden, keeping his gaze on the woman, willing another monk to show up and intervene.

Only then she turned around.

Max wasn't prepared for the shock of her doe-eyed gaze meeting his. She studied him as if she had nothing to hide and everything to offer.

It infuriated him. And then she grinned, and her face lit artlessly.

Inexplicably, his groin tightened.

He shifted, crossing his arms. Damn it—seven years at the monastery should have eradicated these baser needs. And his temper. But it only reinforced Sun Chi's increasingly repeated statement that Max wasn't meant to be a monk.

She gave him one more sweet smile before she followed the dispersing tour back to the bus.

He needed to stop her, but frankly, if he got his hands on her, he didn't trust himself not to strip her bare and sink in deep. His conscience pointed out that he'd seen other women in the past seven years—the tour guide, for example—and not had this strong a reaction.

He told his conscience to shut up.

The bus's engine growled to life.

Max looked around. Still no one. He glared at the bus. No choice. Teeth grinding, he went to head it off.

He'd taken only a few steps before a strong hand caught his arm. Caught off guard, he trapped the hand and automatically arced the wrist in a leverage.

The calloused hand reversed the leverage instantly, letting it go almost as quickly. Max spun around, bringing the knife edge of his hand up to chop. He stopped an inch from his mentor's neck.

The Keeper's peaceful face shone up at him. Its serenity irritated the hell out of him. How could he be so still when his throat had almost been crushed?

When the Book of Water had been stolen?

Max looked over his shoulder to see the bus winding down the mountain road back to civilization. Angry and frustrated, he scowled at the old monk. "Damn it. The Book of Water is riding away on that bus."

Sun Chi stared after the bus. Max waited, expecting a barrage of questions, starting with why he hadn't done anything to stop it. But his mentor just studied him quietly before turning and shuffling away. Motioning with his hand, he said, "Come."

What the hell? Max stalked after the smaller man, wanting to interrogate but knowing he'd get no answers until the monk was ready. As a teenager, when he'd just become a Guardian and was sent to study with Sun Chi, the man's stoicism had infuriated him. As the only child of rich bluebloods, Max had always had everything handed to him when he wanted. Since, he'd learned patience.

For the most part.

Following Sun Chi into the archives room, Max closed the door behind him and watched as the monk kneeled before a shelf in the back. He hadn't realized how much he'd wanted to be wrong about the woman stealing the scroll until he heard Sun Chi's gasp and had a corresponding sinking feeling in his chest.

"Gone." Sun Chi looked up at him, his gaze bright. "The Book of Water. The journal of Wei Lin. And more."

"Why would she take the journal?"

"As a mistake in her haste. For more knowledge of the scrolls. The reasons are numerous." Sun Chi gazed at him levelly. "This is disastrous. You understand, yes? She must not be allowed to learn the mysteries of the Book of Water or locate the other scrolls."

"Yes." The scrolls were distributed to separate Guardians because their powers were so strong. Too corrupting. For one person to possess all five...He shook his head. "I thought the Book of Water was sent to its next Guardian."

"Sent. And refused." Sun Chi stood and walked the room in slow, measured steps, hands behind his back.

Max frowned. "The Guardian didn't accept his duty?"

"Some Guardians are thick-headed." He tapped Max's shoulder before returning to his contemplative stroll. He suddenly stopped and lifted his head, piercing Max with his all-knowing gaze. "You must go after her."

From the moment the bus drove away he'd known this was coming, but a part of him still didn't want to accept it. All he wanted was to go back to his cell and forget he'd ever seen the duplicitous angel. "No."

His mentor nodded as if Max hadn't spoken. "You use your family's diplomatic connections."

"I gave all that up seven years ago. I'm on a different path now."

"You choose the wrong path. Your path is to follow that woman. I feel it here." The monk beat his fist over his heart. "Find who she is. Retrieve the scroll and the journals."

"No," he said again, shaking his head. "Seven years ago—"

"Seven years ago, you came to the monastery to heal," Sun Chi interrupted. "But you stayed in the monastery to hide."

"I haven't been hiding," he said, but even as the words came out of his mouth he knew they were a lie.

"You hide. From the past, from the present, from the future." His mentor's narrowed gaze dared him to contradict those words. "You are letting yesterday kill tomorrow."

"My future—"

"Your future is back in your world." Sun Chi pointed at him. "You are not a monk. You are Maximillian Prescott, Guardian of the Book of Metal. Heir to your own dynasty. Your path"—he pointed into distance—"leads out into the world. After that woman. You must find her," he said, his voice low and insistent.

Max knew from experience that the Keeper's will wouldn't be denied. To fight it was wasting energy. He gritted his teeth. God help that woman when he caught up to her. "What will I be up against?"

The monk had the grace not to gloat. "The Book of Water is not claimed by its Guardian, so the powers are free. They will affect the person who holds it."

Remembering how unprepared he'd been for the onslaught of his own powers, he said, "That could be to our advantage."

"Her powers will be weaker than yours, since she is not a Guardian. Unless she studies the scroll and learns to harness its secrets." Sun Chi shook his head. "You must recover it. And the journal."

Max heard the implied *do whatever it takes* in his master's words. He recognized the chance to redeem his mistake with Amanda seven years ago, but it didn't mean he had to like it. He rubbed his neck, his fingers sliding over the familiar ridges of the burn scar—a constant reminder of that night.

Sun Chi placed a hand on his shoulder. "To heal, you must go. This last step exorcises the ghosts of your past."

More likely this was just going to attract another ghost—one with big doe eyes and lips made for sin.

No, this time he knew better than to let a beautiful woman's appearance sway him. He drew on *jīn ch'i*. His powers settled around him like a cloak, giving him the cool distance he needed from his thoughts. "I'll leave immediately."

His mentor nodded. "I never doubted that you would. Go in peace."

Bowing his head, Max strode out of the room, not happy in the least to be reentering the life he'd left behind.

Chapter Three

Clutching her bag to her chest, Carrie stared at the closed office door and tried to imagine what her doctoral advisor would say when she found out Carrie had proof of the existence of the Scrolls of Destiny. Proof that Wei Lin had used them to, in effect, alter Chinese history.

Leonora Hsu was going to freak. And she'd be ecstatic that one of her students was the one to unravel the mystery of the scrolls.

Not that she'd unraveled all the mysteries yet. Carrie had returned from China only three days ago, and, in between sleeping and her one shift at the Pour House, she'd spent most of her time in the narrow stall of her shower. For some reason, she just craved it—maybe to wash away the long flight and the jetlag. So she'd barely had time to read much more than the first part of Wei Lin's journal. She hadn't even looked at the other scrolls.

But what she had read was exciting. And enough in itself to earn her the position and have her name known as an eminent Chinese scholar.

At least she hoped so.

She took a deep breath and knocked on the door.

"Come in," Leonora's soft voice called. When Carrie opened the door, the older woman's smile shifted, becoming just a touch more friendly. "Carrie, you're back. How did you find your first trip to China?"

"Awesome. Exhilarating." She sat down across from her advisor. Normally, she liked to ooh and ah over the array of antique swords Leonora had hung on the walls—they were so cool. But today she gave them only a cursory glance, her attention on Leonora.

And her bag. Carrie held it snug in her lap. She'd been toting the book and scrolls around with her, and protecting them had become a quick habit.

Well, she couldn't leave them at home. Her apartment was smack in the middle of the worst of the Tenderloin. It'd never worried her before—she was a poor student, and it was cheap compared to the rest of San Francisco. But she wasn't naive enough to think anything she had was safe there.

Tightening her hold on the bag, she leaned forward in her seat. "That's why I came to talk to you."

"About your travels?"

"No, about what I found on my travels."

Leonora's thin eyebrows arched.

When she first met Dr. Leonora Hsu she would have read her reaction to mean disinterest. But in the years she'd first earned her masters and then her PhD, Carrie had gotten to know her advisor well enough to know she was extremely interested, just in her understated way.

In fact everything about Leonora was understated. From her conservative, dark-colored suits to the tight bun

of her hair. She was the most proper and demure woman
Carrie had ever met. So totally different from herself.

Carrie gripped her bag and leaned forward. "You know
how you said the board was reluctant to consider me for a
position here unless I did something to differentiate myself
from the pack? That my dissertation wasn't sexy enough?"

"Of course."

She couldn't keep her silly grin in. "I've found what'll
make it sexy."

"Found what?"

"Well—" Carrie didn't have all the proof yet, and she
didn't want to make claims she couldn't substantiate. But she
wanted so badly to tell someone what she'd found. Someone
who'd understand and recognize the significance. "I have a
source that claims the Scrolls of Destiny existed, and that
Yongle used them to foster peace through his kingdom."

Leonora sat still. She didn't even blink.

Not the reaction Carrie expected. She frowned.
"Leonora? Did you hear me?"

"Of course." Her advisor resettled the glasses on her
face and folded her hands on the desk.

Carrie waited, but when no questions were forthcoming, she gaped in disbelief. "I'm not sure you got it. I said
I have reason to believe the Scrolls of Destiny were reality
instead of myth."

"What led you to this conclusion?"

Finally—some interest. "When I was in China I found
a source that documents their existence and use."

Leonora's brow wrinkled. "You just happened to come
upon this source during your travels?"

"Well, no." She grinned sheepishly. "I kind of went
there on a tip that turned out to be right."

"A tip from whom?"

"I can't say." Because her source—her best friend Gabe—didn't know she'd given Carrie the tip. And Carrie wanted to keep it that way.

"You can't say," Leonora repeated flatly.

"Uh, no. Confidential information." She'd arrived early to hang out with Gabe and accidentally overheard Rhys, Gabe's boyfriend, say he'd read it in Wei Lin's journal while he was at the monastery.

Carrie hadn't known what *it* was, but the second she heard the name *Wei Lin,* everything in her froze. In her research, she'd found several obscure references to Wei Lin and the Scrolls of Destiny tied to Yongle.

The chances that Rhys's Wei Lin and Leonora's Wei Lin were the same person? Fairly slim. Maybe nonexistent. But the more Carrie thought about it, the more curious she got. If she could prove there actually was a historical basis for Wei Lin and the scrolls, a position at Berkeley was guaranteed. Leonora taught a special myths class, and Wei Lin and the Scrolls of Destiny were a particular favorite topic of hers. If her advisor got excited about her thesis, Carrie was a shoo-in for the job.

It hadn't taken much research to find out which monastery Rhys meant—there was a lot of press on him, which shouldn't have been surprising, given how affluent and entrepreneurial he was. She found a mention in one article, complete with the name of the monastery and the province where it was located.

What *was* surprising was that Gabe and Rhys were talking about Wei Lin. Why? Carrie wanted to ask, but she couldn't. Not without revealing that she'd spied on them.

She bit her lip. She'd never been one to lie, and that's

exactly what she was doing. Not to mention the thievery and smuggling, if you wanted to put a fine point on it. This whole thing was turning her into someone she didn't recognize, and she wasn't sure she liked it.

It'd end soon. It'd all work out, and she'd never do it again.

She just hoped her conscience survived intact.

"Carrie?"

Blinking, she returned her attention to her advisor. "Yeah?"

Leonora stared at her with her myopic dark gaze for a long silent moment before she shook her head. "I'm not sure how you expect to prove this if you can't reveal your source."

"My source just led me to the proof. The proof is all that counts. That's what I'll publish." She wrinkled her nose. "This is enough to put me on the map, right?"

"Certainly this is enough to attract the interest of the board. If you can prove that the Scrolls of Destiny existed, even historically, you'll have every major university in the world clamoring to have you."

"It's nice to be wanted." She grinned. "But my first choice is Cal. I love it here."

"How close are you to proving your theory?"

Not close enough, but she'd get there. "I have some reading to do."

"What are you reading?"

Had to be careful here. "I have, uh, a copy of Wei Lin's journal."

Leonora sat bolt upright. "You found a copy of his journal? Where?"

"I can't say." She headed off her advisor before she

could protest. "But don't worry. I'll be able to prove authentication, too." She hoped without getting arrested.

Mark that down as something to work on.

Leonora studied her without saying a word. Carrie thought she'd ask more questions or at least bring up more doubts, but Leonora surprised her simply by saying, "Keep me apprised of your progress."

From Leonora, that was the same as shouting, *Go for it, babe*. "Okay."

"In the meantime, it's probably best to keep your findings quiet."

"I figured that." She stood. "Thanks, Leonora."

Her advisor smiled faintly and nodded before returning to her paperwork.

Taking the hint, Carrie quietly shut the door on her way out. As she turned around, she walked straight into a body. She had to bite back her groan when she looked up and saw Trevor Wiggins. She smiled apologetically. "Sorry. I should pay attention to where I'm going."

"Yes," he agreed in his stern way.

She resisted rolling her eyes. He was such a wet lump. When she'd first met him in grad school, she'd thought he was smart and cute. With his brown hair and Harry Potter glasses, he looked scholarly—an attractive novelty compared to the country boys she'd grown up with in Iowa.

But two minutes in his presence was enough to kill any temptation to set aside her staunch no-dating policy and go out with him. He wore his self-importance like a well-loved pair of jeans. And it wasn't enough that he thought he was better than everyone else—especially her. He was vocal about it, too. Annoying.

If he knew what she had in her bag, he'd turn green
with jealousy.

She glanced at the door and then back at him. How
long had he been standing there? What were the chances
he eavesdropped?

Pretty big. She frowned. "Have you been waiting long
to speak to Leonora?"

"I was on my way to my office." His chest puffed up.
He took every chance he got to work that in—unlike the
other doctoral candidates, he had an office.

But right now she could care less how much he pos-
tured. "Were you listening at the door?"

"Of course not." He recoiled indignantly. "I don't know
how you can accuse me of stooping so low."

Probably because she'd seen him do it before. "I didn't
mean to sound accusatory."

He harrumphed and stalked off. She didn't have to be
psychic to hear his unspoken thoughts of superiority.

And she didn't have to be a genius to know that he was
lying through his teeth when he said he hadn't listened at
the door. Question was, how much did he hear?

She didn't put it past him to rip off her thesis, but she
had Wei Lin's journal. Without it, he had nothing.

With it, he could ruin all her hard work.

Carrie shook the thought out of her head. He wasn't
going to get the journal. She'd never leave it, or her bag,
lying around. It—and her thesis—would be safe.

Floating.
Water lilies caress her skin as she drifts in the
warm pond on her back.

Naked.

Her breasts lift above the surface. The water laps at them, and the bite of the cool air makes her nipples taut—a sharp tingle that shoots straight between her legs.

A shadow falls over her, and she shivers in anticipation, knowing who's casting it.

It can be only one person.

His blond hair is every bit as wild as before, looking more wild for the savage gleam in his eyes. His shoulders are broad and muscular, gleaming in the muted sunlight that filters through the weepy trees. The thin trail of hair down his abdomen lights gold, like a path leading to more treasure.

She hears a soft splash. The waves become more frenzied, as if they know what's coming and anticipate it as much as she does.

Smiling, she looks up. He stands in the water, looking down at her, his gray eyes burning. She feels his gaze travel down her body like a cool blade running along her skin. She gasps, feeling the sharpness of it as it trails over her nipples and down her belly. Between her legs.

Eyes hungry, he leans over her.

She wants him. She wants every promise written on his fierce face. She opens her arms, offering herself to him, but feels herself slip under the water. She surfaces.

He's gone.

Carrie's eyes popped open, her breath harsh in the stillness of her apartment. A dream.

How pathetic was she? She buried her burning face in the pillow. She was having wet dreams about a man whose name she didn't know. A monk, for God's sake.

She groaned and rolled over to check the time. She'd come home from her meeting with Leonora for a short nap before her shift, but now she'd be late for work.

Fumbling to subdue her hair, she grabbed her things and jogged to the BART station. She got to the platform as a train pulled in and arrived at the Pour House in record time.

Gabe looked up when Carrie walked in, a smile lighting her face. "The world traveler returns."

"Hey." Grinning, Carrie ducked behind the counter and grabbed her friend in a hug. Gabe returned it smoothly. Months ago when they'd first started hanging out, Gabe was skittish, especially when it came to affection. She'd relaxed a lot. Carrie knew it was due to not only her friendship but Rhys's love, too.

Carrie valued that friendship. Gabe was the first real friend she'd had since she moved from Iowa. She was so different than anyone she'd known. Not just physically—though tall Eurasian women with blue streaks in their long black hair weren't exactly common in her hometown. Gabe was contradictory. Tough, but a sensitive artist. Street-smart and still compassionate.

Gabe eased back, holding her at arm's length. Lines furrowed her forehead. "Something's not right."

Carrie looked around. "Everything looks okay to me."

"No, just now when you walked in I felt—" Her blue eyes stared so intently Carrie wanted to squirm. Her gaze fell to the messenger bag, and her frown became more pronounced. "Maybe I'm just tired."

Nerves flaring, Carrie pulled away. Gabe couldn't possibly know what she had in her bag. Sure, Gabe had a highly attuned intuition, but she didn't have X-ray vision. Carrie tried to relax as she stowed it under the register. "Were you up late painting again?"

"I was up late." She grinned wickedly, her earlier unease erased from her face. "So was Rhys."

Carrie grabbed an apron and tied it around her waist. "I can't decide if I want all the details or if that'd just make me jealous."

"You could find yourself a boy toy." Gabe held up her hands. "I know, I know. I'm talking crazy, but dusty libraries don't offer orgasmic delights."

The monk from the monastery came to mind. She remembered her dream, the way he stared at her, all intense, like he wanted to eat her up.

Her cheeks went up in flames. Even if she was interested in dating—which she wasn't—he was so out of her league. Trevor was more the type that she usually attracted. Unfortunately. "I'm not sure the type of man I attract can offer orgasmic delights."

"Bullshit," Gabe said in her succinct way. "You just need to get out more. It's not like you're going to meet a sex god among the library stacks."

"I don't have time to get out more." That man's chiseled face flashed in front of her eyes again, and she knew without a doubt that for someone like him she'd be tempted to make time.

But she could resist temptation—all she had to do was think of her childhood and how her mom struggled. That was enough to deter her, even when temptation came in such an alluring package.

She shook her head to clear it and turned to find Gabe studying her, eyes narrowed in speculation.

"Have you met someone?" her friend asked.

"Yeah, a monk," she said truthfully but with self-deprecation.

Gabe rolled her eyes. "A match made in heaven, since you live like a nun."

A couple of construction workers walked in, which stalled any more talk of sex. She and Gabe fell into their usual light banter as they worked, which made the hours fly by quickly.

A few times, she had the distinct impression she was being watched—by the monk. She looked around, knowing she was being silly. No way was he here. It had to be lingering feelings from her dream.

Carrie couldn't believe it when she looked at the clock and saw it was nine. "Shouldn't you be going home soon?" she asked Gabe as she pulled out a couple bottles of Budweiser.

"Just waiting for Rhys. He said he'd pick me up."

As if on cue, Rhys walked in. Tall, dark, and handsome, he was eye candy to the extreme, even with the scar bisecting the corner of his lips.

Carrie paused for a moment to admire his sheer masculinity.

Actually, today he reminded her of the monk. She wrinkled her nose. Strange. By outer appearances they weren't anything alike. Rhys's hair was cut to precision, and the monk had a wild mane tangling around his face. Rhys also looked like he'd stepped out of *GQ*—a far cry from a coarsely woven brown robe.

Must be the intensity. Rhys had the same focused look about him. Maybe he'd learned it while he'd been at the monastery.

He walked up to the bar, took Gabe's hand over the counter, and kissed the inside of her wrist. "Hello, love."

Carrie sighed. That was so romantic. She wanted someone to kiss her wrist.

"Stop drooling." Gabe took off her apron, wadded it, and tossed it under the counter. "He's taken."

Carrie grinned. "He's not my type, anyway."

"You have a type?" Rhys asked as he sat at the bar.

Yeah—brooding and blond, apparently. She looked around. She swore she could feel someone watching her. Maybe she was still jet-lagged. She shrugged. "One who's not in love with another woman is a good start."

Rhys frowned, suddenly alert. He looked around and then settled his piercing gaze on Gabe.

They may have been together for only a few months, but they were so attuned to each other it was scary. Gabe frowned in return and asked, "What is it?"

"I sense—" His eyes narrowed. "Did you raid the safe again?"

"What? Of course not. I promised I wouldn't touch the scr—uh, stuff again without your supervision." She scowled. "Which bites, by the way. It's not like I'm wholly untrustworthy."

"It's not a matter of trust." He took her hand and rubbed her palm with his thumb. "I won't risk you being hurt."

Carrie sighed again. "Be still my heart."

Gabe shot her a look of death.

She grinned. "I love the macho thing. You're so lucky.

The last time a man was protective of me was—well, never."

"It's damn irritating," her friend grumbled. But Carrie could see her melt under Rhys's soothing touch.

"Ready, love?"

"Yeah." Gabe ducked under the counter. "Just let me get my things."

Rhys watched her walk away, and Carrie almost had to avert her eyes to stop from witnessing his hot, I-want-her-bad gaze.

"You must come to dinner one of these evenings." He turned back to her once Gabe disappeared into the back room. "Give your eyes a rest from your dense tomes."

She groaned as she wiped the counter. "The last time I came to dinner, I swear I gained five pounds."

"We'll only serve two desserts instead of five," Gabe promised, slipping into her sweater as she rejoined them.

"Or maybe I could work out with you guys." She waved her arms, trying to look like Jet Li. "You can show me some kung fu moves."

"Dream on, babe." Gabe reached across the counter to give her a one-armed hug. "You're a cute bunny, not a killer, and I like you just the way you are. Get used to it."

"Maybe I can show you a move or two when she's not looking," Rhys said with a hint of a smile. He stood up and stretched to kiss Carrie on the cheek. But as he withdrew, his brow furrowed and his hand clamped on her arm.

"Rhys?" she heard Gabe ask distantly.

His eyes honed sharply on Carrie, and she felt something vague roll through her, disquieting and uncomfortable. His grip tightened on her, and confusion twisted his expression.

He wasn't the only one confused here. Something was going on, but she had no idea what it was. She bit her lip. She only knew instinctively that he needed to let her go—now. But when she spoke, her voice came out thin and wispy. "Don't."

"Rhys, what the hell?" Gabe grabbed his hand and pulled one of his fingers back, peeling him off.

"Bloody shite, Gabrielle." He flexed his fingers as he scowled at her.

"Well, you were being a freak." She glanced apologetically at Carrie over her shoulder as she escorted him toward the door. "See you tomorrow?"

"Yeah," she replied automatically, totally confused as she watched them leave.

What just happened?

She shook her head. Maybe Gabe would be able to clue her in tomorrow.

Rolling her shoulders, she looked around at the semi-full bar. No one seemed to be aware of the drama that had just taken place. She tried to shake it off, but still she felt like someone had her under a microscope.

One more strange thing to add to the assortment of strangeness that had happened today. She shook her head and went to refill pints for a couple regulars at the other end of the bar.

Chapter Four

The blonde knew Rhys.

Max's hands fisted in his pockets. His feet pounded the pavement with each step he took to his rental, an echo of the rage pounding in his chest.

The blonde knew Rhys. Rhys Llewellyn, the man he once loved like a brother. The man who'd betrayed him. The man whom, for the past seven years, he'd hated with every molecule in his being.

He hadn't expected it. Expected it? Hell—he was in complete shock. Reaching the car, he put his hands on its roof, trying to pull himself together.

When he'd disguised himself and gone to her place of employment, he'd thought it'd be a matter of simple observation. He'd get to know her routine, perhaps figure out where she'd hidden the texts, retrieve them, and leave—no one the wiser.

But then Rhys had walked in.

Jīn ch'i swelled in Max, fueled by his fury. He felt it surge through him, leeching from his body. The metal under his hands vibrated, and with a low groan the car's roof began to twist with the force of his anger. When he lifted his head, the top of the Audi was a rippled chunk of steel.

With a grunt, Max clicked to disable the lock and slid in, slamming the door shut behind him. Francesca would deal with the car. He'd deal with the blonde. And Rhys.

Closing his eyes, he gripped the steering wheel, trying not to picture her in Rhys's arms. It was all he could see. Her doe eyes showering affection on Rhys. Her soft body held in Rhys's traitorous hands.

Just like Amanda. Although, inexplicably, imagining the blonde in Rhys's embrace disturbed him far more than actually witnessing Amanda in it.

Through sheer force of will he controlled *jīn ch'i* and tore off down the street, making it back to the Nikko Hotel in record time. Without a word, he tossed the key to the valet and strode through the lobby, to the elevator, and to his suite.

In his room, the curtains were open and San Francisco's lit skyline lay before him in its glory. He barely saw the view. Instead he saw a pair of big brown eyes teasing him with feigned innocence.

He gripped the windowsill, conscious of the groan of its metal frame. He had to discover what they were up to. There was no doubt in his mind that this was planned. Rhys Llewellyn left nothing to chance. Max knew only too well how far Rhys would plot to get what he wanted. In this case, it stood to figure Rhys wanted to finish the job he'd started: to steal Max's scroll.

Max rubbed his palm over the burn scar at his neck. The cut he'd given Rhys still marked him, too, almost as indelibly as the broadsword-shaped birthmark that identified them as Guardians. Rhys as the Guardian of the Book of Fire, and him for the Book of Metal.

Fire controlled metal, melding it, destroying it.

Did Rhys plan to destroy him?

Like hell he would.

Max had to modify his original plan. Destiny had given him the perfect opportunity to pay Rhys back for his duplicity seven years ago. Max would use the blonde to bring him down, just like Rhys had used Amanda.

He pulled the dossier he'd had compiled on the woman—Carrie Woods. His second time flipping through, an idea struck. He extracted his cell phone from his coat pocket and called his assistant.

Francesca answered before the second ring ended. "Sir?" she asked, sounding alert despite the fact that she'd probably started working at dawn and it had to be well after ten now.

But that was why he employed her—she worked tirelessly and efficiently. That and the fact that since her mother was his parents' housekeeper, Francesca had grown up in his household, alongside him. She already knew his habits and preferences—she was the logical choice for the job. He could trust her to keep his affairs in order, as she had during his years at the monastery. And trust wasn't something that came easily to him.

"I'd like you to fly to San Francisco," he said now. "I have business I'd like you to attend to here."

"I'll be on the first flight in the morning," she said without hesitation.

"I'd also like you to open the Santa Monica house."

There was a surprised pause before she said, "When

should I expect you to arrive, and how long will you be in residence?"

"I'll leave in three days for an indefinite amount of time." As long as it took to retrieve the scroll and the journal and to defeat Rhys.

Again that startled pause. "Shall I have one of the cars prepared for you, as well?"

"Yes, the Maserati." He paused. "And prepare one of the guest suites."

"A guest suite?" She didn't manage to keep the shock out of her voice this time.

"I'll provide details when you arrive. And Francesca?"

"Yes?"

"The rental car had a mishap, so the company will need to be reimbursed for the damages. Thank you." He ended the call before she could ask anything more.

His idea was brilliant—he'd hire the woman to work for him, right under his roof. Yes, he'd still recover the stolen documents, but he'd also figure out why and how Rhys was involved. Payback factored in there, too.

He fingered Carrie Woods's file, his mouth set in a firm line. He wouldn't imagine what it'd be like to live with her, to have her at his beck and call.

He didn't have to imagine. He pictured her big eyes and lush mouth and knew what it'd be like. Pure hell.

Chapter Five

Carrie stared at Leonora's door. Ever since her advisor had called that morning and asked her to come by for a meeting, the pit of Carrie's stomach had been gnawed by nerves.

She bit her lip as she shifted her bag higher onto her shoulder. She couldn't think why Leonora would want to see her again, except to tell her that researching Wei Lin and the Scrolls of Destiny wouldn't fly. That the board wasn't interested in hiring her.

Or that they'd hired Trevor instead.

Okay, better to go in and find out what's going on instead of foretelling gloom and doom out here. Carrie swallowed and knocked on the door.

"Come in."

Opening the door, she poked her head in. "I know you wanted to meet at four. I'm a few minutes early."

"That's perfect. We can have a moment to chat before Ms. della Vega arrives." She waved her hand. "Come."

Curiosity eased some of her tension. "Who's Ms. della Vega?"

"I'll get to that in a moment." Leonora studied her, her ever-present pen sliding through her fingers. "It seems you've brought back some luck with you from China."

She had? She wrinkled her nose. "I guess you could say that. Finding Wei Lin's journal was like finding a needle in a haystack."

"And now there's the fellowship."

"Fellowship?" She perked up. "What fellowship?"

"Have you heard of Bái Hǔ?"

She laughed incredulously. The White Tiger was as legendary as the Scrolls of Destiny. "Who hasn't heard of Bái Hǔ? He's got one of the most renowned private collections of Chinese texts and artifacts in the world. He's also the most elusive man in the world. I heard no one's seen him for years. I'm assuming he has something to do with the fellowship?"

"Yes. His assistant, Ms. della Vega, contacted me asking about you. It seems rumors of your competence in translation and archival work reached his ears. He has a special project he'd like to have you work on."

Carrie grinned. "Awesome. Do you have details?"

Before her advisor could answer, someone knocked on the door. Leonora rose to answer it.

A fellowship from the famous Bái Hǔ. Carrie's grin widened. This was a coup—an honor. Having this on her résumé would go a long way in convincing the board she was worthy of a job. Combined with her theory on the Scrolls of Destiny, she was a shoo-in.

"Carrie, meet Francesca della Vega." Leonora gestured to the doorway.

Carrie turned around, not expecting the tall, elegant woman she saw in the threshold. Bái Hǔ's assistant was gorgeous. Perfect features, porcelain skin, and long, slim limbs. Fiery red hair gave her color, even if it was severely restrained in a knot. She looked flawless and expensive.

"Ms. della Vega, this is Carrie Woods, the scholar you've expressed interest in."

Carrie smiled, knowing she was being appraised, too. She also knew she'd be found sorely lacking, in her old jeans and scuffed boots. At least she had a nice shirt on because she was working this evening.

But she was a scholar, not a socialite. They'd be interested in her mind, not her fashion sense. Or lack thereof. "It's great to meet you," she ventured into the stilted silence.

The statuesque woman inclined her head to one side. "Ms. Woods."

Carrie grinned. The lack of enthusiasm wasn't lost on her.

Leonora waved to the empty chair. "Please sit down."

Francesca perched on the edge of the seat as if she was afraid of wrinkling her suit. "I trust Dr. Hsu has informed you of our offer."

"Yeah, Leonora just did. I can't wait to hear the details," Carrie said with an extra dose of perkiness. She felt like she had to compensate for the other two women.

Opening her briefcase-purse, Francesca pulled out a Blackberry and tapped at the screen. In a way that reminded Carrie of her uncle Milton the lawyer, Francesca began reciting from her notes. "The work you're asked to do consists of translation of several undocumented texts from the Ming Dynasty. We understand that time period is your specialty."

"Yes. I—"

"In compensation for your work, you'll receive a modest stipend as well as room and board," she continued. She drew a sheet of paper from a leather portfolio in her bag and held it out.

Curious, Carrie accepted it. She had to blink a couple times to make sure she'd read the amount of the stipend correctly. She looked up and gaped at Francesca, sure there had to be a typo. One too many zeros.

Francesca frowned, a faint wrinkling of her fine brow. "Is the amount adequate?"

"Oh, it's more than adequate." Carrie shook her head. It was more money than she made in four months at the bar. "The fellowship is for how long?"

"I estimate it will take four weeks to complete the translation. However, Bái Hŭ might have other translation work for you, as well. The estate has been without a curator for seven years."

"Wow." Carrie arched her brows. "That's a long time. Is there any reason for that?"

Francesca shifted in her seat and lowered her head as if the Blackberry in her lap required her attention. After a long stretch of silence, she said, "There hasn't been need for anyone until now."

Curious. Very curious. Something was up here, and she wanted to figure out what.

She'd obviously read too many Nancy Drew books growing up. Grinning, she shook her head at herself.

"You aren't interested?" Francesca asked.

Carrie blinked at the tinge of alarm in the woman's

voice. "No, I'm totally interested. I'd be interested even with a tenth of that stipend. It's any historian's dream to work on a collection like Bái Hǔ's."

"Quite." The unease fell from Francesca, leaving her brisk and all business once again. She shuffled through the portfolio again and pulled several pages, which she held out. "You'll want details about the position."

"Of course," Carrie murmured as she took them.

"It begins on Monday—"

"Monday?" Her head popped up. "That's three days away."

"Is that a problem?"

"Uh, no." She mentally reviewed her schedule. Her boss, Johnny, wasn't going to like her leaving again, but Vivian would probably welcome the extra hours—it'd give her extra time to torture Gabe, which was her favorite pastime. "I can swing it."

Francesca continued like that was a foregone conclusion. "The hours you work will be flexible and probably long, and you'll be required to be at Bái Hǔ's disposal. He's set aside a room for your use—"

"In his home? Isn't that, I don't know, odd?"

"It's Bái Hǔ's request," she answered. But her tone said, yeah, she thought it was strange, too. "You'll also have access to a car and any other amenities you'll need."

"I don't need a car in San Francisco. I take public transportation."

Francesca began putting away her portfolio. "You won't be in San Francisco. The collection is in Santa Monica."

"Santa Monica?" Carrie gawked at her before turning to her advisor.

Leonora said nothing, her gaze blank.

What did that mean? Pack your swimsuit because you're headed to Southern California? Working with texts never before documented *was,* after all, the chance of a lifetime.

"Ms. Woods?"

She looked at Francesca and smiled. "When is my flight leaving?"

Chapter Six

"When do you leave? And do you have enough condoms?"

Carrie shook her head and tossed a bunch of her nicer T-shirts into her suitcase. "This is a business trip, Mom. I won't need condoms. And I leave Sunday."

"Oh, honey, that's wonderful."

She paused in her packing. "It is?"

"Of course. I have a great feeling about this. I can almost feel your soul mate waiting for you."

Oh, geez—not the soul mate stuff again. "Bái Hǔ isn't my soul mate."

"Have you met him?"

"No. I only know that he's amassed one of the most impressive private collections of Chinese artifacts and texts. And I've heard his family is pretty rich." She picked up her old bikini. She hadn't worn it since she moved to San Francisco four years ago, but swimming seemed like a great idea. Wondering if it still fit, she threw it in her bag, too.

"He sounds perfect for you," her mom exclaimed. "The same interests. *He* loves Chinese things, *you* love Chinese things—"

"He's probably a perverted old man," she said absently as she folded her only dress. She usually wore jeans, but might as well take something nicer in case she ended up going out to dinner.

"Carrie, honey, I love you like the dickens, but I can tell you're tuning me out."

She laughed and perched on the edge of her twin bed. "Sorry, Mom. I'm preoccupied with packing."

"I think you should make the most of this opportunity. It couldn't have come at a better time in your life."

If only Leonora had been as enthusiastic. She seemed to think that the few weeks in Santa Monica would interfere with her research and discouraged her from leaving. So it was nice that someone was excited.

"I know this is a great opportunity. I'd be a fool to pass it up." Carrie closed the top of her suitcase and pushed it aside.

"I'm talking more than just career-wise, honey. You're going to meet your heart's mate. If he's rich, all the better." Her mom sighed. "My mother's intuition is going off like crazy."

"Mom, I hate to tell you this, but I won't have time for anything but work. And I doubt I'll meet Bái Hǔ. Apparently he's reclusive. I'll probably be working with his assistant."

"Hmm," her mom said noncommittally.

Carrie laughed. "Seriously, Mom. I'm the hired help. We're not going to be hanging out."

"It's not natural going celibate for so long, honey. Not even I've been celibate as long as you."

"*Mom.*" She shook her head. They had an open relationship, but some things she didn't need to know. Like the time she'd gone home for Christmas and found a vibrator in the bathroom cabinet—along with a pair of velvet cuffs.

"Honey—" Her mom paused.

By her tone, Carrie knew she was either going to bring up her dad or ask something invasive. *Please let it be something invasive.* She'd rather say when she'd gotten laid last than talk about the man who'd abandoned them.

"Honey, if you're a lesbian, I'd understand."

She sputtered for a moment before she burst out laughing.

"I love you no matter what. And there's nothing wrong with being a lesbian. I kissed a girl or two in my youth, too."

"*Mom.*" Groaning, she squeezed her eyes shut and forbade herself from picturing it.

"I just wondered," her mom said. "You moved to San Francisco, after all."

"To go to Cal, not to hide my sexuality from you." She shook her head. "I appreciate your understanding, but I'm not gay. If I ever decide to bat for the other team, you'll be the first to know."

"Just so you know I'm always here for you."

"I love you, Mom."

"I love you too, honey." She paused. "You'll be open to the possibilities, won't you? And you'll call me when you arrive?"

"Of course I'll call you. It's not like I'm going someplace foreign. I'm just going to LA."

"Honey, I've been to LA, and it's as foreign as you can

get." She made kissy noises, just like she'd always done when she said good night. "Love you, Carrie honey. And make sure you pack the underwear I sent for Christmas, just in case."

Grinning, she rolled her eyes and hung up. But she opened her drawer and pulled out the underwear.

Yeah—still as naughty as she remembered. A handful of lace and satin in black. Racy see-through panties that revealed more than they covered. She'd never worn any of it, but she didn't tell her mom that. Her mom probably knew—the woman had this weird sixth sense about her that Carrie had never been able to understand.

Why was she even considering packing them? She shook her head. You wore underwear like this for some-one else to see, and she wasn't going to get the opportu-nity to show it off for anyone in Santa Monica. Not with the work schedule she had planned.

"Ugh." She grabbed the undies and tossed them in her suitcase. It wasn't like they took up room, and she could tell her mom she brought them.

She surveyed her suitcase. Mostly packed. She still had to add her laptop, a dictionary, and a couple other refer-ence books she might need. They were piled on her living room floor. She turned to get them and ran into her mes-senger bag, resting at the foot of her bed.

The texts. She needed to take them, too—to do her own research in the evenings. She packed them one by one in her clothes, taking special care so they wouldn't get damaged in any way.

But the last scroll grabbed her attention, just like it had at the monastery. When she ran a finger along its edge, she had that same feeling of dipping into cool water.

"Odd." She untied the leather and unrolled a small portion of the scroll.

The black script was tiny—smaller than in Wei Lin's journal—but elegant, formed with an expert, light hand. She traced the first character of the first line. "Beautiful."

The gentle sound of lapping water followed her reverent whisper. She shook her head to clear her ears and began to read, the words echoing curiously in her head at the same time.

Here begins the Book of Water, wherein lies the truth about man and energy. For energy is but a tool, good or bad determined by he who wields it . . .

Staring at the scroll she held in her hand, she froze. Was she imagining it?

No. She rubbed her fingers along the cool paper. She let herself blink, and then she reread the opening.

Still the same, complete with the disembodied echo.

"Oh. My. God." Her heart began to beat triple time, because the roll of paper in her lap wasn't someone's journal. It was one of the infamous Scrolls of Destiny.

Chapter Seven

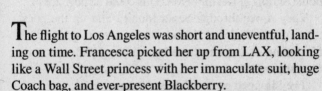

The flight to Los Angeles was short and uneventful, landing on time. Francesca picked her up from LAX, looking like a Wall Street princess with her immaculate suit, huge Coach bag, and ever-present Blackberry.

The woman was as chilly as ever, so instead of trying to make conversation with her, Carrie sat back to enjoy the scenery. At least she tried, but she kept getting distracted by the tug of the ocean. It reminded her of the dream she had last night—yeah, another one. More vivid than the one before and starring the monk—again.

In the dream, she swam out to him and anchored her legs around his waist, his erection rubbing against her intimately. The water seemed to join in their play, and it created this weird, erotically charged threesome. She woke up moaning, the sheets tangled around her legs.

What was her problem? Why couldn't she be normal and dream about Brad Pitt? On dry land. Heck, in a bed, even. Maybe her mom was right—maybe she really did need to get lucky.

Of course, she'd been obsessed with water lately. It didn't escape her that her strange water fixation could be tied to finding the Book of Water. Probably a subconscious acting-out of her guilt.

She'd return it. As soon as she studied it a little. She'd tried taking photos of it, but every attempt came out blurry. She couldn't send it back without reading it. They probably wouldn't notice its disappearance as long as she didn't keep it overly long.

She clutched her bag, where she'd tucked the scroll away. There hadn't been any record of anyone documenting one of the Scrolls of Destiny. Ever. This could be huge for her.

They drove through Santa Monica and up the coast, turning off Highway 1 and onto a scenic drive. Traffic became sparser as the houses dotting the gentle hills became larger.

They stopped at one of those houses.

Though *house* seemed an inadequate description. Small mansion maybe. It was a Mediterranean style home, something you'd expect in Greece. Or Southern California.

"Not in Kansas anymore," Carrie murmured to herself, opening the car door. The ocean stretched vast just beyond the house. She inhaled its salty tang and started toward it.

"Ms. Woods," Francesca called crisply.

Oh, right. Maybe later. She could go for walks on the beach every day—anything to keep her butt from reaching epic proportions (drat her love of carbs). She glanced at the water longingly again before turning around.

Francesca was already clacking up the wide porch steps to the front door. "We're behind schedule. He expected us fourteen minutes ago."

"Fourteen minutes should be forgivable," Carrie said, hurrying to catch up.

The woman stopped and frowned at her.

Carrie practically tripped over her feet to keep from running into Francesca. "I mean, neither air travel nor LA traffic is predictable."

Does not compute was written clearly on her face. But she didn't say anything, instead pulling out her keys and continuing for the door.

Carrie sighed and skipped up the steps.

The door opened before Francesca reached it. Standing in the doorway was a tall, broad, barefoot man in jeans and a flowy white linen shirt. He had wild blond hair that needed a cut—

She froze on the top porch step. The monk.

Woo-hoo—it was him! Her girly parts tingled in anticipation. Maybe her sex dreams didn't have to be just dreams. Thank goodness she packed her sexy undies.

Oh, God—wait. Why was he here? Did he know about the journal and scrolls?

What was she thinking? He had to know she'd stolen from the monastery. She bit her lip. Would he believe her if she handed over her bag and told him she didn't mean to do it?

She studied him, but she couldn't read anything from his gaze. Maybe he was waiting for the police to show up before he made a move.

Oh, God—her mom was going to flip out if she ended up in jail.

Stop acting like a spaz. She drew in a deep breath, and the smell of the ocean soothed her.

And cleared her mind enough to think logically. If he thought she'd taken something, he would have just found her and demanded it back—he didn't have to hire her. This had to be a coincidence. So she relaxed.

Only then she remembered her dreams and tensed again. It didn't help that he was watching her so closely.

Shifting her bag, she glanced at Francesca, hoping the woman would break the awkward moment with an introduction, but Francesca just stared at him with single-minded focus.

He didn't seem aware of the woman whatsoever. She wondered if he was gay, because Francesca was the kind of beautiful that deserved to be on the silver screen.

Carrie looked at him, at the intense way he watched her with his hooded gaze, and shivered. Definitely not gay. The guy had woman-attracting pheromones oozing from every pore.

Which was going to make sticking to her all-work/no-play philosophy over the next four weeks that much more difficult.

As Max held the door open wide and moved aside to let her into his home, he saw it again—that damned little-girl twinkle in her eyes just like at the monastery.

She hesitated on the threshold, as if debating turning around and walking away. But then she stepped in and grinned—half innocent, half imp, and wholly fallen angel—and said, "If you're going to offer me an apple, I'll have to pass."

Max crossed his arms, suspicious. "An apple?"

"You know, like Eve in the Garden of Eden."

He studied her, adding a touch of frost to his gaze. "That can mean only one of two things."

She tipped her head to the side and studied him right back. "What two things?"

"That you're likening me to the serpent."

She nodded thoughtfully. "And the second?"

It didn't escape his notice that she didn't deny it. "Or that you think I'm offering you temptation."

A muffled cough made both of them turn around. For the first time he noticed Francesca standing next to Carrie Woods. He leveled a cool stare at her, not pleased that she interrupted before he got an answer.

Francesca took a small step back, paling under his admonishing look. To her credit, she gathered her composure and, as she closed the door, said, "Sir, this is Carrie Woods, the historian who will be working on the translations. Ms. Woods, this is Maximillian Prescott, also known as Bái Hǔ."

The little thief swung her wide-eyed gaze back to him. "*You're* Bái Hǔ?"

If the situation had been any different, he might have been amused. But there was nothing amusing about this situation. He was here to return what she'd stolen to the monastery and exact his revenge from Rhys. Period. "Is that a problem?"

"Of course not." Her brow furrowed. "I just wasn't expecting—"

"A white man?"

She grinned again. "Oh, that's the least of it."

He would have given anything to know what was going through her head, but then he noticed the bag she clutched onto her shoulder and stilled. A bolt of awareness shot through him—one that had nothing to do with sex and everything to do with the presence of the scroll. She had it in there. The journal, too, he'd bet.

She must have sensed his scrutiny, because she tightened her hold on the bag.

Too little, too late, he thought. *You're already in my snare.* "We should get you situated."

Francesca rushed forward. "I've had Don take her bag to the first-floor guest room. I'll show her—"

"Have her things transferred to the gold room," he cut in.

Francesca started in shock. "But—"

He simply stared at her.

Ducking her head, she took a step back. "Of course. I'll see to it right away."

He turned to find Carrie Woods frowning at him. He gestured to the stairs. "I'll show you to your room."

She opened her luscious mouth to say something but, in the end, closed it and nodded. Without a word, she began up the marble steps.

He followed behind, watching the sway of her hips. She was lush there, too—nothing innocent about the way she filled out her jeans.

Was she trying to lure him on purpose? He'd noticed the attraction in her stare—maybe he could use that to his advantage.

She glanced over her shoulder as if she felt his gaze. The slight frown still marred her forehead.

Max strode past her, wondering who was offering whom the apple now. "Your room is this way."

Without waiting to see if she followed, he stalked down the hall to the gold room and opened its door. He stood in the doorway and inhaled her as she brushed by him. Fresh, like wild strawberries.

"This is fabulous." She laughed, a golden tinkle that matched the shimmery drapes covering the windows.

"It's bigger than my studio. I'll be totally spoiled by the time I leave."

He watched her drift to the window and run her fingers along the silk before pushing it aside to look out. He knew what she saw: the Pacific Ocean lapping at the isolated beach.

"There's no one down there," she said so softly he had to step forward to hear her. "If I lived here I'd be on the beach every chance I got."

"The beach below is private. But you're welcome to use it in your free time." It'd give him the opportunity to search her things.

"Thank you." She turned a brilliant smile on him.

He stared at her lips, caught by the urge to lay claim to them. His body tensed, desires long buried fighting to rise to the surface.

Puzzled by his reaction, Max took a step back. Distance brought clarity, and he needed that—now. "Your bath is through the double doors to the left. I'll have Francesca send up a tray for your dinner, as I'm sure you're tired from your travels."

"It was only an hour-and-a-half flight."

Ignoring her protest, he headed for the door. "If you need anything, dial zero on the house phone and you'll reach Francesca or the housekeeper. I'll leave you to get settled."

"Where—"

"I'm sure Francesca left you details on the layout of the house. I'll see you at eight in the library." He left before she could say anything else...and before he gave in and found out whether her lips tasted as sinful as they looked.

Chapter Eight

He waits for her in the surf.

The gentle waves break around him, on him, but he lies still, propped on his elbows. Stretched on the sand, his naked body glistens in the sun, and he watches her approach with hooded eyes.

He appears unaffected and calm, but she knows he wants her. The hard evidence is right in front of her.

She walks faster, shedding her clothes with each step. She reaches the water's edge, the waves tickling her feet, encouraging her closer to him. Until she stands over him.

He runs a hand over his hardness, invitation and dare smoldering in his eyes.

She drops to her knees, following the path he blazed with her own hand.

He hisses at her touch, drawing her up until she straddles his head. Her heart beats hard, seeing the intent in his cool gray eyes. She widens her stance in encouragement.

Lifting his head, he thumbs her open. One gentle kiss, and then his tongue lashes at her, firm but languid. She gasps, and she gasps again when he latches on to the most sensitive part of her.

The water laps at her, echoing his sucking rhythm. With his hands, he guides her, encourages her to rub herself on him—over and over until she wants to scream.

The water rises, and a wave engulfs them, pushing them apart. She looks for him, reaching— needing him. But he drifts away, his gaze sharp and wanting.

Carrie woke with a groan, turned on beyond belief. Not another one. She shifted under her covers, blushing when she realized her hand was inside her panties, clutched between her legs. Unable to stop herself, she glided her fingers over her wetness.

She groaned again and let her legs fall open. Imagining Max's tongue working her, it took only several frenzied strokes before she came, calling out to him wordlessly.

She buried her face in her pillow, her face flaming. How embarrassing. The wet dreams were becoming more and more vivid. It just wasn't like her. She had to get herself under control. Lusting after the boss was a no-no. Especially when he had the power to ruin her reputation and career.

She rolled over and tried to go back to sleep, but every time she closed her eyes she pictured Max lying before her, naked and spread out like a feast.

"This is so not like me," she murmured, glancing at the clock. Three a.m. Too early to start her day, especially when she'd had only three hours of sleep.

What she needed was warm milk. Her mom used to give it to her when she woke up from nightmares and couldn't sleep. Plus, there was nothing sexy about milk. It should take the edge off of her libido.

Hopefully.

Shoving the covers aside, she slipped out of bed and pulled her extra-large T-shirt down. For a second she debated putting on pants, but no one would be up at this hour. Besides, her shirt was longer than some women's dresses.

Just in case, she opened her door and poked her head out to check. Seeing no one, she padded down the dark hall and to the stairs.

Max gritted his teeth as Carrie moaned. Again.

It was her moaning that woke him up. At first he thought she'd sneaked someone in. That Rhys could be in there with her almost had him knocking down the wall between their rooms. But after he'd calmed from the cold haze summoned by that thought, he realized he would have heard someone entering, and he definitely would have sensed Rhys. Guardians felt each other's presence, and he and Rhys had been especially close.

No, she was alone, and it didn't take much imagination to know what she was doing.

A faint rustle of her sheets.

He glared at the wall, wanting to block it out, needing to see through. In his mind, he pictured her kicking aside the covers and baring her body to the cool night air. She'd run a hand over her breasts, teasing the pink tips until they were hard, swollen nubs. Her other hand would steal down to bury itself between her legs.

Another groan filtered through the wall.

He fought the urge to palm his hard-on. He wasn't above using sex to get information from her, but he'd be in control of the situation. Right now, control was beyond him.

She cried out, loud and clear. He imagined her head thrown back, her graceful neck bared, as she stroked herself to orgasm.

His cock surged in reply to her cry, the rasp of the Egyptian cotton sheet unbearable. He pushed the covers aside and paced his room. "Damn it."

He waited, hoping she'd go to sleep so he could return to bed. He knew he was out of luck when he heard her get out of bed and open her door.

He stilled. Where was she going? To meet someone? He remembered catching Rhys red-handed with Amanda, and his blood went cold. Putting on a pair of pajama pants, he stalked to the door and silently opened it.

Carrie tiptoed down the stairs, her body obscured by the railing.

He ducked behind the door when she paused and looked over her shoulder. He saw her shrug and continue down the stairs.

Max glanced right. Her door was open.

He strode into the room and stiffened. Energy from the Book of Water crawled over him, making the mark on his shoulder prickle. His gaze swung to the bag on the floor next to the bed, and he walked toward it.

He didn't have to open it to know the scroll was in there. He considered taking it, but he needed to figure out what Carrie was up to first.

He glanced at the bed, the covers twisted and rumpled. A hint of strawberries overlaid by musk flirted with his nostrils. Carrie's scent. It reminded him of summer and sex, and his cock stirred again.

Cursing under his breath, he strode out of her room and downstairs to find out where she went. The thought that she could be meeting someone made his chi flare wildly.

He searched the library, his office, and the living room. He was about to step outside to check the grounds when he noticed a faint light from the kitchen. He crept down the hall and looked around the corner.

She sat on a stool at the counter, her feet swinging as she drank a glass of milk. She wore a thin, oversized shirt that rode up her thighs and showed the outline of her nipples.

The combination of sexiness and innocence grabbed him low. He could see the shadow of her panties underneath, and he wondered if they'd be wet from her earlier arousal.

He breathed deeply to center himself and stepped into the kitchen.

She looked up, and her eyes widened as they roved down his bare chest, to his pajama bottoms, and back up. Her cheeks went up in flames.

He crossed his arms, standing across the counter from her. "Couldn't sleep?"

"Um, no." She held up the glass. "Warm milk never fails. Want some?"

Milk was not what he wanted. He shook his head.

"My mom used to warm milk for me when I couldn't sleep as a kid. I think she brainwashed me into believing it worked." She smiled, cradling her glass.

"Do you have trouble sleeping often?"

"Not at all. I think it's the change of environment." She looked out the window. "The water's been plaguing me all day."

He frowned. "Excuse me?"

She waved toward the ocean, though it was invisible in the night. "The water. It's everywhere. I've lived in San Francisco all these years and I've never been so *viscerally* aware of it. It's like I can feel the condensation of the mist in the air, even."

Effects of the scroll, without a doubt. If she were a Guardian, the effects would be magnified. He just wished he knew how much she was being affected. How much had she read? What did she know?

"It's so weird," Carrie went on. "I've been having these dreams about the water and—" She gasped, gaping at him.

With guilt? No. With embarrassment—mixed with heat? Intrigued despite himself, he took a step closer.

She downed her milk and slid off the stool. Her shirt caught on the seat, revealing creamy thighs and a peek of white panties. She tugged her shirt so forcefully the stool teetered.

He reached to steady it at the same time she did, and his hand brushed the outside of her hip. *Jīn ch'i* surged, and he stilled, stunned by its intensity.

With a yelp, she jumped back. "I, um, need to get to bed. I mean, go to sleep. Good night." She edged backward. At the doorway, she turned and scurried down the hall, holding her shirt down to cover her ass.

Max heard the shrill protest of metal bending. Looking down, he saw the rippled metal, melted by chi. He cursed, shoving it aside.

It teetered unevenly before toppling over. As unexpectedly unbalanced as Carrie had left him.

Chapter Nine

Max stood at the edge of the ocean, his sword held out loosely in front of him. He closed his eyes and took a deep breath to clear his thoughts. He wiped away last night and his uncontrolled reactions to one woman with big innocent eyes and soft moans.

He reached out with his chi the way Sun Chi had taught him years ago. He let *jīn ch'i* gather at his core, build, and fill his body. He directed the flow out his arm and into his sword.

The metal warmed instantly. He felt the familiar vibrations echo in his body until there was unity—until he and the sword were one. No beginning, no end to either of them.

Usually, that was when he felt the most peace—when he wielded his element. But today restlessness drove him. And frustration. He hadn't been able to sleep after his encounter with Carrie last night. He'd lain in bed, conscious of her in the next room, wondering if she was touching herself. Picturing her beaded nipples and imagining how they'd feel under his tongue. His chi pulsed in time to his need.

With a low growl, he made a sweeping block followed by a slash—the opening move of his practice form. He methodically went through each movement, decimating imaginary foes at a brisk pace.

When he finished, the energy still pushed him, so he launched into another form. He was just regaining his equilibrium when he felt someone at his back. Whirling, he swung the sword around his head and brought it down in a slashing cut.

And then he saw Carrie, standing there looking like a teenager in her jeans and fitted hoodie, her loose curls dancing with the wind.

It took all his strength to pull back from the strike. His sword's jarring protest resonated through his body. He managed to stop an inch away from slicing her chest open.

She blinked up at him with her guileless eyes, but her pale face told him he'd scared her. However, all she said was, "That was close."

"Close?" Anger overrode the horror of almost having cut into that soft flesh. "I almost ran you through."

"You have too much control not to stop in time," she said simply. As if she knew him.

Before he could yell at her that her faith in him was misplaced, he saw a bead of blood well on her lip, where she'd obviously bit it. The faint metallic tang hit him, calling to his element. He closed his eyes against it, willing himself to ignore its temptation.

"Are you okay?"

He opened his eyes and stared at her. A moment ago

he'd almost killed her, and now he wanted to jump her. *Okay?*

Damn it, she didn't even have shoes on. He glared at her, trying not to notice the way her pink-tipped toenails peeked from the sand.

"You aren't okay. You're pissed because I interrupted your practice," his doe-eyed nemesis said, fidgeting with the zipper on her sweater. "But you have to admit you practically invited me over."

"How is that?" he asked, knowing he did no such thing.

"Well, it's not every day you see a guy with his sword out on the beach. And it's a big one." Her eyes traveled over his scar, his bare chest, and then lower. Cheeks flushing, she quickly raised her gaze. "Um, your sword, that is."

His groin stirred at her visual caress, and he tamped the reaction. "What are you doing out here so early?"

"Walking. Despite the milk, I had trouble sleeping after I left you in the kitchen. I just couldn't help..."

He waited for her to finish, but she just shook her head. For some reason he had to know what she was going to say. "You just couldn't help what?"

She turned to face the ocean, her forehead lined with a frown. "Coming closer to the ocean. I thought it might soothe me."

More effects. He studied her profile, trying to find a hint of the treacherous, stealing female he knew her to be. But all he saw was purity. He gripped his sword so hard he could feel the steel protest.

She looked back at him, a rueful smile flirting with her lips. "I've never slept so close to the ocean. I didn't realize how loud the waves would be. I was conscious of them all night."

He noticed the dark circles under her eyes and pushed away concern. He hefted his sword in front of him, telling himself he didn't need to feel concern for her.

"Well, I guess I better head back in. I'm not getting paid to walk on the beach, am I?" she asked, pushing her hair from her face.

"No, you aren't." He turned around, holding his sword in front of him as he closed his eyes and began to refocus his chi.

Behind him, he felt a shift of energy and heard her gasp softly, close to him. Before he could turn, he felt the faintest brush on his shoulder blade.

Over his birthmark—the broadsword-shaped mark of a Guardian. As fleeting as the touch was, he felt it deep. It cut to his core.

Whirling around, he growled through gritted teeth. "What are you doing?"

Carrie snatched her hand away. "I don't know what came over me. I—um, that's cool. Is it a tattoo?"

Narrowing his eyes, he pinned her with his most intimidating look.

She blinked, but—damn it—she held her ground. "Right. It's a birthmark, then?"

"I thought you were going to work?"

"Yeah. On my way." She offered him a tentative smile. "Can I expect you to join me—"

"No," he said curtly. Actually, he'd planned on working with her this first morning to observe her, to get to know her better. But now he needed to regroup. He could still feel the ghost of her fingertips—his mark pulsed with it.

Disconcerting.

"Oh. Okay." Her smile faded and she took a step back. "I'll see you later, I guess."

Max stood there, gripping his sword, watching her walk back to the house. He waited until she'd stepped up all the stairs and disappeared through the door before he gave a warrior's yell, slashed his sword through the air, and launched into his form all over again. This time he fought Rhys—Rhys, who got to Carrie first.

It took doing it three times before he felt a measure of his previous calm. Grabbing the shirt he'd taken off earlier, he wiped the sweat from his body. Shirt in one hand, sword tucked under his other arm, he strode to the house—with purpose. He needed to find Francesca. Now.

As always when he needed her, she appeared moments after he entered the house.

"Good morning." Her eyes widened for a second as she looked at his bare chest, but when she lifted her eyes there was nothing in them to betray any hint of emotion. She gave him the cool smile she'd perfected in the years he'd been away.

"Where is she?"

A faint frown lined his assistant's forehead. "Ms. Woods? She's waiting for you in the library. I had Don take in a breakfast tray for the two—"

"You go." He strode to the staircase.

"Excuse me." Her rapidly tapping heels followed him across the marble. Even in her haste to catch up to him, she sounded perfectly cool. "I don't understand. What do you want—"

He stopped on the fifth step and faced her again. "What I want is for you to work with her."

No mistaking her frown now. "But I thought—"

He gazed at her coldly.

Visibly recoiling, she took a step back. "Of course, sir. Excuse me. I'll work with her until further notice from you."

He nodded and ran up the rest of the stairs. With Carrie occupied, he could search her room, for both the texts as well as any clue as to what she and Rhys were planning.

The thought of her plotting with Rhys should have been enough to kill the feelings she stirred in him. Should have been, but wasn't. Probably the reason Rhys had chosen her. Rhys knew his weaknesses. Rhys had always known him better than Max knew himself.

It made Rhys's betrayal that much more cutting.

After a brief stop to deposit his sword and shirt in his room, he went next door to hers and pushed open the door.

As he stepped in, he was assailed by the scent of strawberries. He looked at the bed and inhaled deeper, trying to catch a hint of the sex redolent in the room last night.

Get a grip. He shook his head, disgusted with himself, and let his senses search the room to guide him to the Book of Water again.

Nothing.

He frowned. He didn't feel it in the room. Did she take it with her?

Possible. He continued his search, looking for any information. He started with the bed, in and under it, not allowing himself to wonder whether she slept clothed or if the sheets touched her naked body.

Searching the dresser yielded nothing, as well, unless the knowledge that she haphazardly tossed her clothes in there counted for something. He opened the top drawer of the dresser last.

A sea of black lace.

Max froze. His fingers brushed a pair of panties almost of their own accord. Her pale skin would look creamy in black.

"Stop," he ordered himself ruthlessly. He slammed the drawer shut and did a cursory search of the bathroom, knowing it wouldn't yield anything.

And it didn't. Worse, by the end of his fruitless search, he had a raging erection that ached for attention.

Entering his own suite next door, he slammed the door shut and headed straight for the shower. Half an hour in the icy cold should do it. Maybe.

Chapter Ten

Based on her encounter with Max (she just couldn't bring herself to refer to him as Mr. Prescott) on the beach, Carrie decided it'd be prudent to go to work, even if it was a little early.

After retrieving her bag from her room, she went in search of the library. It took her a couple tries before she found it. And, really, mostly it was her curiosity that caused her to wander a bit. Curiosity about the Western man who was at home both in a monastery and twirling a sword, had a killer Chinese collection, and was called the White Tiger.

Though the White Tiger part totally made sense. He prowled. And watching him twirl his sword this morning she knew it wasn't faked.

The library had austere furnishings like the rest of the house. Every room she'd been in was sparsely decorated with modern furniture in cold tones, framed by lots of metal. Even the gold in her room was cool rather than warm. The high ceilings and expansive windows lent to the cavernous feel.

She plopped down on a low chair, setting her messenger bag at her feet, and looked out the window to the spot in the sand where Max had been practicing with his sword.

He didn't look like a cold, unapproachable billionaire as he'd battled his invisible foe. He'd looked fierce, intense, and so amazingly virile. As he'd swung the sword in an arc around his head, his shoulders and pecs had rippled, and the sweat glistening on his tan skin had highlighted each ropey bit.

His arms had looked elegant despite being so thick. Carrie sighed, then blushed as she remembered the golden line of hair leading down into the waistband of his loose workout pants.

The brown monk's robe hadn't done his body any justice. Neither had her dreams, though she'd pictured that golden trail pretty accurately. She didn't have to try very hard to imagine kissing down that trail. He'd be taut there, his hair would be soft, and she didn't doubt he'd be pretty impressive just below, just like he'd been in her dreams. She'd started to look, but his surliness distracted her.

Not that she could blame him for being surly. She'd breached his inner sanctum. She had the feeling she'd seen something very, very few people had ever seen.

And—God—she'd *touched* him. What the heck was she thinking? On her first morning here.

Her phone ringing startled her. She answered, still distracted by thoughts of him. "Hello?"

Silence hissed over the line.

"Hello?" When there was no answer, she looked at the screen to check for coverage. Full bars. The call was from a restricted number, so hanging up and calling the person back wasn't an option. "Hello? Is anyone there?"

There was a crackle and then a buzz. Then an electronic voice said, "You have something that doesn't belong to you."

Carrie froze, the pit of her stomach twisting. "Who is this?"

"I know you have it," the masked voice said.

The only thing she had that didn't belong to her was what she'd taken from the monastery. She swallowed. How did anyone know what she'd done? And what did he mean by *it?* The journal, the Book of Water, or one of the other scrolls?

Either way, total denial was in order. She tried to sound unshaken—completely the opposite of how she felt. "I have no idea what you're talking about."

"Holding on to it will be...detrimental...to your health."

"Are you—"

The call ended.

"—Threatening me," Carrie finished limply. She looked at her cell phone, as if there'd be some kind of clue as to who the caller was, but that was futile. She tried to tell herself it was a fluke—a wrong number—but she couldn't convince herself that this was a random crank.

Someone knew what she'd taken.

Impossible. She shook her head. Who would know?

Max. He'd been at the monastery. He'd seen her. Would he stoop to devious terrorizing like this? He seemed more the type to charge forth and take what he wanted. She was in his house, for God's sake. All he had to do was corner her and use brute force to take them away from her. She wasn't delusional enough to think she could fight him off.

Or that she'd stop him from strip-searching her. If he wanted to. Ahem.

The library door opened. She startled, jerking to face it.

Just Francesca. "Thank God," Carrie murmured under her breath.

"Excuse me?" Francesca said in her proper way as she set her big bag at the foot of an upright chair.

"Uh, nothing." It struck her that this could possibly be one of the few circumstances in which she'd been happy to see the woman. Anyone was better than a stalker. Even chilly, aloof Francesca.

It was just a crank call. Or the wrong number. She shook off her residual skittishness and smiled. "How are you, Francesca?"

"Fine, thank you, Ms. Woods. I trust you slept well."

She muffled her snort. She hadn't lied to Max. Last night, after running into him—the object of her desire, live and in glorious, hard flesh—she hadn't been able to sleep. So she'd stayed up studying the Book of Water. It read in metaphors, but she had a feeling the metaphors were layered to hide some fascinating stuff.

Oddly, the overlaying voice wasn't a product of her imagination. Whenever she started reading, it started, too. And even more oddly, it said things not written in the scroll.

She tried to rationalize it by jet lag or as some extended dreamlike delusion, but she couldn't convince herself that she was insane. Except she had to be insane—she was hearing things.

Add the phone call to the mix, and she felt jittery. Like she'd had six straight shots of espresso—intravenously.

She'd meant to photocopy all the documents and send them back. Then no one would have reason to threaten her. But she couldn't return them—not just yet. Not before knowing the Book of Water's secrets.

"Ms. Woods?"

Carrie looked up to find Francesca staring at her impatiently. Oh—right. How did she sleep. Not wanting to seem like a princess (or paranoid, for that matter), she decided to avoid the question. "My room is really comfortable, thanks."

Francesca nodded, seemingly satisfied by that nonanswer. She moved to the sideboard. "Can I get you coffee or tea?"

"I'll help myself, thank you," Carrie said, standing up. As she poured her tea, she watched Francesca add a couple cubes of raw sugar to her cup and stir, each rotation careful and precise, before returning to sit properly in her chair.

Carrie looked at the sugar longingly, thought about all the hours she was going to be sedentary, and then sipped her tea. Grimacing at the bitter taste, she reached for a piece of whole-grain toast—plain—and tried to ignore the scones, fresh croissants, and apple pastries.

Pretending her toast was dripping in butter and jam, she sat back down and gestured at Francesca. "So Max said he won't be joining us."

"No, *Mr. Prescott* won't," the woman said succinctly. "He has other matters to attend to."

What kind of matters? She'd ask, but she instinctively knew Francesca wouldn't take kindly to it. She seemed very protective of her employer.

It made Carrie wonder if there was something going on between them. Or if they had history. Sexual history.

She scowled at her dry toast. The picture of them

entwined in each other's arms, naked, was entirely too easy to imagine.

And she didn't like it at all. Surprising in itself, because she wasn't one given to fits of jealousy. But even a blind person could see Francesca wasn't thrilled with Carrie's presence there. Sure, she'd been hospitable, but it'd been the bare minimum and probably mandated by Max.

Could *she* have made the crank call?

Carrie studied her, frowning. She didn't look like a woman who'd just made a threatening call, using an electronic device to mask her voice.

Picking up her tea, she hoped her tone was nonchalant. "How long have you known Mr. Prescott?"

"All my life."

She waited for something more but decided as the woman began tapping at her Blackberry that nothing more was forthcoming. So Carrie said, "You started really young."

Francesca paused, her gaze full of distrust. "My mother was in the ambassador's employ."

"The ambassador?"

"Mr. Prescott's father," she said shortly, pulling out her portfolio.

Max's dad was an ambassador? How could an ambassador spawn someone so antisocial? "So you grew up together?"

She frowned at the papers she sifted through but didn't look up. "Yes."

Then they did have history. And now Francesca worked with him, so she must know him inside out.

She wanted to ask if Francesca had ever played doctor with Max. Not that she should care. She was here to work.

She cleared her throat. "Where did you grow up? If Max's dad was an ambassador, I assume you guys lived out of the country."

"Asia," was the answer she got. Then the woman stood up, went to a locked drawer, inserted a key (God knows where she pulled that out from—her bra?), and extracted a large, obviously ancient book. She carried it over to the desk closest to the windows overlooking the ocean. "This is what Mr. Prescott wishes to have translated."

"The whole thing?" Carrie tried not to gape, but she wasn't sure she was successful. It'd take the better part of a year—maybe two—to translate the whole thing.

"No, there's a specific chapter." She consulted her papers and nodded as she found the one she was looking for. "Here are the details."

Carrie took the proffered page and glanced at it. Then she went to the book and picked it up to move it to the table in the corner. "Not good to have it in direct sunlight," she explained at Francesca's puzzled look.

"I see."

She set the book down and carefully flipped through some of the pages. She started to get excited as she touched the crinkled vellum. She loved old texts. "I'm looking forward to this project."

Francesca didn't look like she believed Carrie, but she nodded. "Supplies are in the other desk. Help yourself to anything you need. I'll have Don bring in a tray for lunch. Is there anything you'd prefer?"

A bacon cheeseburger. Or fried chicken and mashed potatoes. She sighed as she pulled out a stool to perch on. "Maybe just some cottage cheese and fruit."

"The cook is an experienced French chef. You can have anything you like."

She shook her head. "But my butt can't."

"Oh." Max's assistant frowned like she couldn't comprehend such a thing. Then her expression went back to its normal placid blankness. "If you need anything else, I can be reached through the house phone."

"Great. Thanks." She watched Francesca glide out of the room, wondering if the woman would ever warm to her.

Seemed unlikely. But if someone had told her she'd find one of the Scrolls of Destiny and end up working for the famous Bái Hǔ, she'd have scoffed at that too.

Chapter Eleven

The apple pastry was ogling her, she just knew it.

Carrie glared at the tray of food. Each morning Max's butler Don delivered breakfast for her, and each morning the tray included that killer apple pastry. Tuesday, she'd broken down and tried one. She'd had one every morning since. Three in total.

Okay, four, because she had two on Thursday.

Her butt couldn't withstand another twenty-five days of fatty carbs. This morning, she'd been determined to resist and had a piece of whole-grain bread instead. When the cinnamon aroma of the apple pastry taunted her, she'd moved the tray to a table across the room.

But the smell still wafted over to her.

Like she wasn't having a hard enough time concentrating as it was. She set Max's ancient text aside and stretched her arms over her head.

She never knew she had such a problem with temptation. Probably because she'd never come across anything so tempting.

Nor *anyone.*

Her problem wasn't temptation—it was Max. He was not only fattening her up but weakening her will. Not that she'd seen him in person since that first morning on the beach. But, man, had she seen him in her dreams. Every night. In living color and tumescent flesh.

Not only did her dreams interrupt her sleep, but they made her restless in a way she'd never been before. Working on her dissertation didn't even soothe her anymore.

"Rather annoying, really," she muttered, pushing her things aside. She ambled around the room.

And ended up in front of the food tray.

"One more won't hurt," she told herself. She wouldn't eat any after this. Plus she'd gotten into the habit of taking a walk on the beach each morning. There was a pier at the end of Max's property where she liked to sit and think. Or, these days, sigh over her boss.

"Pathetic." She reached for the apple pastry and paused. Thinking of her thighs, she turned her back on the tray and headed to the kitchen for a banana.

At least that's what she'd planned—until she heard a rhythmic *whack-grunt-whack* farther down the hall. A female someone, by the tenor of the grunt.

Curious, Carrie went to investigate. The noise came from the last room down the hall. She peeked around the corner.

A rec room, bright with sunlight and airy because of the high ceiling. Instruments of torture, otherwise known as workout equipment, were arranged in half the room. The other half was covered with a series of interlocking, thick mats. A super-long piece of blue silk dangled down from over one end of the matted area.

A punching bag hung in one corner, and beating the bag was Francesca. She wore a sleek sleeveless catsuit that didn't leave anything to the imagination, its femininity incongruous with the ferocious attack. She rained a series of left–right punches that set the bag spinning. Then she backed up and delivered several kicks for good measure.

Carrie meant to leave Francesca to her workout—really, she did—but when the woman turned, running and launching herself onto the silk, she had to watch.

Catching the fabric a few feet off the ground, Francesca maneuvered it until it wrapped around her leg, the silk a bright contrast to her fair skin. She anchored it at her ankle with her other foot, reached higher overhead, and pulled herself up like it was a rope. Higher and higher until she was almost to the ceiling.

Francesca stopped and began a complicated series of twists and turns that resulted in the silk wrapped around her waist, her body a straight plank perpendicular to the fabric. Slowly, with utter control, she opened her legs into the splits.

Awesome. Carrie wondered if the woman would show her how to do that. She studied the move. It didn't look too hard.

Then Francesca dropped, her legs spinning like a windmill as her body rolled down the silk.

Carrie gasped and stepped forward to help.

But despite the crazy speed, Francesca was still in total control, her grip secure. Several feet from the bottom, she let her hands go and dropped backward, suspended from the silk by her legs. Her upside-down gaze zipped directly to Carrie.

Brow furrowing, Francesca twisted until she was free from the fabric and flipped into a cat-crouch on the mat. "Did you need me? Is there a problem with your work?"

"No, I was going to the kitchen to get a snack and I heard a noise." Not able to contain herself, she walked to the mat and fingered the silk. "That was so amazing. You were like Catwoman. Where did you learn to do that?"

"In an aerial dance class."

"Maybe I'll try it sometime." She ignored the woman's look of doubt. "You looked like you knew what you were doing with the punching bag, too."

"I've studied kung fu," she said briskly as she picked up her Blackberry from the sidelines.

"I've always wanted to study a martial art. Have you trained for a long time?"

Francesca gave a noncommittal grunt that was reminiscent of her boss.

"Well." Carrie rolled her eyes. "I don't want to get in your way. I'll just get back to work."

Missing the sarcasm in her tone, Francesca nodded. "I'll join you shortly."

Cool—something to look forward to. Shaking her head, Carrie went in search of her banana.

In the kitchen, she pushed aside a mangled stool—how odd—and leaned against the counter to eat her snack, her mind whirring with what she just saw.

Doing something like that would be so cool. How intriguing would a guy find her if she could wrap and unwrap herself with silk at will?

"Not that I have any guy in mind," she lied to herself.

Francesca's skills sparked a little flame of jealousy in her. She didn't have any kind of interesting hobbies.

She'd always thought she'd be great at martial arts, but even if she could squeeze classes into her already overfull schedule, she couldn't afford them. And for some reason Gabe wouldn't teach her.

Because no one expected little Carrie from Podunk, Iowa, to do anything so awesome. She was only ever supposed to be a housewife with two-point-five kids, have a fluffy dog named Sparky, and drive a station wagon.

Well, she didn't want a station wagon. She wanted more from life. She wanted to be a professor, teaching arcane Chinese history at a prestigious university. And she wanted to climb the freaking silk.

Carrie dropped the banana peel in a garbage can, strode back to the rec room, and peeked in.

No Francesca.

Excellent. Anticipation tingled in her belly as Carrie sneaked in, heading straight to the shimmering and enticing length of silk.

Raising up on her toes, she gripped the fabric overhead with both hands. She wiggled to get the silk around her leg. Impossible. She let go, wrapped the silk around with her hands, and grabbed the fabric again. Securing it at her ankle with her free leg, she lifted.

And moved up an inch.

Determined, she tried again. More successful this time, but still nothing like Francesca.

She wasn't sure how long it took her, but she finally got five feet off the floor. She looked down, hoped the mat was as cushy as it looked, and began to work the silk around her waist.

It was great until something went amiss and she got tangled.

"Not so bad, really," she assured herself. She was stuck, but she was secure. If only she could get her leg—

"What are you doing?" a gruff voice barked.

She tipped her head back. Max stood in the entrance to the room, wearing white *gi* pants. His chest a chiseled work of art, just like on the beach Monday morning.

She eyed the arrow of golden hair on his six-pack, lost her grip, and yelped as she slipped and the silk yanked her.

Muttering under his breath, Max stalked to her. He spun her several times and then set her on the floor.

"Whoa." Dizzy, she reached out to steady herself. Except the only handhold she had was his biceps.

Rock solid. She surreptitiously felt them up as she blinked to refocus. She told herself she leaned into him because she was off-balance from the aerial stunt. "Maybe I should have had a spotter."

Cold anger radiated off him in waves. "At the very least."

"It didn't seem that hard." God—his mouth was *right there*. All she had to do was get up on tiptoes to reach. Even set in an angry line, it was enticing.

She recalled everything those lips had done to her in her dreams, and her face burned. She glanced at his abs, and her mouth went dry with the desire to nibble at the dips and grooves of the muscular ridges.

Not a good idea. She tried to edge away—from him and the urge to run her hands over his shoulders, down his chest, and into his pants. "I should get back to the library."

His gaze dropped to her lips, and she swore she felt some of his iciness melt. He took a step toward her. "Next time, come to me."

"Come to you," she repeated lamely.

"If you want to try something new," he said, his voice husky.

That spot between her legs zinged, and her body screamed at her to take him up on his offer.

But she slipped around him and hurried for the door. "Thanks for the offer, but I should keep my feet on the ground from now on."

She headed back to the library, glancing at him once from the hallway. He watched her. She shivered, tempted to return to him.

Next time, she'd stick with the apple pastries. They were definitely less dangerous to her thighs.

Chapter Twelve

Max stared at his ringing cell phone. The Keeper.

Not answering was only going to put off the inevitable. But he wasn't looking forward to telling his mentor he still hadn't made any progress.

Seven days since she arrived, and instead of recovering the documents or figuring out what Rhys's part in this was, he'd succeeded only in driving himself insane with desire for her.

Every morning he searched her room. He told himself it was for information. But the way he'd greedily seek out her scent—the way he was repeatedly drawn to the drawer housing the black lace—made a liar out of him. And a pervert, damn it.

Grunting in self-disgust, he opened his phone. "*Sifu.*"

"Your progress?"

"None," he said without preamble.

The long-distance line crackled with the silence.

"There's more. She and Rhys have a—" What did he

call it? He settled on "liaison," though the thought of it made him go cold with fury.

He could almost hear Sun Chi thinking. Max wasn't entirely surprised when his mentor said, "Still this enmity with Rhys. Is it not time to let go of past differences?"

Even though he expected this response, it still angered him. The phone cracked in protest of his tightening grip. "What's between Rhys and me is hardly a difference."

"Are you certain?"

Hell, yes, he was certain.

Sun Chi sighed. "It's a shame to lose one's brother."

Max gritted his teeth. "A brother wouldn't lie and betray you. He wouldn't try to steal your most prized possession."

"Is that what Rhys did?" Doubt weighed each word.

"Didn't you call to talk about the stolen documents?"

"Your focus does you discredit at times, Bái Hŭ. Yes, tell me your plans."

Max settled on a leather chair in the suite attached to his bedroom. "I hired her to do a translation for me so she'd be on my territory, but I haven't reclaimed the scrolls. She has them with her, however. I felt the Book of Water when she arrived."

"Is it wise inviting the enemy into your home?"

"It's the only way. I need to find out what her connection with Rhys is."

"I see."

Max frowned at the meaning loaded in those two words. "It's not like that."

"If she turns your heart, carrying through on your mission will be difficult."

"I won't let that happen." His heart wasn't engaged—
his body was.

But he wouldn't let another distraction get in the way of
his duty. One Amanda in a lifetime was one too many. He'd
get close to Carrie, but only as a means to bring down Rhys.

"Bái Hǔ?"

"Yes." He shook his head, pinching the bridge of his
nose. "I know what I have to do."

There was another one of Sun Chi's pregnant pauses
where he was obviously thinking. But whatever was going
through his head, he didn't reveal it. Instead he said only,
"Keep me apprised," and then he hung up.

Max closed his phone and pressed it to his forehead.
He knew what he had to do.

He turned, running his hand along his sword, and
strode out of the safe haven of his room. It was Saturday,
but he knew his adversary would be downstairs with her
head buried in an ancient Chinese text.

As he walked down the stairs, he knew he couldn't simply take the documents back and get rid of her. Sun Chi
may not be concerned, but his mentor had always refused
to believe the truth about Rhys, his favorite student. Rhys
was relentless—he wouldn't stop simply because Carrie
was no longer a resource to him. He'd find another way to
realize his plans, whatever they were.

Carrie was the key to cracking Rhys.

Stopping in front of the closed library door, Max
roused *jīn ch'i*. Cool and sharp, it spread from his core out
to every corner of his body. The power vibrated under his
skin, a steely encasement to fortify him.

Ready, he opened the door.

As he stepped into the library, he felt it—the Book of

Water. The room undulated with its power, and his head swam.

He zeroed in on the source. He wasn't surprised to find it coming from a bag at Carrie's feet.

She worked, huddled in the darkest corner of the bright room, completely engrossed. Her hair was pulled back into a haphazard mass, revealing the pale nape of her neck.

He shook himself once he realized he was staring at that bit of skin. He quickly took in the rest of her—from her brow furrowed in thought to the loose tendrils framing her heart-shaped face. Sweet.

But treacherous. He glanced at the bag to remind himself just how much. He cleared his throat.

She jumped, jerking around to face him. But the moment she saw him, she smiled. "Good morning."

He scowled at the flicker of warmth in his chest.

"Actually, you don't look like you had one," she said after a moment.

"One what?"

"A good morning."

"How do I look?" he asked before he could stop himself.

She tilted her head. "Like you're battling demons. And the demons are winning."

He made a noncommittal sound and dropped onto a chair facing her. The better to keep an eye on her.

"Not that you want to talk about it with me. After all, I'm only your employee." She shrugged and returned her attention to her work, albeit writing more slowly than her previous rapid-fire pace.

As chatty as she was, it shouldn't be hard to get her

talking. Only he hadn't willingly conversed with anyone since—in seven years. Rusty on the art of conversation. He frowned at her bent strawberry-gold head and wondered what he could say to get her going. He cleared his throat. "Are you settled?"

"Yeah."

He narrowed his eyes. He had the distinct feeling she was being difficult on purpose. "I hope Francesca has been helpful to you."

"Francesca's been great," she replied without looking up. "You're lucky you have her."

It bothered the hell out of him that he couldn't see her eyes. It made it harder to determine if she was lying. At least, that was what he told himself. "Francesca is an asset."

Carrie dropped her pencil and turned around in her seat. "Francesca is more than an asset. She's completely devoted to you."

"I know." He noticed she was barefoot again, her worn tennis shoes kicked off and forgotten under her chair, and her feet peeked from the legs of her jeans.

Those jeans hid the most gracefully curved legs he'd ever seen. He hardened, thinking how they wrapped around his waist in his fantasies every night.

"No, you don't know," she said, distracting him out of his sexual reverie.

He frowned at the bite in her tone. "What is it?"

She opened her mouth but then snapped it shut and shook her head.

She was disappointed in him. He blinked, taken aback. He didn't know whether to be annoyed or impressed. But he was undeniably fascinated, despite himself. No one had ever dared express disappointment in him—except Sun Chi.

Before he could command her to tell him what she was thinking, she relaxed back in her chair and said, "I've been taking a walk on the beach every morning. I haven't seen you practicing with your sword."

The whiplash of subjects made him pause. "No."

"Afraid you'd have to talk with me again, huh?"

He glanced at her lips. Talking wasn't what he was afraid of. "No."

Her glance called him a liar. "You're good with the sword. Have you been doing that long?"

He shrugged.

"It was really cool. I couldn't tell where you started and the sword stopped. It was like you were one."

Partly his training with Sun Chi, and partly his affinity with metal. It occurred to him she could be fishing for information, but his intuition said no. They didn't have to research his weaknesses—Rhys knew everything about him.

"I wish I could do that." She sighed wistfully.

"What?"

"Wield a sword like you do. It'd be so awesome." She held her hand up. "I know. Not the most useful skill in the modern world, and it must be tough getting your sword through airport security, but it'd still be really cool."

"Maybe."

"If you aren't careful, you'll talk my head off. I've never met a more loquacious man."

He regarded her implacably. "Are you sassing me?"

"Me? Of course not. I would never sass." Her eyes sparkled. "Especially you."

"Why don't I believe that?"

"Have no idea." She crossed her legs Indian style on her seat. "How long have you been studying kung fu?"

"Since I was seventeen." When he'd received his scroll on the passing of an uncle he didn't know existed. His parents had been—still were—caught up in their political whirl of entertaining, so he'd left to find a mentor. Just like Rhys had. He felt the metal armrests of the chair meld under his clenched fists and forcibly tried to relax.

"Then you've been studying kung fu for some time."

He heard the caution in her tone and knew she'd picked up on his discomfort. He had the feeling she didn't miss much. "Fifteen years."

"No wonder you're good." She gazed at him like he was a god. "I want to learn kung fu. My friend Gabe is really good, but she won't teach me anything. But Rhys, her boyfriend, said he would."

Rhys has a girlfriend?

Relief swept through him, followed by irritation—with himself. It shouldn't matter if Carrie was romantically tied to Rhys—same difference if she was working with him.

Strangely, he found that it did matter.

Could he trust that she was telling him the truth?

He wanted to. Badly.

Pushing those renegade feelings aside, he forced himself to relax, hoping she'd continue to talk about Rhys. He needed to know exactly who Rhys was to her.

"Although I don't think Rhys will risk her wrath. And I can't afford to take classes. So I'm stuck. I bet I'd be a really good martial artist. I think I was a kung fu princess in a previous lifetime. Maybe you could show me a move or two while I'm here. When I'm not working."

"*No.*"

She blinked. "That was rather emphatic. Why not?"

He imagined sparring with her, taking her to the ground and covering her with his body. Taking her, period. He clenched his jaw. "You're not suited."

"I've got two hands." She stood up, bounced back and forth on her toes, and swiped her fists around like she was a boxer. "I learn fast."

Unable to help himself, he stood up, too, and walked to her. "You're too—"

"What?" She stopped moving and eyed him with pursed lips. "Old?"

Hardly. He shook his head.

"What, then?"

Knowing he shouldn't—but damn it, he couldn't help himself—he stepped in close. He inhaled her strawberry scent, and his gaze fell on that vulnerable soft spot at the crook of her neck that her upswept hair revealed.

She swallowed audibly. "Am I too uncoordinated?"

"No." The cold metal in and around him went molten. Against his will, he brushed that creamy skin with one finger. The iron in her blood reacted to *jīn ch'i,* her cheeks flushing pink. "Too soft."

He heard her gasp, and he couldn't mistake the heat in her eyes or the way she swayed toward him.

Her gaze fell to his lips. "Is that a bad thing?"

He reminded himself that she was the enemy—in league with Rhys. She'd stolen the Book of Water. God knew what she planned inside that beautiful head of hers.

But it would be strategically wise to use her attraction to draw her into his confidence. "It could be a very bad thing."

"Do you do bad things?" she asked.

He wanted to—dark, illicit things that would make her writhe in pleasure. That would make her moan the way she had that first night. This time for him.

For a moment, he wondered what taking her would be like. Sweet. Exquisite.

Dangerous. Given the opportunity, he knew he could lose himself in her—and that wasn't something he could afford.

He reinforced *jīn ch'i* like a barrier around him and stepped back. "I don't. Do you?"

"Sometimes doing a bad thing is necessary for the best outcome."

"The best outcome for whom?"

She shrugged and settled back on the chair, her knees drawn up against her chest. "We're just speaking hypothetically, aren't we?"

"Are we?" He headed for the door, not unaware that he was trying to outrun temptation. "I'll see you tomorrow."

"Tomorrow? You're working with me?"

Hearing the nerves in her voice, he glanced over his shoulder. "Is that a problem?"

She swallowed. "No. I just thought Francesca—"

"Francesca is busy tomorrow." Yes, she was definitely nervous. Hiding something? Without a doubt. Disappointment clung to him as he nodded at her and left.

He was doing the right thing. He pulled out his cell phone and texted Francesca to meet him ASAP. It was time to press his advantage. And he knew just how to do it.

Chapter Thirteen

I need you to befriend Carrie Woods."

Max knew he must have shocked Francesca with his request, because her usual blankness slipped to reveal surprise. He settled on the corner of the desk in his private study, watching her as she sat primly on the couch, wearing her signature suit. She worried the strand of pearls his family had given her for her sixteenth birthday.

But her hand stilled and lowered to her lap, her expression returning to its normally placid state. "May I ask why?"

"I need information from her."

"And you believe that if I deceive her into friendship, she'll reveal all to me?"

Max frowned at the sharp edge to her tone. "Specifically, I want to know how she knows a man named Rhys Llewellyn. But I don't want her to suspect you know of her association with him."

"Hm."

He shifted on the desk, eyes narrowing. "Is this assignment going to be a problem?"

Francesca opened her mouth and closed it, her mouth forming a firm line. She shook her head. "Not at all. When haven't I done what you wanted?"

Before he would question her, she stood up. "Will that be all?"

For a moment, anger made her eyes sparkle and her face flush, but then her usual placid mask was back in place. Max blinked, remembering the vivid little girl who used to follow him around. It hadn't occurred to him how she'd changed over the years. He wondered why he noticed it now.

"Sir?"

He shook his head. "That's all."

With a tip of her head, she stalked out of the room.

Odd. She'd never balked at one of his requests before, no matter how unorthodox.

He frowned. She'd never failed him. That was all that mattered.

Max decided that the best way to increase Carrie's longing for him was to make himself scarce, so he stayed in his office all day. He needed to study the dossier his private investigator put together on Rhys, as well as review the reports on his holdings.

It appeared to be true—Rhys was living with a woman. Gabrielle Sansouci Chin, an artist who bartended with Carrie.

Did Carrie introduce her to Rhys, or vice versa? He e-mailed some questions to his PI, including a request for a background check on Gabrielle Chin.

It was late when he finally quit for the day. He left the office, intending to go to his room to meditate before bed. His intentions went out the window when he saw the light seeping from under Carrie's door.

He stared at the thin line of illumination. She was in her room. Awake.

He pictured her, lying across the top of her bed, wearing nothing more than one of the scraps of lace he'd found in her drawer. He imagined her luscious ass, her curves barely covered. The way she'd look over her shoulder and lick her lips—beckoning. She'd be warm and accepting, taking all of him in—including the broken bits.

His cock stirred, and he stepped toward her door.

No. He stopped abruptly, fists clenched. He couldn't. With a growl, he turned around, jogged down the stairs, and headed outside to the beach.

The vigorous walk did him no good. He still throbbed with need—physically and mentally—so he stripped his clothes and dove into the ocean. He cursed as the chilled water closed over his head. Stupid, going swimming in the Pacific alone at night. A pathetic act of desperation.

Max let himself flow with the current before he propelled himself forward at his own pace. Forcing the thoughts from his mind, he let *jīn ch'i* warm him as he dove in and out of the waves. When he felt his muscles tire, he dragged himself out of the water and back to shore.

Using his shirt to dry himself off, he slipped on his underwear and carried the rest of his clothes back to the house. With any luck, she'd be asleep, and he could rest in peace.

Only as he reached the stairs from the beach up to the house, something felt wrong. He stilled, looking up at the house.

Nothing.

No. Max shook his head. Something wasn't right.

Then he saw the person, clinging to the side of the house. Climbing up.

To Carrie's room.

His eyes narrowed. An accomplice, or an intruder?

What was he thinking? It had to be an accomplice, going to meet with her. Was that what she was waiting for, still awake? Was it Rhys?

Fury riled *jīn ch'i*. It took a moment to get himself under control and back into a logical state. If it were Rhys, he would have felt it.

If it wasn't Rhys, then who was it?

"One way to find out," he muttered under his breath, running silently up the steps.

Stopping at the edge of the garden, Max focused his chi. He envisioned it sharp as his sword's blade, cutting through the intruder's layers of dark clothing. With his hand, he made a swiping motion.

The prowler grabbed his leg and lost his footing. He quickly corrected, holding firm to the railing of Carrie's balcony, and looked down.

Max unleashed another razor-sharp burst of energy.

A low moan of pain. Part of his pant leg shredded, revealing lacerated white skin. He lost his grip again, dangling precariously, but regained control and quickly shimmied back down the side of the house.

Dropping his clothes, Max ran to intercept him. Damn, the guy was nimble. Even having the two wounds didn't stop him from jumping the last ten feet from the house and hopping over bushes to make his escape.

The bastard wasn't getting away. Steeling himself, Max aimed his chi for a stunning blow guaranteed to drop the person. Chasing him around the corner of the house, he let *jīn ch'i* burst forward.

To hit emptiness.

"Damn it." Max looked left and right. He had to be somewhere.

But there was nothing. No signs of anyone. No footprints in the sand below. No sounds disturbing the night, except for the dull murmur of the ocean.

Chapter Fourteen

Carrie dragged herself out of bed and tried to force some enthusiasm for the day's work as she tugged on her jeans. She loved the work. It was the early hour that she wasn't thrilled about.

Okay, eight wasn't especially early. Unless you stayed up late reading, which was what she'd done. But she'd been making good headway into Wei Lin's journal, and she couldn't pass up studying the Book of Water. There seemed to be a correlation between certain meteorological events and that particular scroll. In fact—

"Stop," she told herself, opening the dresser for a shirt. She needed to concentrate on Max's translation for the next eight hours. She could come back to her own research this evening.

Maybe after a nap. And a walk—she'd overslept and missed her usual morning stroll on the beach.

Yawning, she settled on the first T-shirt she touched. She was still having trouble sleeping—the dreams hadn't abated.

In fact, every night they just got stronger, with Max doing unspeakable things to her, always in and around water. With his hands, his mouth—even his toes. She woke up in the wee hours of each morning, twisted and tormented. Worse, the ache remained no matter how she tried to relieve herself.

If the dreams weren't bad enough, two nights ago she woke up thinking she heard a sound outside. When she looked, there was nothing. Until she looked closer and saw a half-naked Max prowling in the night.

The sight of him in his white boxer-briefs was forever burned on her eyelids, more fuel for her sex dreams. She didn't know how she was going to face him without imagining his powerful legs and impressive—

Her phone's ringing startled her out of the lascivious thoughts. She pulled her shirt over her head on her way to grab it from the nightstand.

Her mom? Probably. Carrie had forgotten to call when she'd arrived. Mom was probably calling to see if she'd had sex yet. She picked up her phone. Restricted caller. Was Mom calling from the clinic? She flipped it open. "Hello?"

"*I'm watching you.*"

The electronic voice caused a chill to go up her spine. Carrie froze, hand on her zipper, her heart thumping wildly in her chest. She looked around the room, up at the ceiling, and out the balcony window. "Who is this?" she asked, wincing at the lame question. Like the guy was going to answer.

"You can't escape me," the person went on, every breath a Vader-esque hiss. "I know where you are."

Fear raced through her system. She stumbled over to the windows and drew the curtains tightly shut. "What do you want?"

"What you have. What doesn't belong to you."

Carrie glanced at her bag, which held Wei Lin's journal and the Book of Water, as well as the other scrolls she hadn't inspected yet. Which one did he mean?

The Book of Water. It had to be.

"Give it up and you'll be spared. Refuse to cooperate and I'll make you regret taking it."

Was risking her life worth this?

This *was* her life. Anger surged through her, stronger than the fear before. She wasn't going to let some punk dictate how she lived her life. "Listen, you—"

"I'll wait until you're alone and catch you unaware."

"No, you won't," she replied with more assurance than she felt.

"Are you willing to die for this?"

The call ended.

Carrie stood there, stunned. He had threatened her.

Who? Who could want the scroll so badly that they'd be willing to kill for it?

She snorted. Anyone. She herself had risked everything to get her hands on it. Of course, she wanted it for scholarly purposes, not the nefarious.

Maybe she'd done a bad thing, unearthing all this.

No, she'd make sure it all worked out. She'd cite the journal for her proof and make sure the Book of Water was returned to its safe haven.

She rolled her eyes. "Piece of cake."

At least she was ensconced in Max's citadel. He probably had all kinds of security—the fancy high-tech kind of systems that even experienced burglars couldn't crack. She was probably safer here than anywhere.

Unless he was the one after her. Then she was in the spider's web.

But he seemed to go out of his way to avoid her—except those few times he hovered close, like he wanted to kiss her. If he wanted the scroll, why didn't he just make a move?

In any case, whoever was threatening her appeared to be all talk and no action. Maybe she didn't have anything to worry about, after all.

The realization was reassuring, but the situation was still sobering. She gathered her things and went down to the library. If she finished the work she had scheduled for today quickly, she could get to her own research earlier. The sooner she got what she needed from the journal and Book of Water, the sooner she could return them.

Francesca arrived shortly thereafter, settling onto a couch next to Carrie instead of the stiff chair she typically used. "Good morning, Ms.—uh, Carrie. You look nice today."

Carrie glanced down at her worn jeans and plain black T-shirt. What kind of crack was the woman smoking?

"I trust you slept well," she said, setting her laptop on the coffee table.

Don't encourage her—she'll give up and let you work. "Hmm."

"Did you enjoy your walk this morning? The pier at the end of the property is a pleasant lookout, don't you think?"

"I didn't go this morning."

"Perhaps you can go out this afternoon," Francesca said, pulling out her ever-ready Blackberry. "The weather promises to be pleasant."

Shrugging, Carrie bent her head over her work, figuring the woman would understand she wanted to be left alone.

But that didn't work. In fact, the quieter Carrie got, the more insistent Francesca's questions became. They seemed almost timed—in fifteen-minute intervals.

"Do you also take walks on the beach in San Francisco?"

"Maybe you have a walking buddy?"

"What do you do for fun, Carrie?"

Carrie looked up from her notes. What was up with the nonstop chatter?

Maybe nonstop was an exaggeration. She thought about it and then shook her head. No—for Francesca, Ice Queen of Santa Monica, the multitude of awkward questions she'd asked this morning equated to nonstop. Today, of all days, when all Carrie wanted to do was buckle down and finish her work.

"You must do something for fun. Perhaps movies." Francesca's brow furrowed as she picked up her beeping Blackberry. "Perhaps you have a boyfriend."

Carrie tapped her pencil against the desktop and studied the woman. "You're awfully talkative today."

"I'm not sure what you mean."

"You've spoken to me more this morning than the entire week I've been here."

"I'm sure that's not true." Francesca motioned to the carafe on the table. "Would you like more tea?"

"No, thanks." And it was true. Since when was the woman interested in *her?* She'd been frosty from the beginning, and Carrie couldn't think of anything that would have changed that.

Eyes narrowed, she watched Max's assistant take a gulp of tea as if it were a shot of whiskey. The woman set the cup down and looked up. "You must meet many men working in a pub. Many foreign men."

"Okay, that's it." Carrie tossed the pencil down and sat up at attention. "What's going on here?"

"I don't understand. Did my question offend you?"

"They're almost the type of questions a friend would ask. Only we're not friends." Carrie frowned, confused. "You don't like me, and I can't help but wonder what's going on."

"Maybe I'm lonely," the woman said after a moment of silence.

Carrie noted she didn't deny the "not liking her" part.

"We should do something. Something girls do together," Francesca said, her lip curled as if the thought itself was as distasteful as actually doing it.

She closed her laptop. She didn't know what was going on here, but obviously Francesca wasn't going to let her get anything done. "I'm taking a break."

"Now?" Francesca clicked a few buttons on her phone. "If you wait forty-five minutes, I have—"

"No, I need a break now. I'm going swimming," she improvised, gathering her notes and shoving everything in the desk.

Francesca stared at her like she'd lost her mind. But then she shut her mouth, snapped her portfolio shut, and stood ramrod straight, as if she was on her way to face a firing squad. "I'll change and meet you on the landing."

Carrie mentally groaned as she picked up her bag. "You're coming, too?"

"Yes," the woman said with determination rather than enthusiasm.

"Fine." At least submerged she wouldn't have to listen to Francesca's stilted attempts at conversation. "See you in a sec."

Booking it up the stairs, she tore into her room. The thought of warm water all over her made her skin tingle in anticipation. It'd wash away all her apprehension—about her dissertation, the threatening calls, Francesca, and Max.

She contemplated her bag. Leave the scrolls here, or take them with her?

"To the pool?" She shook her head. Kneeling next to the bed, she pulled out her suitcase. Taking all the texts out of her messenger bag, she tucked them away in the luggage and stuffed it back under the mattress.

"Not a Swiss bank vault, but the best I can do for the moment." Hurrying, she changed into her old bikini, wrapped a bath towel around herself, and went to the landing down the hall from her room.

Francesca waited for her there, a shell-shocked look on her face. She wore a short robe that hit her midthigh, showing off miles and miles of leg. But even as fabulous as Francesca was dressed, she didn't look like she wanted to be there.

Carrie sighed. "You don't have to come along if you're worried about missing work."

"No, I want to come," she said halfheartedly, casting a glance at the door next to Carrie's.

"What's in there?"

"You don't know?"

"No." Carrie glanced at it. "Is it where he hoards his treasure?"

"I thought—" The woman swallowed whatever she'd

been about to say. Then she frowned. "He didn't tell you?"

"Why would he?"

Francesca shook her head. "This way."

Carrie looked back at the door. Would it be impolite to check it out later? With Francesca acting this way, she had to know what was in there.

Francesca led her down the stairs out to the back and pushed open a door, holding it open for her. Carrie followed, sighing at the tropical paradise.

Max's pool area rocked. Right off the house, the pool was long and rectangular. Lush plants filled the space around it, and a couple of reclining lounge chairs and low tables angled toward the ocean. To one side was a round pool, too small to be a swimming pool.

"The whirlpool," Francesca said. She walked to one side and kneeled down. With the push of a button, jets began to agitate the water. "The controls are here. Feel free to use it whenever you'd like."

Carrie wanted to point out that the tub in her bath had Jacuzzi action, but she supposed she should embrace the luxury of having two whirlpools at her disposal. Taking out her elastic, she shook her hair. She sure wasn't in Kansas anymore. Or Iowa, as it were.

Dropping her towel, she turned to the pool and dove in.

The water welcomed her, engulfing her in its warmth. She surfaced, letting it buoy her. Her hair floated around her like seaweed, alive and free, and she luxuriated in the sensation.

So it took her a moment to realize she was still alone in the pool. She glanced up.

Francesca looked at her like she'd lost it, but the woman was too reserved to comment.

"Aren't you going to come in?" Carrie asked halfheartedly, propelling herself forward.

She didn't think Francesca actually would, but then the woman took a deep breath, peeled off her robe, and crouched at the side of the pool.

Carrie admired the expensive-looking sky blue bikini. She knew it—the woman had a body to die for. With her hair done up in its twist and the jewelry, Francesca looked like she'd stepped off the set of a magazine shoot.

Okay, she officially hated the woman. Francesca was smart, successful, had a great wardrobe, perfect legs, and Max. Plus, she could eat all the pastries she wanted and not agonize over the size of her butt.

Some women had it all. Shaking her head, Carrie went under, paddling for what seemed like ages before coming up to the surface and doing lazy laps. She hadn't realized it before, but she'd felt parched. It'd been ages since she'd done any swimming, but with each stroke she felt more invigorated. All her worries faded, and she felt peace. She came back to the top and floated on her back.

"Ms.—uh, Carrie, do you get the opportunity to go swimming in San Francisco?"

So much for peace. "No."

"Of course. It's fairly chilly year-round, isn't it?" Pause. "Maybe a friend of yours has an indoor pool?"

"I work all the time." She rolled onto her stomach and dog-paddled. "I never have time. Playing hooky isn't a habit."

"It isn't?" Francesca asked as if it was hard to believe.

Stopping at the lip of the pool, Carrie rested her head

on her folded arms. Maybe if she humored Francesca
and answered the questions, the woman would leave her
alone. "All I do is research and work. I've been here eight
days, and instead of taking advantage of the amenities
I've holed myself up in my room each night reading an
obscure Chinese text for my thesis."

"Do you enjoy your work?"

"I knew the first time I saw an ancient text that I'd
found what I was meant to do. Something bigger than
myself. So I'm not sacrificing anything with all the work."
At least she didn't think so, despite what her mom said.
"Is that how you feel about working for Max?"

Francesca's brow furrowed. "Of course."

She didn't sound so sure. Carrie almost pointed that
out, but then she decided it wasn't any of her business. If
the woman wanted to talk about it, she'd listen, but she
didn't feel like dragging information out of her.

The question seemed to have done the trick. Francesca
sat at the edge of the pool, quiet and introspective.

Finally. Carrie lolled onto her back and drifted free.
Arms spread out, she felt the water caress her, over and
under her suit—all over her body, like a lover's touch.

She heard footsteps but didn't bother to look up. "Don't
tell me you're leaving already, Francesca."

"She is, in fact," a masculine voice growled.

Her eyes popped open. Not just any masculine
voice—Max's.

Chapter Fifteen

Max stepped onto the patio and into a dream. Or a nightmare, depending on how he looked at it.

And he looked. He couldn't help it. Carrie floated in the pool, her face registering bliss—the kind of bliss that, in the dark of night, he imagined giving her. The only thing wrong with the image was her bikini. In his dreams, she wasn't covered by anything but his hands and mouth.

"Sir."

He glanced right.

Francesca stood, as regal and composed as if she were in one of her power suits, and slipped into a robe. Interesting how the sight of her didn't rouse him. At all. But seeing Carrie's glistening skin, he craved her—inside and out. In a way he'd never desired anything or anyone.

"Sir," Francesca said again. Her hands fumbling at her sash were the only things that gave away her agitation. "I didn't—"

"Leave," he ordered. "Now."

Without another word, Francesca gathered her things and strode back into the house.

He heard Carrie mutter, "Traitor," and turned to look at her. She'd swum to the side of the pool and awkwardly climbed out. He stifled the urge to help her, not trusting himself to touch her. Not with the way her bikini clung to her curves.

"You didn't have to bark at her," she said, grabbing a towel from the edge of the pool and rubbing the wet-ness off herself. "It was my idea to come out here. You shouldn't treat her that way."

"You're hardly in the position to tell me how to treat my employees." He stepped forward, clenching his hands so he wouldn't be tempted to shake her.

"There's no reason to get so worked up." She held the towel in front of her like a shield. "We were just taking a break. I'm making good time on the translation work, and you never said it was against the rules to take an hour off."

"I've been searching the house for you for the past half hour." He grabbed her arms and lifted her to her toes. When he couldn't find her, it'd driven him crazy, first wondering if she was meeting someone, then wondering if she was safe. The only saving grace was that he'd found the Book of Water stashed under her bed in a half-assed hiding job. He didn't think she'd leave without the scroll. "Didn't you think that maybe I'd wonder if something happened to you or if you'd run off?"

She blinked, her big dark eyes shining innocence. "Don't worry. I won't leave before finishing the work."

"I couldn't give a damn about the work," he growled. He wanted to know what she wanted. He wanted to know who Rhys was to her. He wanted to know why he just wanted to get closer when every bit of common sense told him to run. Damn it.

He hauled her up and crushed his mouth to hers.

Dropping her towel on the ground, she wrapped her arms around his neck and pressed herself to his hard, wide body. She melted against him, as if it didn't occur to her to fight him.

Why not? Damn it, didn't she understand he was the enemy? He clasped her closer, his kiss savage. Not enough. Reaching around, he palmed her ass before pressing her against his hardness. They both moaned.

For one insane second he toyed with the elastic of her bottoms, his finger just barely under, wondering how she'd feel if he slipped to her center.

Insane was right. He stepped back, withdrawing his hand from her damp skin.

Carrie panted, letting her arms fall from around him to hug her body as if she was chilled. When she spoke, her voice was all sex. "At least now I know."

"What?"

"That you do kiss like the Viking god you resemble."

Max stared at her. A bead of water rolled down her neck and into the valley between her breasts. He swallowed, wanting to lick after it. He wanted to untie the strings of her bikini and let his tongue roam free.

Fucking insane. He shoved his hair back, regulating his breathing. He needed to get it under control. He needed information from her—not mindless passion.

Because mindless it would be. He'd have every intention of kissing the secrets out of her, but if he got her under him, the scroll, Rhys, and everything else would be the last things on his mind. His focus would narrow to the feel of her hands and mouth on him—to see the fire in her eyes—all for him.

He hardened painfully, just thinking about her eyes gazing at him in passion. *Damn pathetic.* With coolness he was far from feeling, he nodded. "Until tomorrow."

Max caught a glimpse of her incredulous stare before he returned to the house, as if she couldn't believe he didn't stay and make good on the promise in his kiss.

Frankly, he couldn't believe it, either. He didn't have promises to give. But as he walked away, he found himself wondering *what if.*

Chapter Sixteen

So much for doing my own work tonight." Carrie shoved the Book of Water aside and sat up on her bed. As much as it drew her, all she could think about was the way Max had kissed her earlier.

She'd felt that kiss all the way to the soles of her feet.

Her mom used to say that the right man could make you weak in the knees with his kisses. She'd humor her mom by nodding politely, but she'd never believed.

Well, she was a believer now.

Only the kiss had left her restless—like she was too big for her skin. She needed more. She needed him to touch her again, to slip his strong fingers over her and finish what he started by the pool.

"Not going to happen." Even if she wanted it to. A little.

Okay—a lot.

She flopped back on her pillows. It'd be so easy to forget her no-personal-attachment vow with him. God, he was tempting—a once-in-a-lifetime kind of guy.

But, remembering how her mom got derailed by a man, she shook her head. Pleasure was fleeting. Entanglement wasn't worth years of regret, and she didn't doubt Max could ensnare her.

Outside the ocean roared, like it agreed with her.

The ocean. Carrie sat up, staring out the billowy curtains. A walk by the ocean would make her feel better.

She returned the scroll to its hiding place under the bed, grabbed a jacket, and slipped out of her room. The hallway was totally still—no one in sight. Not that anyone would stop her from taking a walk.

At least, she didn't think anyone would. She thought about yesterday's phone call again and shuddered. Maybe a walk alone at night wasn't a good idea.

No—she wasn't going to let some jerk affect her life. Determined, she tiptoed past the door next to her room—

And stopped. Staring at it, she wondered what was in there. Francesca seemed shocked that she didn't know. Would it hurt to look?

Carrie pressed her ear to the door. No noise. She put her hand on the doorknob and twisted.

It opened with a soft click.

She paused. If there was something in here she shouldn't see, it should have been locked. Right?

For some reason, she had a brief flash of herself sneaking into the documents room at the monastery.

"Silly," she murmured, pushing the door open. "I'm not going to take anything this time."

It was dark inside, the only light from the moon shining in through the wall-to-ceiling windows along one side. It took a moment for her eyes to adjust.

Then she saw The Bed.

It was the biggest bed she'd ever seen—plush and silky and mysterious. Beckoning her like she was Goldilocks.

It was *his* bed—she knew it without a doubt. This was his room.

Heart pounding, she looked around, expecting Max to be lurking in a dark corner, ready to pounce on her.

Unfortunately, he wasn't there, lurking or ready to pounce. The stillness in his room was too absolute.

"Bummer." She trailed a hand along the soft, cool comforter on his bed. She wondered what he'd do if he found her here. Most likely fire her.

Sighing, she turned to leave even though she wanted more than anything to snoop around. But she knew it was better to leave before she found something that'd upset her—like a half-used box of condoms or something.

She turned to head to the door when a gleam caught her eye. Looking left, she saw a sword mounted on the wall.

His sword.

She grinned, trying to keep all the obvious innuendos out of her mind. Hard, though. No pun intended.

Drawn to it, she lifted her hand to touch it. She shouldn't—she knew that—but she couldn't help dragging one finger across its surface. She imagined how Max would react if he saw her touching it.

With a shiver, Carrie hurried out of the room and away from temptation.

Tangled in her thoughts, she stole through the house and out the back to the steps that led down to the beach. She walked straight to the edge of the water, letting its coldness lap at her ankles like an eager puppy. She matched her breathing to the tide, a slow in and out until all the tension—sexual and otherwise—melted from her body.

Be not lulled by its beauty, for as it soothes, so does it sting. So is the nature of all things.

"Strange." She started walking slowly, hands in her pockets. Why did that verse from the scroll come back to her now?

And why did it leave her feeling like something wasn't right? Huddling in her coat, she tried to pinpoint what was wrong.

Someone was out there.

She lifted her head and looked around. It wasn't Max. It didn't feel like his stare—he'd stared at her enough that she'd know if it were him. He always left her feeling a little weak, kind of shaky, and a lot turned on.

That wasn't what she was feeling now. Not even close.

Go back to the house. The urge was sudden and irrefutable. Picking up the pace, she hurried back to the stairs.

In high school, her friend Marie always dragged her to horror movies. Carrie used to make fun of them—the heroines were so stupid. But suddenly she felt like one of those idiot heroines. She knew that if she didn't make it to those stairs she was a goner.

So she ran. The sand made her legs feel like lead, and the steps to the house seemed never-ending. She ran through the garden, past the pool, and straight in through the door she'd gone out from.

Shoving it closed, she rammed the deadbolt shut and sagged against it, trying to catch her breath. Only she didn't feel safe—like whatever was out there followed her inside.

"Is everything okay?"

With a small yelp, she whirled around.

Francesca stood there, that faint disapproving frown lining her widow's peak.

Pressing a hand to her chest, Carrie wilted back against the door. "You scared the *crap* out of me."

The woman looked outside, beyond her, her frown deepening. Lifting her hand, she played with the pearls of her necklace. "Were you out walking?"

"Yeah. I—" She shut her mouth, her gut telling her not to let on about the creepy feeling she'd had out there. Trying to smile, she slipped past the woman. "I'm going back to my room now."

"Are you okay?"

"Fine." She waved a hand over her shoulder and practically jogged through the house, up the stairs, and to her room. When she got there, she locked her door, too—the first time she'd bothered since she moved in—and turned on all the lights.

Someone had been in here. She felt it like the residual ripples from an unseen disturbance in a pond.

Something was wrong.

She shimmied out of her jacket and let it drop. Grabbing a figurine from the dresser, she inspected every nook and cranny where someone could be hiding.

Nothing.

The documents. *The scroll.*

Kneeling by the bed, she pulled out her suitcase and exhaled in relief when she found the texts safe and sound inside. Except were they in a different spot inside her bag, or was she hallucinating?

"You're being silly," she told herself. She zipped it up,

tucked it back deep under the mattress, and stood up. "It's just your imagination."

But she couldn't make herself believe it. Her imagination wasn't *that* active, and she certainly hadn't imagined the threatening calls. Plus, she knew what she felt. Someone had followed her outside, and someone had been in her room, too.

Chapter Seventeen

The next morning, Carrie walked into the library and straight to Francesca, who perched primly on the edge of the couch, a laptop balanced on her legs. "One question," she said.

"Good morning, Carrie," Francesca said without taking her eyes from the screen. "How are you this morning?"

"Puzzled, which leads me to my question. Why was someone in my room last night?"

Francesca looked up, her brow furrowed. "What do you mean?"

"That I think someone's been through my stuff." *Specifically you,* she wanted to add.

"It was probably just the housekeeper." She arched an elegant eyebrow. "You do know there is a housekeeper, don't you? It was probably her."

"Yeah." She'd considered the housekeeper, but why would the housekeeper wait until she left the house and then enter her room? That late at night? Didn't make sense.

Of course, she was hearing a several-hundred-year-old piece of parchment talk to her, too, which made even less sense.

What did make sense: that Francesca had been in her room. She had, after all, been roaming the halls last night. Carrie didn't put it past her to go through her things, looking for stolen silverware or anything else incriminating that would get her in trouble. Despite Francesca's recent attempt to be friends, she'd probably jump at the chance to have Max to herself again.

Probably? Most likely.

"Was anything taken?" the object of her suspicions asked.

"No." That was the weird part. It wouldn't have taken a rocket scientist to find the scroll. The thing was hidden under her bed, for goodness' sakes. And a poor doctoral candidate with ancient texts under her bed? Total red flag.

"It was the housekeeper, and I assure you that the staff is highly screened and would never take anything that didn't belong to them."

Right. Carrie knew that. And if it weren't for the calls, she would have agreed. But, as much as she could see Francesca going through her things, she couldn't picture the woman threatening her with anonymous phone calls.

She studied Francesca, who was engrossed with her Blackberry. There was more going on here—Carrie felt it in her gut. She just hoped she'd figure out what before anything bad happened.

The rest of the week was uneventful. Carrie got up, went for her walk, worked on the translation, and then retired to her room to hammer out her thesis. There were no phone calls, no feelings of someone invading her privacy, and no sensations of being watched. Francesca was scarce, probably doing Max's bidding. And God knew where Max had gone.

It all made Carrie quite nervous.

After another restless night, Carrie got up early Saturday morning, dressed, and quietly left her room for her morning walk.

She paused outside Max's door. Was he in there? Hovering, tempted to check, she hurried down the stairs and outside before she could give in to temptation.

The salty sea air greeted her. Alert, she walked through the yard and down the wooden stairs to the beach, relaxing once she realized she didn't feel anything strange. She glanced at the spot where Max had been practicing with his sword, disappointment stabbing her. He wasn't there.

"Silly." She shook her head and began to trek. She wished she'd stop thinking about him so much. She should be concentrating on her work. Editing her thesis to include her new findings on the Scrolls of Destiny required total focus.

She was focused, all right—not on her work but on Max.

The kiss by the pool should have soured her fascination with him, but it'd only added fuel to the fantasies inspired by her dreams. She hadn't thought reality could compare to the lush eroticism of her dreams, but that kiss had proved her wrong.

If he could do that with just a kiss, maybe her dreams weren't so far-fetched.

She trudged unhappily through the sand. That was just

what she didn't need—some insanely great kiss that was going to mess with her and her future.

"I won't let that happen," she promised herself, kicking a hunk of seaweed. She knew what she wanted, and a distracting man wasn't part of the equation.

Assuming Max even wanted her. Note that he'd disappeared this week.

Her frown turned into a scowl, and she walked faster to work out her frustrations. By the time she reached the other end of Max's beach, she had a sweat going but didn't feel any more tranquil.

Wiping her forehead and readjusting her ponytail, she headed to the pier. The sturdy wood platform extended well into the ocean, but no boats were moored to it. It seemed to serve no practical use except as a place where she could sit and think. Odd, since it appeared to have been recently built.

"Maybe Max's boat is in the shop," she mumbled as she stepped onto it. The planks were so solid, they barely even creaked. The sea rolled violently today—as restless and gray as she felt. She watched the waves break below, large and aggressive, spraying her with a thick mist.

Halfway down the pier, a loud crack sounded.

And then she fell.

Carrie screamed, her hands scrabbling to grab hold of something. Her fingers hooked on the part of the pier that was intact. Her feet dangled, as heavy as lead.

"Don't look down," she told herself. But she couldn't help it.

Churning waves swept over craggy rocks ten feet below her. One wave rose up, soaking her jeans, trying to drag her under.

"Oh, God." Her body began to shake, her muscles both freezing and twitching uncontrollably.

Stop. You can get back up.

In her head, she heard

Water is ever-determined. It yields, yet still moves forward, undeterred from its path. It does not understand defeat, but searches another course to advance its flow.

"Doesn't understand defeat," she said through gritted teeth. She took a deep breath, concentrating on the ebb and flow of the water. She stilled her shaking limbs and swung her legs. *Gain momentum. Hook them back onto the pier.*

But each sway of her legs caused her hands to slip. Her palms burned, and her fingers fought for purchase. Afraid she'd fall, she stopped moving and tried to pull herself up with her arms.

They quivered with the effort. She yelled, hoping her cry would give her extra oomph.

Her muscles gave out. Hanging by the tips of her fingers, she looked down again.

Big mistake.

Her shoulders and back screamed in protest. She started to feel them giving out. "*No.*"

Suddenly, hands gripped her wrists and yanked up.

Instinctively, she struggled against them.

"Stop, damn it, or we'll both fall in."

Max. She looked up to find him standing above her, his chiseled jaw set with determination. She relaxed her body and let him pull her up.

Her arms wrenched, and her body scraped against the

jagged edges of splintered wood. She heard a tear and hoped it was her clothing and not a muscle.

Max hauled her up and back until she sat with her legs dangling through the broken planks. She scrambled back, wanting to put as much distance as possible between her and the crashing waves below.

Raking his hair back, Max inspected the broken slats. His shoulders tensed as his fingers ran over one edge. He muttered something under his breath and returned his attention to her.

"Are you okay?" He leaned over her, his hand brushing her hair so her head tilted back and he could look into her eyes. His gray gaze was searching and cold with anger.

"Why are *you* angry?" Her teeth chattered so strongly she could barely get the words out. "I'm the one who almost plummeted to a certain death."

"I'm not angry at you." Then he cursed—quite audibly—and hauled her up into his arms.

"What are you doing?" God, his body heat felt good. She curled into him despite herself.

He glanced down at her with a fierce scowl. She didn't think he was going to reply, but then he said, "You're in no shape to walk."

She would have liked to argue, but she didn't think she could be convincing—not with the way she was shaking.

The sand didn't seem to impede his strong stride, and he made it back to his house in no time. He rounded the corner of his home and took her inside through an entrance she'd never seen.

It led straight into the kitchen. Max set her down on a cold marble counter and pointed a finger at her. "Stay."

She huddled into herself. She wasn't sure she could

walk away if she wanted to—she was still shaking pretty badly. A combination of the adrenaline crash and her soaked clothes. Still, his bedside manner needed some finesse.

His butt needed nothing, though. Even in the loose cotton pants he wore it looked good. She tried to see if he wore those sexy boxer-briefs underneath, but she couldn't tell.

Now is not the time to ogle him. Instead, she looked at her hands. They were red, scratched, and starting to get puffy. She could see a few large splinters lodged under the skin. Working today was going to suck—if she could even hold a pencil.

Max returned to her side, setting a large first-aid kit next to her. He opened it and pushed her hands away. "Let me take care of this."

"I—"

He lifted the torn flap of her shirt, and his hand brushed her bared midriff. She hissed as a shock of pleasure shot through her.

Max must have taken it for pain, because his frown deepened. He looked closer, inspecting the thick vertical scrape from her bra line to her waist.

She stared at the top of his golden head, confused—and worried because, frankly, she didn't trust herself with him so close.

His cool fingers traced over her ribs, more gently than she would have thought he'd be capable of. "Does it hurt?"

Hardly. Carrie sat rigidly, wondering how far up his hand would go. Her nipples tightened as she imagined his large hand cupping her, and she bit her lip in an effort not to arch up and offer herself to him.

"Not bad. Let's look at your hands." He lifted hers, palms up, in his own.

She tried to tug them back. It stung. Worse, it gave her ideas she didn't need. "I can—"

"*I'm* going to extract the splinters." His voice brooked no argument. "You're going to tell me what happened."

She shrugged, trying not to whimper when he began poking her with a pair of tweezers. "I was out for my morning walk. I usually sit on the end of the pier before I come back. This morning the planks just gave out."

He looked up at her, his gaze steely and intense. With suspicion?

No, it had to be reproach. "I know it was my fault. I should have known there was a reason the pier wasn't in use. The wood must have been rotted. You don't have to worry that I'd blame you or anything."

He stared at her for another unnerving moment before he returned to tending her hands. She felt a curious zing, followed by soothing coolness. Then he withdrew a ball of gauze from the first-aid kit and gently wrapped the worse of her hands.

"Thanks," she said, looking at the expertly done job.

"It should be better by tomorrow." He put the first-aid kit back together. "Don't use them today."

"But the translation—"

"Can wait," he finished for her, facing her with narrowed eyes that dared her to defy him.

Fine. She'd just work on her thesis. She shifted to scoot off the counter, hoping her shaking legs would support her.

He must have noticed, because he cursed and lifted her again.

"Hey. What are you doing?" She steadied herself on his chest. And, okay, she may have done a little gratuitous feeling up, too.

"Taking you to soak in the hot tub."

"I can just use the whirlpool tub in my room," she said, trying to squirm free of his hold.

"Your tub will take ten minutes to fill and heat, and the Jacuzzi is ready now. You need warmth immediately." He set her on her feet at the edge of the whirlpool and bent down to turn it on.

She couldn't argue with that—she was freezing—but her swimsuit was upstairs, and she wasn't going to parade around in her underwear. And naked? No way. "But—"

"You'll need help getting out of your clothes. You shouldn't get your bandages wet."

True. Still. "I'll just wear my jeans into the hot tub."

He stared at her like she was insane. "Why would you do that?"

Because the thought of him stripping her had her shaking, and she couldn't blame it on being chilled. She pictured him baring her inch by inch, and it made her breathless. Tingly.

And nervous. She shouldn't be picturing him undressing her. She shouldn't picture him at all. She was here to do a job—not get freaky with the boss.

He stepped up to her, challenge in every line of his face. "I'm going to help take your clothes off."

Gulp.

She tried to come up with a reason to keep them on, but he reached out and undid the top button of her pants before she could say anything. Putting a wrapped hand over his, she said, "My jeans only. The rest stays on."

He cocked an eyebrow but didn't argue. He unzipped her pants, slipped his hands into the waistband, and got to his knees. Slowly, he peeled the wet denim from her legs.

Very slowly.

Carrie held her breath. His fingers glided over her skin as he worked the jeans down her legs, and his mouth hovered so close to ground zero that she swore she could feel the heat of his breath through her underwear.

Swallowing a moan, she stepped out of them as soon as they puddled on the ground. She tried to smooth down her too-short, shredded shirt, but it came only to her waist. Her white cotton bikinis glared below the hem. Like a beacon.

She became conscious of the burbling water. The sooner she was in, the sooner she'd be hidden, so she stumbled over to the pool and awkwardly eased herself in.

"Oh, God, that's good." The heat seeped into her, and the chill melted away. Propping her hands on the lip so her bandages wouldn't get wet, she closed her eyes and let her head fall, trying to forget Max was there.

It occurred to her that was like living in the shadow of Kilimanjaro and trying to ignore its constant looming presence.

Then the mountain came to her. Feeling the water rock with the motion of him slipping in, she squeezed her eyes tight. She would not look. She wouldn't wonder if he got in fully clothed or if he'd stripped down to bare skin dusted by that faint golden trail of hair.

Yeah, right.

She opened her eyes.

Chapter Eighteen

Max knew without a doubt that the image of Carrie bending down to get into the water, wearing white underwear and a T-shirt, would be forever ingrained in his memory.

The only thing that had kept him from palming her round ass was how much discomfort she was in. She didn't complain, but her movements were stiff and awkward.

Small wonder.

The burst of emotion in his chest when he saw her dangling from the broken slats on the pier surprised him. He'd run faster than he thought possible and arrived just in time. Any later and he would have had to scoop her bruised body off the rocks below.

Not that she would have been killed. Another several feet out along the pier and it would have been a different story. Where she had fallen, the drop wasn't far. The worst that would have happened was bruises. Farther out, the water was deeper, the rocks more jagged, and the waves more relentless. She would have fallen, broken her legs, and drowned.

Jīn ch'i flared, echoing the pang he felt at the thought of losing her.

Frowning, he untied his pants, watching her close her eyes and relax. She was remarkably composed for what just happened. He might have thought she'd manufactured the situation, but the terror in her eyes had been real. She also believed the planks had been rotted. He could tell she hadn't been lying—she truly believed it.

Was someone—Rhys—after her? Max was inclined to think so. He just needed to figure out what part she played in all this.

He stepped out of his pants, his gaze on her. Her T-shirt had gone translucent, showing the plain bra beneath it.

And her small, swollen nipples. He bet if he looked lower, he'd be able to see the shadow of her sex revealed by her wet panties.

Getting in with her wasn't a good idea, but he couldn't help himself. He had an inexplicable but driving need to make sure she was okay. Leaving his briefs on, he stepped down into the whirlpool. He knew she was aware of him by the way her body tensed. He wondered what was going through her head.

Her eyes popped open, panic making them wide. "I can't afford to take time off, even a day. I just made a breakthrough on my dissertation, and I have to pull it together if I'm going to get a professorial position at Berkeley." She swallowed loudly. "I really want that job. More than anything."

He frowned, trying to understand what her nervous babble was about.

Shifting uncomfortably, she rushed on. "That's why I work all the time. I've got to focus in order to make it happen. I can't afford distractions, even if my mom thinks I should be distracted more."

Was she saying he was a distraction? He took in her blush and found himself hoping so. "You and your mother are close."

"Yes, she's one of my best friends. I miss her, living out here. I haven't seen her in too long. Do your parents live close by?"

"No."

She blinked. "Where do they live?"

"China, Europe, D.C. My father is a diplomat, so they move around."

"Oh." She bit her lip, obviously processing the information. Then she said, "This feels really good. Thank you for making me soak."

He nodded.

"I can't believe I fell through the pier." Her brow furrowed. "I've been walking there every day since I got here. It never seemed unsafe."

"It wasn't." He thought of the evidence he'd found and felt cold anger all over again. "Someone cut into the wood so it would break with enough weight."

She gasped. "Are you kidding? Of course you're not kidding. You wouldn't joke about that."

He watched her closely, assessing her reaction. She was genuinely surprised that someone had rigged the pier. "Who knows you walk along the pier every day?"

"You think someone set me up deliberately. Like to scare or warn me." Her surprise became contemplative, as if someone wanting to scare her wasn't shocking. Before he could question her, she said, "I haven't made a secret of where I walk. Even Francesca made note of it."

Francesca had no reason to harm Carrie.

Rhys would, though—especially if it meant securing the power of another scroll.

There was the prowler scaling the house, as well. Carrie hadn't attempted to get away to meet anyone, and no one had tried getting to her since. If that was an aborted assignation, they would have tried again.

Had Rhys sent someone else to do the job, knowing Max would sense him?

Carrie worried her lip, lost in her own thoughts. He waited for her to say what was running through her mind. He willed her to confide in him, not wanting to analyze why that felt so important.

She shook her head, as if physically shaking off her thoughts. "I was lucky you came to my rescue."

Disappointment stabbed him. He almost asked her about Rhys right there, point-blank, but he couldn't risk sending her running.

"How can I thank you?"

Despite himself, his gaze fell to her mouth. He should be quizzing her about her agenda and who else knew she had the scroll. But he watched her worry her lip, and the only thing he could think about was nibbling it himself.

Her eyes widened, as if she could read his thought. He also knew from the way her nipples tightened that she liked it. His mouth watered—*watered*—thinking about tonguing those tips.

"I don't do this," she blurted. "This isn't like me."

"This?"

"This." Swallowing audibly, she waved a hand between them. "I probably shouldn't admit this, but I haven't been with a guy like this in, um, forever."

"Forever?" He waded across the Jacuzzi to her side.

"I mean, it's not that I don't like sex. In theory. It's just I don't usually feel compelled."

He faced her, gently bracketing her wrists, elevating her hands to keep them from getting wet. "Are you feeling compelled now?"

"I'm feeling something," she whispered as he lowered his mouth to hers.

Eyes open, their lips glanced—once, twice. Then, with a low moan, she opened to him. Her leg hooked on his hip, and he groaned into her as his cock, hard and ready, pressed against her thigh.

He felt her—warm and soft and so alive—and every broken and worn instinct told him to keep her in his arms.

And he would have, if she hadn't pushed on his shoulders. Easing up without letting her go completely, Max stared down at her.

Her chest heaved with each breath. "This is *not* a good idea."

It seemed like the best idea he'd had in a long time. "Why not?"

"I work for you."

He was tempted to fire her.

"And I just had a traumatic experience. We're both probably still experiencing heightened emotions from it. Near-death experiences make people come together like this, right?"

He looked at her dampened curls and wide eyes. *This,* whatever it was, was not the result of an accident. A cosmic joke? Maybe. But definitely not a fleeting, adrenaline-induced reaction.

She licked her lips, gently kissed him one last time—an angel's kiss—and wiggled out from his arms. "You'll thank me in the morning."

He doubted that, especially as he watched her climb out of the hot tub, her underwear clinging sexily to her curves. He had to force himself not to follow the glittering trail of water she left as she picked up her jeans and padded into the house.

Like a trail of crumbs, leading to paradise.

Max hauled himself out of the Jacuzzi and into the pool. Laps would help him cool off. He cut through the water with a vigorous stroke. Hopefully the trail would be dry by the time he finished. That was one path he needed to avoid.

Chapter Nineteen

Carrie glanced at the library door for the thousandth time since she started working that morning. No sign of him. She hadn't seen him since he'd pulled her to safety on Saturday. Two full days. She didn't know if she was relieved or disappointed.

She shouldn't be either. She should be freaked because of the pier incident. The phone calls weren't cranks. Someone was out to get her—or at least to scare her. She had no clue who it could be, either. Disconcerting, that. It was hard protecting yourself against an unknown predator.

Her skin broke out in goose bumps every time she remembered how close she'd come to falling. Thank God Max had come to the rescue.

Max. How did he happen to show up there just in time to save her? She tapped her pencil against the notepad. He was the only person who could know what she'd done— he'd caught her right after she left the monastery's documents room. Did he suspect? Was he the one terrorizing her?

If he was, then why didn't he say anything? And why did he kiss her like he wanted to eat her up?

What did he want? In the Jacuzzi on Saturday it sure didn't seem like some old Chinese texts were on his mind. He'd seemed especially concerned, too. Was he faking it?

One thing he hadn't been faking: the enormous erection. It was a supreme act of willpower not to explore that territory.

Francesca cleared her throat.

Carrie looked up, saw Max's assistant eyeing the pencil pointedly, and stopped the nervous drumming. "Sorry."

The woman placidly went back to answering her e-mails, or whatever she did on her Blackberry.

Carrie stared at the work she hadn't done. She was a couple of days behind. If she buckled down she could catch up, but with Max on her mind getting any work done seemed like an impossible goal.

Sighing, she lowered her head and tried to concentrate.

The door opened and she looked up, expecting to find Don bearing more food. If there was a perfect time for an apple pastry, it was now.

But it wasn't Don. Instead, Max stood in the doorway, fixing her with his unyielding gaze.

Her breath caught in her chest. He looked feral, his hair wilder than usual. And masterful. She remembered the way he'd slid across the hot tub to her on Saturday and felt her body swell and moisten.

"Come with me," he ordered.

She should have said no, but curiosity got the better of her. She stood up without a question.

At the door, she caught Francesca watching, her expression closed. Bitter? Before Carrie could reflect on that any further, Max placed his hand on the small of her back.

A current shot through her, and she held her breath. Was he going to keep it there? Would he hold her hand?

She mentally chastised herself as he removed his hand as soon as she stepped out of the library. *Grow up, Carrie.* She had to stop acting like a teenager.

He closed the door behind them and headed down the hall.

Whatever he was up to had to be indoors, given he was barefoot. She admired the way his loose linen pants showcased his butt. Too bad he had a top on—a bare torso would have completed his beachcomber look nicely.

Grinning, she hurried to follow him. Maybe he wanted to give her some other work. Maybe he wanted to ask her to return what she took from the monastery. Maybe he wanted privacy so he could chastise her for her behavior and tell her what happened Saturday would never happen again. Maybe he wanted to take her to a private alcove and ravish her until she was a puddle of goo on the floor.

The fourth option appealed the most.

He glanced behind at her and scowled. "Keep up."

She rolled her eyes. He interrupted her work for some reason and then he barked at *her.* Typical.

He jogged down a set of stairs and disappeared through a door.

Curiosity totally piqued, she hurried after him. "I've never been down here. I'm not sure I realized there was a lower level." She paused in the doorway and looked around.

"Media room," he muttered, walking around to a fancy-looking desk and computer setup in the back.

She glanced at the huge screen in front and the cushy seats with cup holders. Needing to try one out, she sat down and leaned back. The seat reclined and a footrest popped open underneath. "I knew it would recline. If my uncle Bob could see this he'd die. I don't think he realizes his La-Z-Boy is actually a low-end model."

Max grumbled something indistinct.

Lolling back, she propped her head on her folded arms and stared at the screen. The chair was big enough to accommodate two people, but no way would she imagine him sprawled next to her, feeling her up as they watched a film. "This room is bigger than some movie theaters I've been to. I didn't picture you as the type to like movies. What do you watch?"

She listened to the rapid tap of his fingers against what she supposed was a keyboard. She wasn't sure why, but she hadn't associated him with being computer savvy. Maybe it was his caveman-esque demeanor. "I bet you watch classic Chinese movies with lots of action and fighting."

When he didn't reply, she flopped onto her stomach and watched him over the top of the chair. He was entirely focused on whatever he was doing at the computer. His brow furrowed and his eyes looked all intense, and she was overcome with the most inappropriate desire to kiss him on the forehead. "And romance," she added. "I bet you like your action tempered with a touch of love."

Scowling, he looked up. "Are you done?"

"I'm just waiting to see why you interrupted the work you're paying me to do."

Adorably irritated, he motioned her over.

Carrie rolled off the recliner and headed to him, drawn by his magnetism. Knowing it wasn't a good idea to get too close—harder to keep her hands from trailing over his impressive shoulders—she stopped just short of the desk. "What are you doing?"

He pressed a button and she heard a dial tone. Something clicked, and she heard a tinny voice call through the computer speakers. "I'm here," said a voice that sounded an awful lot like—

"Mom?" she exclaimed, rushing close and trying to edge in front of Max.

"Wait," he said in his usual commanding way. He pushed a few keys and suddenly her mom's face lit up the huge screen. "Are you still there, Irene?"

"Yes, thank you, Max."

Carrie frowned at him. "Since when do you two know each other?"

He, of course, didn't answer her. He stood up and gently pushed her into the plush leather seat he just vacated. The heat of him still lingered there, and she couldn't help burrowing into it.

Gruffly, he pointed at a small camera on the desk. "Stay in view or your mother can't see you." Obviously disgruntled, he cursed, raked his hair back, and stalked out of the room.

She stared after him. What was going on?

"Honey, you're gaping."

Shaking her head, she returned her attention to the big screen. Surreal seeing her mom larger than life. And amazing. "I can't believe this. How is this possible? Did you buy a webcam specially?"

"Max set it up. He had a webcam delivered and installed this morning, and then the nice delivery boy walked me through using it. Isn't it neat?" Her mom laughed.

The familiar sight and sound of that laughter untwisted a knot Carrie hadn't realized she'd had. "Yeah, it's neat."

"You're thinking, sweetheart. What's wrong?"

"I just don't understand why he'd bother doing such a thing."

"Don't you?" Her mom's eyes twinkled.

"It's not like that, Mom."

"He's a fine specimen of a man." Her mom leaned closer to the camera and whispered. "If I were a few years younger, I might be tempted—"

"*Mom*." She glanced to make sure Max wasn't lurking in the doorway. "I work for him."

"Men like that always fall for their assistants."

She wasn't his assistant—Francesca was. And the woman already had feelings for him.

"How do you explain the webcam? He wouldn't have gone through the trouble so we could talk face-to-face if he wasn't interested in you. Think about it, honey. He's a wealthy man. Why would he bother unless he cares?"

Exactly. "Maybe he has ulterior motives. What if he's just doing this to get my body?"

"All the better." Her mom nodded. "I'll send you a sampling of my favorite little toys and a box of condoms."

"No toys, Mom," she said quickly. That was all she needed—for him to discover her importing sex toys into his home. She shuddered, thinking of Francesca sorting the mail.

"You're so repressed, honey. I can't believe you're a product of my loins." She held a hand out. "I know. I'll drop this now. Tell me how you are. Are you eating enough? You look skinny."

Carrie smiled. "I'm not skinny, and I'm eating like a horse. Max's chef makes these apple pastry things that melt like heaven in your mouth."

Her mom's eyes lit. "Tell me more about *Max*."

Crap. "No."

"He looks like a strapping lad. Certainly not the decrepit old man you led me to picture." Her mom leaned close again. "Is the camera lying?"

No, the camera wasn't lying. But she also wasn't going to tell her mom that she'd gotten intimate with Max's muscles forty-eight hours ago. The woman didn't need that kind of encouragement. "How's work? Any interesting new patients come into your clinic?"

"You can't distract me. You know I have the tenacity of a bulldog."

"I'm making great progress on my paper. I think I might pull it together yet."

Her mom leaned in. "Have you kissed Max yet?"

"*Mom.*"

She shrugged. "You've been there for how long, alone with a red-blooded man, and you haven't kissed him? Are you sure you aren't lesbian?"

"We haven't been alone." Except for Saturday. And that time he'd unwound her from Francesca's silk. And when he was on the beach with his sword. Oh—and the first night, in the kitchen, when she'd flashed him her panties. She rushed on before her mom tricked her into admitting any of it. "The man is my boss. Kissing is sexual harassment."

"Only if he protests." Her mom frowned. "*He's* not gay, is he? He didn't look gay."

Max wasn't gay. At all. But if she said that, her mom would want to know how she knew for sure. So she just said, "I don't think he's gay, but he did wear a pink polo shirt."

"*Oh.*"

Carrie bit her lip to keep from grinning. "I'm so happy I got to see you like this. I've missed you."

"I know, honey, I've missed you, too." She reached out to the screen. "I'm so proud of you and the way you're going after what you want. Just don't forget to have fun along the way, or else it's not worth it."

"I won't, Mom."

"Also, don't forget to use a condom when you get it on with Max."

She rolled her eyes. The woman never gave up.

"I love you, honey." Her mom waved, and then the screen went blank.

Carrie sat back in the chair and stared at the blank screen. She had fun. She did.

Fine—she had less fun lately. But life was like that. Sometimes it was great, and sometimes it wasn't. She'd been focused on her career, and it wasn't like she'd met anyone worth the trouble of dating.

She thought about Max and the way his muscles rippled under her hands.

Maybe she could make an exception. She let her head fall back and imagined what it'd be like to date him. She'd shower him with affection, and he'd grunt at her.

Okay, she was being unfair. He *had* done this really great thing for her after she told him how much she missed her mom.

What did it mean? All his motives were unclear. Was he after the documents, or did he really want her?

The first option chilled her. The second thrilled her more than she wanted to admit.

Chapter Twenty

Working the rest of the day was impossible. Carrie couldn't concentrate with Max's sweet but perplexing gesture hanging out there like a white elephant. When she started drawing hearts all over her notes, she knew it was time for a break.

Recognizing she needed space to think, she decided to take the Maserati Francesca said she could use for a drive. Getting the keys from Max's butler, Don, she climbed behind the wheel and inspected the controls.

"No big deal," she reassured herself. Even though she hadn't driven a car since she left Iowa. And even though this car cost more than she made in a year.

But the Maserati was the least expensive of the bunch. She'd checked. Don had blinked at her in confusion when she asked if there was a Civic or something she could take out instead.

"I'll be careful." She turned it on, listened to the engine roar to life, and put it in reverse to back out of the garage.

She wound through the twisty road that led from Max's

house, driving ten miles below the speed limit. Ignoring the occasional car that zipped around her on the two-lane road, she managed to get herself down the hill.

The pier incident fresh in her mind, she checked the rearview mirror constantly as she toured down Highway 1. It didn't seem like anyone was tailing her, but just in case, she parked next to a busy fish-and-chips place close to the Santa Monica Pier. The more people, the safer she'd be.

Looking around as she walked on the warm sand, Carrie wondered how safe she really was. Even with her vigilance, she still had that queasy feeling of being watched. She looked around. Lots of people riding bikes and rollerblading. No one stood out.

"You're being paranoid," she told herself. It was probably only someone wondering what such a pale, bookish-looking woman was doing among the chic, sexy Santa Monica crowd. Besides, as long as she had the scroll and journal, no one would seriously hurt her.

In theory.

The more pressing issue at the moment was Max. Carrie strolled for a while until she found a quiet bench to sit on. She watched the waves, which looked deceptively gentle. Underneath she knew the tide was fierce.

Like Max? She wrinkled her nose. He just didn't seem like the sneaky sort—stepping in and taking what he wanted was much more his style. He would have been more upfront if that was what he was after.

Well, she'd know soon enough. She'd left all the documents in plain sight on her bed, along with a note informing him she was going out for a bit.

But if he really did want her... Well, that was trickier.

She didn't want to end up like her mom.

She winced. Not that her mom wasn't great. Her mom was fantastic—the best mom ever. She was so lucky to have her.

But her mom gave up everything—being top of her class at Johns Hopkins and a brilliant medical career—for a man. She met Steve Woods, got married, and moved to Iowa.

Carrie kicked at the sand. Her mom gave all that up for a husband who, in the end, didn't stick around. And then Irene had her, which meant returning to school was impossible.

Now her mom was an acupuncturist. A great acupuncturist, but that seemed like such a poor compromise.

Max was the kind of guy who'd seriously interfere with your life. Look at her—Carrie was already having trouble keeping her nose to the grindstone, and they hadn't done anything more than kiss.

When she'd left Iowa, she'd sworn she'd be someone. She didn't want to fade into anonymity. Her work was who she was, and she didn't want to lose that.

She needed a voice of reason. Someone who was more cautious than her mom. Someone like Gabe. She shifted and pulled out her phone.

Gabe answered on the second ring, sounds of the bar prominent in the background. "Where the hell have you been, stranger? I've been worried about you."

"If you've had time to worry about me, Rhys isn't doing his job right."

Gabe's sigh gusted over the line. "He had to go out of town on business. But forget Rhys. Tell me what's going on with you. How's Santa Monica?"

Biting her lip, she tried to pin the right word. She finally settled on, "Confusing."

"Work is confusing?"

"No, my boss is confusing."

"The Chinese guy? Are you having a hard time understanding him? I thought your Chinese was pretty good."

"My Chinese is really good, but my boss isn't Chinese."

Gabe paused. "Wasn't his name Boo Hoo or something?"

"Bái Hǔ," she corrected. She wondered how Max would take it if Gabe called him Boo Hoo to his face. "That's his name, but he's not actually Chinese."

"What is he, then?"

"Hot," she said without thought.

Gabe laughed.

"It's not a laughing matter. He's hot, and I haven't, you know, *dated* anyone in forever."

"Are you interested in *dating* him?"

She thought about the way his hands molded to her in the pool and sighed. "Would dating involve wild monkey sex, do you think?"

Gabe laughed again. "I think it might in this case."

"Crap. I'm screwed, aren't I?"

"Not yet, unless you're omitting pertinent facts."

"Well…" She bit her lip.

"No freaking way. Hold on." There was some rustling, some mumbled words, and then silence in the background. "Okay, I'm in the office where it's private. Tell me."

"You left the bar unmanned? Or is Vivian working with you?"

"Vivian," she said with distaste.

Carrie laughed.

"Sure, laugh it up," Gabe said with exaggerated bitterness. "You've abandoned me to deal with the witch on my own, and she's been especially insufferable since you've been gone."

"I'm surprised you haven't put her in her place."

"I'm turning over a new leaf."

"I recognize that tone of voice. Just promise you won't do something where she can't work. She's covering a lot of my shifts while I'm gone."

"Forget Vivian. Tell me about Boo Hoo."

"His name is Max."

"And you like him."

"What do you mean?"

"Oh, come on. Don't try that with me. I can tell you're totally into him by the tone of your voice. You talk about hot guys pretty often, but your voice doesn't go all soft and melty."

"Did I go soft and melty?"

"Like Velveeta over an open flame."

She sighed. "He's all cold, but then he's all *hot*. I don't see him for days, then suddenly he's all over me. And *then* he does something like arrange a video phone call with my mom. He had the webcam equipment shipped to my mom's house and had it installed and everything."

"Whoa. He wants to do you," Gabe said with an air of authority.

"No, he doesn't." Carrie frowned. "Does he?"

"Hell, yeah, he does. No man goes through that kind of trouble for a woman unless he wants into her panties."

"Charming."

"Just stating it like it is." Gabe's shrug was evident over the phone line. "Have you sampled the goods?"

"What constitutes sampling the goods?"

Gabe's laugh tinkled loud and delighted. "Babe, you're a goner."

"I know." Groaning, she dropped her head into her hand. "I keep remembering how he felt when he kissed me in the hot tub—"

"The hot tub?" Gabe interjected. "You hung out with him in a hot tub?"

"We weren't naked." Though they might as well have been, for all the good wet cotton did.

"But he kissed you?"

"Um, yeah. Among other things."

Gabe gasped. "No. You? Little miss goody-goody from Iowa?"

"I know! Can you believe it?" She shook her head. "I don't know what came over me. One minute it was all innocent, and then he was slinking toward me with that look in his eyes and I was hit by some weird compulsion that I couldn't resist."

"Any other weird compulsions you need to confess?"

She remembered how his erection pressed against her, and her cheeks flushed. "I plead the fifth."

"Oh, boy." Gabe laughed. "I can't wait for the next installment of *The Young and the Horny*. Will Carrie get freaky with her boss, or will she continue to long for him in silence?"

"That's the thing. He's my boss."

"Only for a couple more weeks."

"Thirteen days. And he's one of the most prominent collectors of Chinese artifacts in the world. What if word gets out that I slept with him? I'll lose credibility."

"I see your dilemma. Would he kiss and tell?"

"Max?" She snorted. "He's a man of few words."

"There you go."

"What if he gets in the way of my plans? I'm so close to achieving all the goals I set for myself."

"You're thinking too much, babe. This is just about fun, right? It doesn't have to be complicated."

"Hmm." If *complicated* didn't describe Max, Carrie didn't know what did.

"And I vote for fun. How long has it been since you've had sex?"

"I think my hymen's grown back."

"Weren't you the one who told me I should seize the day and have as much fun with Rhys as my body could stand?"

"Yeah, but you were in love with him. You just wouldn't admit it." She didn't know how she felt about Max. Not that it mattered. This was probably a moot point. "My mom offered to send me sex toys to use with him."

Gabe guffawed. "I have got to meet your mom."

"And have you guys gang up on me? I don't think so." She sighed. "I miss you."

"I miss you, too. But you'll be back soon, and we'll have tea, and you can tell me how great he was in bed."

She laughed.

"Love you, babe." Gabe paused. "If you want this, you should go for it. I don't know anyone who deserves happiness more than you, even if it's only for a short time."

Carrie hung up, not sure she believed happiness was what Max wanted to offer her.

Her phone rang again. She pressed talk. "Hel—"

"The pier was just a warning," the electronic voice hissed.

The line went dead.

Carrie blinked, holding her phone away from her. Cold dread filled her, but then a crazy rage thawed her. If she got her hand on whoever was terrorizing her, she'd teach them that she was no pushover. She may not have the moves Gabe or Max had, but she could hold her own.

She stood up, hands fisted at her sides, and searched the crowds. He was here—she just knew it. She narrowed her eyes, daring the jerk to come out and face her.

No one rose to her challenge, and slowly the fight drained from her, leaving her feeling vulnerable. Dusk approached, the sun already beyond the horizon, and the dim light cast an eerie shadow on the beach. The lapping of the ocean, which had been so comforting before, began to sound menacing. As if it warned her to move.

"You're just overreacting," she muttered to herself, but she snatched up her bag, slung it over her shoulder, and strode quickly toward the car. The sooner she got back to Max, the safer she'd be.

Ironic, given he was pretty dangerous himself.

The parking in front of the fish shack was dim, but the lot was reassuringly full even if there was no one in sight.

It was okay. She was overreacting. The car was right there—a hundred yards away—and soon she'd be inside it, locked securely and on her way home.

Keys in hand, she strode toward it. Thirty feet. Fifteen. Five. She could hear her tense breathing in the unnatural stillness. She fought to find some of the peace she'd felt earlier, sitting on the edge of the surf, but it wasn't working. The only thing in her head was the dead electronic voice telling her time was up.

Here. She sighed in relief as she clicked the car door open. She put her hand on the latch and pulled—

Someone pushed her from behind and her forehead hit the side of the car. She felt a tug on her messenger bag and then lightness where it'd hung heavy across her body.

Shaking her head to clear it, she reached out for it, turning around in time to see her assailant run off, her bag clutched in his hands.

Fury coursed through her, and she let out a scream that would make her Celtic ancestors proud.

An answering yell sounded behind her.

She whirled, seeing two guys running toward her. She palmed the house key, ready to defend herself.

But they ran past her, chasing the mugger. Knowing her bag was lost, she exhaled and leaned against the car to regroup. Thank God the scroll was safely tucked under her bed.

The two guys returned a few minutes later, panting.

"That was crazy, man," one said after he recovered. "You okay? That kind of shit shouldn't happen here. This is freaking Santa Monica. The worst thing that happens here is paparazzi."

His friend shook his head. "Dude, you should totally, like, report this to the authorities."

"Not that it'll happen again," the first guy interjected. "What would be the chances of that?"

Menacing phone calls, a sabotaged pier, and now a mugging? She wasn't going to answer that. "Thanks for the assist, guys."

"You okay to drive?"

"Yeah." She smiled as reassuringly as she could. "I had my phone in my pocket, so I'll call for help if anything happens."

Her heroes waited until she was securely in the car.

She waved to them as she rushed back to Max's, impatient to get to her room. Although she already had a feeling she knew what she'd find.

Sure enough, there on her bed lay all the documents she'd borrowed from the monastery.

She plopped on her bed, relieved and worried at the same time. It meant Max wasn't behind the attacks.

Except then, who was?

Chapter Twenty-one

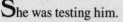

She was testing him.

Max stared at the library door, arms crossed. What other purpose could she have had for leaving the Book of Water in plain sight and sending him a note?

He, of course, hadn't taken the bait. He wasn't ready for the game to end. He wished he could believe it was because he hadn't gotten what he needed to bring down Rhys, but that wasn't what he wanted from her.

On cue, he remembered the feel of her legs wrapped around him and the touch of her lips.

Damn it. He glared at the door. He couldn't even claim setting up the videophone was to get Carrie to let her guard down with him. Sure, that was his original excuse, but he'd been lying to himself. He knew it for sure when she gave him that adoring look as he left. His damn heart expanded in his chest.

Worse—he was *worried* about her. He couldn't shake the feeling that Carrie was in trouble and that she was hiding more than the scroll.

It infuriated him. It infuriated him more that he wanted her confidence.

What the hell was that about?

Ridiculous, the way he hovered outside his own library. Gritting his teeth, he shoved the door open.

She jumped at the intrusion, quickly lowering her head and going back to work. But not before he saw the fear in her eyes and the bruise on her forehead. "What happened to your head?"

"I bumped it." She angled herself away, giving him a view of her creamy nape and bound hair.

She was lying. Why would she lie about hitting her head? He frowned, torn between wanting to know what she wasn't telling him and kissing his way down her neck.

"Are you going to say anything, or are you just going to stare at me?" she said without glancing up.

He had the frightening thought he could have stared at her for the rest of his life. He looked around. "Where's Francesca?"

Her sinful lips twitched as she continued to type into her computer. "Why? Are you checking to make sure she's still keeping an eye on me?"

"What do you mean?"

With a sigh she dropped her pencil and whirled the chair around to face him, arms crossing in an imitation of him. "We need to get something straight. You aren't going to intimidate me, so you might as well give it up."

Her arms pushed her breasts up like an offering. As he wondered if she wore black lace under her tattered sweatshirt, he conceded that Sun Chi had been right. Inviting her into his home was his downfall. "I'm not trying to intimidate you."

She snorted. "You live to intimidate people. But that's not what I want to talk about. I want to talk about what happened. Why did you do it? I'd expect it of someone, say, nicer. But I didn't pin you as the thoughtful type. Especially not the thoughtful type who'd go to the trouble of having equipment sent to my mom so I could see her when I talked to her."

"You don't think I'm nice."

"*Nice* is not an adjective that comes to mind when I think of you, no."

"What comes to mind?" he asked despite himself.

Her knowing gaze seemed to peel away layers that hadn't been disturbed in years. "Overbearing, arrogant, and stubborn. Off the top of my head."

"I'd hate to see what you came up with if you had time to think."

She shrugged. "You asked. So why'd you do it?"

He'd been asking himself the same question. "Did you enjoy speaking with your mom?"

"You know I loved it. You're evading the question." She frowned. "You're probably going to avoid my next question, too."

"Which is?"

"Why'd you jump in? You didn't have to."

He didn't have to ask to know that she meant in the Jacuzzi. "You need to ask?"

"I think I do," she replied, her expression serious.

And he needed to ask about the scroll, why she took it, what Rhys meant to her, and who would want to hurt her enough to sabotage the pier. But with her staring at him so intently, her lips within reach, her body's scent warping his senses, he couldn't think of anything but pinning her to the floor and running his mouth over every creamy inch of her.

She stood up and took a step forward.

Prey—that was what he felt like. A unique experience, since he'd always been the hunter.

Reaching out, she cupped his cheek, her guileless eyes unwavering. "Is it that difficult to just say it?"

He held himself still, waiting to see what she would do. He told himself it was to extract information from her, but staring into her eyes he wondered how long he could continue to deceive himself. To hell with Rhys, the scroll, and everything else—he wanted this. She made him feel unbalanced and confused, and he still gravitated toward her like she was his personal lodestone.

"I can't decide if this is the best idea I've ever had or the biggest mistake," she said, stepping close.

Her innocent scent wrapped around him, and the tension in his body melted. His chi woke, recognizing her. Her body brushed his, and his cock, already alert, went on the offensive.

Carrie felt it, too. Her gaze flickered down. Her eyes widened when they reached his crotch. He thought she'd retreat but instead she lifted her chin with new resolve and stood on her tiptoes.

He looked down at her, the dewy pursing of her lips. He wanted to push her against the wall and have her. He wanted to wrap her in his arms and protect her.

"See?" she whispered.

"See what?"

She glanced at his mouth. "You didn't combust."

Not yet, but he was close.

As if she couldn't help herself, she touched her lips to

his once—twice. She swayed against him, and a bolt of desire shot through his body.

His hand gripped her arms, holding her away yet holding her close. Trying to regain his equilibrium. "I haven't combusted *yet*."

"Is it a threat?"

"Could be," he said, his voice hoarse with needing her.

"Hmm." She lifted her hands, slowly—deliberately—unbuttoning his shirt until it hung open. Her hands stroked inside, around his shoulder, and smoothed over his mark.

A wave of heat crashed over him, rolling heavy through his body. Before he could adjust, she pulled his head down to mash his lips to hers.

This time the kiss was anything but chaste. Wholly unexpected in its unpracticed enthusiasm. Oddly right. Which scared him as much as it excited him.

It made him want more.

Snaking his hand into her gathered hair, he tipped her head for a better angle and showed her how much. He almost wished he would scare her with his need—a last measure of self-preservation. But, moaning softly, she melted against him and he was lost.

He walked her backward until he felt the edge of the desk. He lifted her on top, his mouth never leaving hers, but as he followed her down he kicked something under the desk.

They both looked down.

A FedEx box. He frowned, not aware that anything had been delivered.

She pulled at him. "Come back here."

Something in her tone made him pause. She was trying to distract him. He shifted off her, studying the box. "What is that?"

"Nothing," she said too quickly, blushing.

"If it's nothing, why are you acting guilty?"

"I'm not acting guilty." She propped herself up on her elbows. "It's just a private thing."

"A private thing?" From Rhys? Max wanted to shake her. Couldn't she see her trust in Rhys was misplaced? He'd bet his inheritance—his Guardianship—that Rhys was responsible for the pier.

The library door swung open. "There's an incoming call from—" Francesca pulled up short, a brief flash of emotion on her face before it went carefully blank.

Carrie gave a small yelp and scooted farther away from Max, which irritated the hell out of him. He glared at her as she straightened her clothes.

Francesca cleared her throat. "Sir? It's long distance."

Damn it. He wasn't done here. But he followed Francesca out, unsatisfied in more ways than he could count.

Carrie paced back and forth in her room, biting her lip as she kept an eye on the door, remembering earlier in the library and how Max had kissed her like he couldn't get enough of her.

Cautious hope bloomed in her chest. Maybe this *was* about her and not the texts.

Maybe he'd come up.

Talk about delusional. He wasn't coming up. He was busy with Francesca now.

She grabbed a pillow off the bed and threw it. Then she kicked it for good measure.

"Just as well. Probably," she told herself, returning it to its place. So much for the condoms. She glanced at the bedside table, where she'd stashed them away.

Although—God—she would have liked to have him make love to her. Just once. It seemed like the type of memory you'd pull out years later and sigh over.

"Face it." She punched the pillow. "Not going to happen."

Sigh.

Glancing at the door one last time, she headed for the bathroom. A bath would settle her.

Pulling off her sweatshirt, she tossed it aside as she entered the bathroom. She turned on the faucets to the tub, tossed in some bath salts she found in a cabinet, and stripped the rest of her clothes off. While she waited for the bath to fill, she studied herself in the mirror.

God, she was a mess. The bruise on her forehead was a putrid shade of green. Her hands were completely healed—maybe Max used some special ointment?—but she still felt the occasional twinge in her back and arms. The scratches on her side were faded to thin pink lines crusty with scabs.

She ran a finger over them, and then up to the tip of her breast. Turning to the tub, she ran her fingers back and forth over the hard tips. She watched the water and imagined it running over her as Max touched her, and she shivered.

In. She needed to be in the water, so she climbed into the bathtub.

The hot water eagerly welcomed her. As she sank in, she had the impression of being embraced—the embrace of a seductive lover.

Carrie sighed and settled back, her eyes closed and her arms propped on the edge of the porcelain. The water engulfed her, caressing every inch of her skin. It invaded her, filled her. She could feel its touch all over her, and she stretched out to luxuriate in it.

The motion caused the water to ripple over her, lapping at her body. The water seemed to penetrate her. She could feel it from the inside, where Max had never touched her. Letting her legs fall open, she moaned and slid deeper into the tub.

"Delicious." She closed her eyes on a sigh and let her arousal grow. Only soon it wasn't enough. Because she couldn't help it, she rolled a nipple between her fingertips. She trailed her other hand into the water, across her thigh, and over her rigid clit.

Her back arched at the first touch, and she bit her lip to keep from crying out. The second touch was no less intense. She dragged her finger slowly the third time, acutely aware of the water caressing her, too.

If only it were Max instead of water. She pictured him watching her touch herself, leaning down to lick the same trail her finger was taking. She gasped, surprised at how turned on the thought made her. Surprised at how vividly she could imagine him being there. In her mind she could see his molten eyes trained on her as he urged her with his touch to come.

She wanted to come. Bad. She rubbed faster, her hips thrust upward, imagining she was offering herself to him—needing to offer herself to him. Her breasts broke above the water, and the cascading drops teased her like trailing fingers on her skin. The cold air stiffened her nipples, making them ache sharply, so she pinched one with her free hand, knowing Max would do the same to her.

"Max." She moaned, feeling her orgasm rising, a

distant tide rushing toward her. It broke over her and she cried out.

Wave after wave hit her until she didn't have the energy to keep going. She wilted in the tub, limp with release but oddly not satisfied even though she couldn't remember ever coming that hard for so long—even with a guy.

It would be different with Max.

Shaking her head, she let it rest against the tub, her eyes still closed to savor the lingering tingles. She had to give up on that fantasy. It was a no-win situation for both of them.

Something rustled near the bathroom door.

Her eyes popped open, her breath catching in her throat. It took her several tries before she could speak, and even then she couldn't croak anything more than, *"Max?"*

Chapter Twenty-two

He looked like a Viking god come down, bent on conquering, and—heaven help her—Carrie was totally willing to let him start with her.

If only she weren't so mortified. She sank lower into the tub, wishing she'd had bubble bath instead of salts—the better to cover her nudity.

How long had he been there? Did he hear her call his name when she came? Her cheeks burned at the thought. She glanced at him to see how he was reacting to this. If she saw revulsion—or a total lack of interest—she was going to drown herself right there.

Wide and muscular, he filled the doorway. Not able to help herself, she looked down his body, noting that he still hadn't buttoned his shirt from their earlier escapade in the library. She saw the ripple of his pecs, the ridges of his abs, and—

Oh, God—he was turned on. Big-time, *big* being the operative word there. Her mortification melted away and her eyes latched on to his erection, not able to look away.

If only he'd come closer so she could get a better look. And perhaps—maybe—a taste.

He shifted, and her eyes lifted to his face. She inhaled at the combination of desire, need, and intense focus she saw there. He wanted her—it was written on every bit of his face.

Tensing, she wished she could have channeled an inner vixen and let herself tease him by opening her legs and asking him if he liked what he saw. But the stakes were too high.

He stepped forward, his eyes roving over her. Intense.

She shivered, wanting all his intensity focused on her.

He took another step, and another, until he towered over her at the side of the bath. "I shouldn't be here."

Swallowing thickly, she nodded. Couldn't argue with that. This was totally unprofessional, and if it got back to someone in the department she'd be branded with a scarlet letter for life.

But she heard her mom tell her she had to let herself have fun sometimes. And Gabe telling her to go for it. Her eyes searched his, and she knew this was inevitable.

She stood up. Water sluiced over her skin, a thousand little touches that inflamed her all over again.

His gaze flickered down. She swore she could feel it like a physical touch on her skin, over her nipples, down her belly, and between her legs. Especially between her legs. Swallowing thickly, again, she widened her stance—just enough to let him know he'd be welcome if he wanted entrance.

His gaze shot back up to hers, and before she could say anything, he scooped her into his arms.

Throwing her arms around his neck, she kissed the side of his neck, right over the burn scar.

He paused to stare down at her, his gaze perplexed. His grip on her tightened, and he strode to her bed and gently lowered her onto the covers.

His eyes never wavered from hers as he stripped his shirt off and dropped it. He undid his belt and whipped it out of the loops, letting it fall next to the shirt.

"Wait a second." She scooted to the drawer, ripped the condom box open, and pulled one out.

On second thought...She took two more. Then she propped herself against the pillows. The better to watch the show. "Okay. You can continue."

His brow lifted in his adorably arrogant way. "Are you certain?"

"Yes." God, yes. Any more certain and she'd combust. "Actually, I'm dying of anticipation. I've been waiting for this, it seems like, forever."

His expression sharpened, and he quickly undid the fly.

Carrie blinked. "No underwear?"

"No."

"Can I touch?" she asked, rolling to her knees.

He dropped his pants.

Guess that meant yes. She ran a finger along all of him. His hard-on pressed straight up against his belly. She brushed along his leg, smiling when he groaned, and wondered what he'd do if she actually touched *him*.

Time to find out. She let her fingers play over his hardness.

His hand clamped down on hers, and she glanced up to find his eyes squeezed tight.

"Do you like it, or are you in total agony?" she asked.

"Both," he said through gritted teeth.

"Oh. That's good, then."

He half groaned, half snorted. "It's too good."

She didn't think there was any such thing. Of course, she hadn't had sex in so long she didn't think she was qualified to make any sort of judgment. She tried to move her hand, but he held it still right there. "What—"

"Wait." He breathed deeply.

Carrie frowned. "Are you trying to get yourself under control?"

"Yes," he hissed. "Hold still."

"I don't want you under control. I want you totally wild and wanting me."

He laughed without humor. "Trust me, I want you."

She stopped struggling to free her hand. "Really?"

"Yes, really."

"Oh." She blinked at the force behind his words. Then she leaned forward and ran her tongue along the top of his erection.

"*Carrie.*" His grip tightened on her hand. "What are you doing?"

"Hopefully making you want me more." Before he could do anything to stop her, she licked the bulbous head like a lollipop.

He made a strangled sound, which she translated as *that was good.* She nuzzled his belly and then kissed her way back to the tip of his hard-on.

As she nibbled and licked and sucked—which he seemed to like, given the way his entire body tensed—she started to get more turned on herself. She felt herself grow warm and wet, imagining him returning the favor. Oh, yeah, she wanted him to return the favor in a desperate way.

"Carrie." He let go of her hand and speared his fingers through her hair.

She paused. That was the first time he'd called her by her name, and the way he said it sounded like an endearment.

Okay, don't get carried away here. Afraid he'd make her stop if she let up, she gripped his butt cheeks—God, they were firm—and tongued all around the head of his penis.

Instead of pulling her away like she thought, he held her closer. A go-ahead if she ever saw one, so she began to place sucking kisses all around.

He groaned, and his hands pulled her hair in a way that would have been painful if she weren't so turned on. She went at it in earnest, licking at his wetness. He was trusting her with his body, and maybe just a little of his soul for a moment in time.

A heady feeling. And humbling.

Suddenly she felt a change—a gathering of energy—and she knew he was close. Power surged through her. A shock wave zapped through her body, head to toe, flushing with heat. It tingled, as if every molecule in her was suddenly alive and radiating.

Looking up, she saw he watched her, his gaze dark and intent. Passionate. His jaw clenched as she took as much of him into her mouth as she could and sucked. She let go and did it over again, and again, and again, until his hips surged forward, seeking her mouth.

He growled, and with a sudden burst he came.

She rode him out, going softer as the waves of his orgasm receded, until his body relaxed.

Well, most of his body. His penis was still half hard.

She lapped at him one more time and then lifted her head. She couldn't stop a grin from stretching her lips. "So I guess you kind of liked that, huh?"

In answer, he flipped her onto her back, covered her

with his body, and ravaged her mouth. His hands seemed to be everywhere at once, and still it wasn't enough. She squirmed to get closer, wanting to feel more of his skin pressed against her.

"Easy," he murmured, nuzzling her neck.

"Yeah, right." She arched her back as he started nibbling his way down her chest. *Oh, yes.* "You can say that. You've already had your pleasure."

He kissed the inner curve of her breast. "I seem to recall you had your pleasure, too."

Her face went up in flames. "You, um, noticed that?"

"Yes." With his tongue, he traced a path around the tip of her breast. "You called my name when you came."

She laughed to cover her embarrassment. "You starred prominently in the fantasy I was having."

He glanced up, and his normally cool eyes blazed with heat. "I want you to tell me your fantasies, and I want to watch you touch yourself while you do it."

Even though her cheeks were still red with self-consciousness, the idea of teasing him by playing with herself made her hot. "Right now?"

"No." He lowered his mouth to lick her nipple. "Another time. Right now it's my turn to taste you."

"Okay." Her body went limp, and a gush of warmth flooded between her legs.

Max sucked her nipple for a second—hard—and then let it pop from his mouth, repeating it on the other side and then back and forth until she writhed on the bed, her legs wrapped around his waist. She wanted more. She *needed* more.

She started rubbing herself against his erection—fully hard again. He felt perfect. But he shifted away from her and began biting his way to her belly. His hands trailed from her hips to her thighs, which he pressed wide open as he settled between them.

She lay open before him, bared and vulnerable. Swallowing, she looked at him, wondering what was going through his mind but afraid if she asked she'd ruin the moment. So instead she said, "Need pointers?"

He cocked his brow. "Do you have much experience with women?"

"Uh, no. None at all." She grinned. "But I'm pretty sure I know what I like."

"Pretty sure?" He leaned down and licked a trail up her inner thigh. "You aren't positive?"

"I don't have all that much practical experience." She sighed and let her leg fall open more. "But that's not too bad."

"Tell me what you know you like."

She hesitated. But she felt Max's breath on her skin and wanted him so badly, she couldn't hold back. "Sometimes I like it slow and soft. So I can barely feel it."

She felt the most delicate stroke—a whisper of a touch that had her straining to feel more. He brushed her again, and when she felt the nibbling of his lips she realized he used his tongue. *Oh, God.* Closing her eyes, she clenched the covers, hoping she wouldn't pass out and miss it all.

"What else?" he asked, his voice hoarse with desire.

"Sometimes I like it hard and fast. To be completely filled." She gasped and arched as his finger slid inside her. His mouth joined in, lapping at her like he couldn't get enough. She cried out, wanting to tell him all the secret little fantasies she'd been having, but her orgasm hovered so close she couldn't find the words.

He removed his finger and went back to the barely there, cotton candy licks. With a low, frustrated moan, she tried to inch closer to him but he held her still.

"More?" he asked with a swipe of his tongue.

"Oh, yes, please."

He slid a finger inside her again fast and hard, making her buck off the mattress. She clamped her hands on his head and said, "I want your mouth on me, too."

"Show me where."

His dark tone made her entire body coil. Or maybe it was the way he was pushing in and out of her, each time hitting that spot inside just perfectly to make her gasp. But she wanted more, and she knew he wouldn't give it to her unless she played along. So she let go of his hair and slipped her hand between her legs.

She watched how he stared at it so intently. First she let her fingers caress his hand, still pumping slowly and deeply. But her orgasm hovered so close, she couldn't hold back. She dragged her index finger through her wetness, right where she wanted his mouth.

"Again," he ordered, watching like a hawk.

"You're so pushy," she replied, but she did it anyway. Not going to cut off her nose to spite her face—not now. She rubbed herself up and down, feeling it build.

His tongue followed her finger, and her eyes flew open wide on a gasp. He did it again—and again—lapping her finger and around it. The incidental glancing caresses drove her insane. Panting, she held his head close even while she continued to rub herself. "Harder."

One finger became two, and the friction was delicious. It felt like he was trying to touch her core—her heart— and combined with the duet of her fingers and his mouth, a massive orgasm rolled over her. Distantly she heard herself cry out.

It seemed to go on forever, but finally the earthquakes settled into minor trembling. She realized she was still gripping him—tight—and she let him go with a small murmur.

His tongue circled her one last slow, shuddering time before he placed a kiss on her hip. "Okay?"

Closing her eyes, she laughed weakly. *Okay* was such an understatement. "Why? Can you do better than that?"

"Perhaps."

She felt him slide up her body and lay next to her. She was so boneless she couldn't move anything more than her fingers, which she rested on his muscular thigh. "I may need to see that. I doubt I'll live through it, but at least I'd die a very happy woman."

Max tucked her so he spooned her back. His hand roamed possessively over her breasts, idly skimming over the tips. "Are you sleepy?"

Stretched languidly into his caress, she felt his erection prod her butt. Only as she shimmied against it, she couldn't repress a yawn. "Not if you want to try making me very happy."

"Sleep now," he whispered into her ear, smoothing her hair back. "I'll make you happy later."

She smiled lazily and cuddled against him. "I must be really sleepy, because I swear I just heard you make a joke."

His arms felt so comforting, she started to drift off. So she wasn't sure if she dreamed it or if he actually murmured, "The only joke here is on me."

Chapter Twenty-three

He was going to hell.

Max looked down at the angel in his arms. Tucking her hair behind her ear, he traced a finger down her soft cheek to that beguiling mouth that had driven him insane.

Correction: he was going to hell after a short detour through heaven.

But what had him reeling was the way he'd almost lost control of *jīn ch'i*. For a moment, it had burst from his body and mingled in her. She'd felt it—he'd seen that in her eyes—even if she didn't know what it was.

He hadn't lost control of *jīn ch'i* ever. Not even when he'd just received his scroll and powers.

The scroll was still under the bed. He could feel its pull through all the layers separating them. Uncomfortable. His birthmark itched at its closeness, and—

Max stilled at a faint noise, turning to look out the windows to the balcony. It seemed to come from outside.

There it was again—a light scrape.

Common sense told him he was overreacting, but

intuition insisted he get up to check. He eased Carrie off his shoulder and padded to the windows. As he reached for the latch, a dark figure vaulted onto the balcony. Max recognized him—the same prowler from last week.

Shock rooted them in place for a second before they both jumped to action. The intruder grabbed the railing and hopped over as Max slid open the glass door.

Picturing the railing twist, he drew his chi and unleashed. With a sharp creak, the metal snapped and cuffed over the intruder's hand.

A masked head popped up and met his gaze over the barrier.

Max felt the anger and determination in the bastard's dark gaze. "Who are you?" he demanded, striding forward.

The prowler growled, teeth glaring white in the darkness, and tugged on his hand.

Max's gaze narrowed, and he focused his chi to tighten the bond. The bastard was going to tell him why he was after Carrie.

But with a low grunt, the intruder yanked his hand from the twisted iron and scrambled back down over the edge.

Damn it. Max hurried to the railing and looked down in time to see the prowler drop the remaining ten feet. Rolling out of the fall, he jumped to his feet and swiftly ran away.

Max gripped the metal, feeling it bend under his rigid hold. He waited until the night—and *jīn ch'i*—calmed again before untwisting the railing to its former shape and slipping back into Carrie's room.

She was still asleep. Blindly, foolishly, trustingly asleep.

He stared down at her. He'd felt her, filled her—tasted her. Her innocence wasn't an act. He didn't know why she took the scroll and the journal, but it wasn't because of any evil intent on her part. There wasn't an evil bone in her body.

It was the only thing he was sure of at the moment.

Rhys had to be the one behind everything. He'd probably misled her, used her, and was now trying to clean up any path leading to him. Would he harm Carrie? Without a doubt. His onetime best friend was ruthless.

The thought of Carrie in danger caused a twinge in his chest. Somehow she'd burrowed past his defenses, and the need to keep her safe felt crucial.

Even if he had to protect her from herself.

Max was going to end this. To hell with revenge on Rhys—to hell with whatever reason Carrie had for stealing the documents in the first place. He wasn't going to stand by and wait for her to get hurt.

He'd take the scrolls and return them.

Carrie mumbled and nestled into him. Her back pressed to his chest, and he slipped his arms around her, inhaling her.

Mine. His fingers glided down her belly, combed into her curls, and hooked at the base of her clit. It firmed under his finger, eager. Whatever her reasons for stealing the scroll, she wanted him as much as he wanted her. Her body didn't—couldn't—lie.

She stirred again, her leg falling open, as if giving him permission. He dragged over her again, slowly and softly.

Her moan fired his blood. She arched back into his hard-on. He hissed at the sharp pleasure. Unable to help himself, he concentrated the rough pad of his finger directly where he knew she liked it most.

Her hips began to roll and thrust. A masculine triumph surged in him, something prehistoric and elemental in a way he'd never felt before.

Her legs shifted, and his erection slipped between them. Her wetness bathed the head of his cock, and he involuntarily surged toward it. He froze when he slipped into her body.

He shut his eyes and tried to get control of himself. She was asleep, and he was acting like a randy teenaged boy copping a clandestine feel. He should pull away. Or wake her up at least, for Christ's sake.

Sighing, Carrie rubbed her ass against him and pressed a hand over his. "What are you waiting for?" she asked in a sleep-husky voice.

Reaching for a condom, he covered himself and pushed into her. All the way.

She gasped, her body tensing. He held her in place, trying to regulate his breathing, trying to keep from thrusting into her until she'd become accustomed to him.

Tight. And hot. Like metal in a flame, he felt her give and mold to him. With a low moan, she curled her fingers over his, urging him to rub her faster.

Rolling on top of her, needing to be closer, he thrust into her as he pinched and plucked at her. She bucked against him, her cries driving him on.

His chi crested inside him, pushing to be let loose. This time, he gave it free rein.

They both gasped as it flowed from him into her. He felt the connection between them—strong and solid, but fluid and hot at the same time.

He could already feel himself on the verge. Knowing

he wasn't going to be able to hold out, he softly bit her neck. "Come."

The pillows muffled her scream, but he heard her clearly. "*Max.*"

Hearing her call his name set him off. With a growl, he pushed into her one more time, trying to get deeper, trying to bury himself in her, as he came.

Both breathing heavily, he rolled to the side, cradling her tightly in his arms. She sighed, a content sound aimed straight at his conflicted heart.

Chapter Twenty-four

Carrie woke up in love.

What else could the warm feeling be that swelled from her heart all the way to the tips of her fingers and toes as she watched Max sleep? She'd never been in love before, so she could be wrong, but she was pretty sure this tingly, apprehensive, bubbly feeling was the real deal.

And no, it wasn't the sex.

She could see how such incredible sex could be mistaken for love. When you connect with someone that deeply, when you give all of yourself like that, you want to believe it's some deep emotion.

But she wasn't mistaking great (really great) sex for emotion. Yeah, she liked myth and story, but she was a realist first and foremost. She'd waited this long to fall in love—she was hardly going to confuse it with a lesser thing.

And she knew the exact moment last night when it hit her that she loved him. He came inside her and something changed. It wasn't just physical anymore—he'd given himself over, and they connected on a completely different level.

Propped on her side, she smiled as she watched him sleep. Careful not to wake him up, she pushed back his hair and brushed a kiss over his scar. He was so gruff, so blunt, but underneath he was a big softie. As desperate as he'd been for her, he'd taken care to make sure she was right there with him, seeped in pleasure and begging.

She loved him.

Did he love her? Her smile faded a little, but then she shook her head. He wouldn't be able to give himself like that if he didn't feel something. She doubted he'd admit any sort of feelings—he was so skittish—but she knew deep down that he felt something.

The real question was whether he'd go running or if he'd step up and admit he liked her. Although if he did that thing with his tongue and his fingers again, she'd definitely let him off the hook for another day or two. She shifted her legs, wondering if she should wake him up the way he'd woken her up last night.

His eyes popped open.

She tried to read his gaze but it was guarded, just like usual. She would *not* let that get her down. Instead of letting her heart sink, she pictured her love breaking over him, like gentle warm waves, just like how she read in the scroll.

Instead of lightening, his gaze went even colder. Not what she expected at all. But before she could ask what the matter was, he rolled on top of her and kissed her.

She gave a muffled groan and grabbed his butt. "Closer."

Pressing his hardness against her thigh, he nibbled at

her mouth, sucking her lower lip before releasing it to press a kiss to the hollow at the base of her neck.

She arched, sighing. "I could get used to being woken up this way."

He shook his head, his stubble rasping her skin deliciously. "I believe I was the one awakened."

"Semantics." She tugged on his hair, lifting his head so she could see his eyes. She had to know. "Is anything wrong?"

"What could be wrong?"

"Do you regret it?"

He settled over her, nestled between her legs. "Would I be here if I did?"

That wasn't an answer. Call him on it, or not? She was leaving in just over a week. What could she expect from him? What right did she have to expect anything? They'd spent only one night together. For all she knew, this was it.

He stroked down her body, watching his hands mold her.

If this was all she got, then she was going to make it something to remember. She stretched into his hands, speared her fingers through his hair, and kissed him, over and over until they both panted wildly.

Lifting up, he took a condom off the side table, slipped it on, and rolled them over so she sat on top of him. In one smooth move, he was inside her.

Balancing herself with a hand on his chest, she kissed the base of his neck, right over the raised skin of his scar. "I wonder how you got this."

His hands clenched her hips. She didn't think he was going to answer, but then he said, "I was betrayed."

She blinked. No wonder he was so prickly about everything. She wanted to ask who betrayed him and what had happened, but his scar ran more than skin deep, and now wasn't the time to delve into it. Because she couldn't stand the shadows that returned to his eyes, she leaned over him and made love to his mouth.

Just like that, everything went from being pleasurable to being crazy intense. He groaned, and she felt something in him change. Open. She felt a wave of cool strength blow through her, just like the last time they'd had sex.

She smelled a metallic scent and lifted her head to make sure she hadn't bitten him too hard with her teeth in her enthusiasm, but she didn't see any blood. Weird.

He speared his hand in her hair and brought her mouth back to his. His kiss left her dizzy and writhing and moaning. She could feel her orgasm rushing over her, and she cried out, rocking against him.

His head reared back, and she lowered her mouth to his scar, nipping it with her teeth. He roared and his body bucked as he started to climax. She couldn't hold back if she tried—she went headlong into the pleasure with him.

She wilted on top of him, panting. She didn't want to move—she would have given anything to stay here all day with him. But she had work to do, and she didn't know how he'd take the suggestion. She didn't want him to think she was a slacker or using him in any way.

His arms tightened around her. "You're thinking."

She grinned. "You can see the smoke churning from my head, huh?"

"It was fairly obvious," he said mildly.

Turning her head, she kissed his chest before resting her cheek on his heart. "I was just thinking it was going to take a monster breakfast to get me ready to work. Something that involves French toast, eggs, bacon, and maybe even one of those apple pastries your chef keeps supplying me, even though I've told Francesca not to serve them anymore."

He rolled her onto her back. "I was under the impression you liked them."

She wrapped her legs around his to hold him close. "I do. Too much. My butt can't handle that kind of love."

He stared at her, obviously puzzled. "You're worried about gaining weight?"

She rolled her eyes. "What woman isn't? Well, except Francesca, but secretly, I think she's part of the Borg, so she doesn't count."

His hand slipped under her and gripped one of the butt cheeks in question. "You could stand a little more weight. You're tiny."

"Only compared to you." She laughed. "You must like your women rotund."

"Hmm." Burying his head against her neck, he shifted his weight off her, just enough so she didn't smother but so their bodies remained connected.

The mark on the back of his left shoulder caught her eye. How cool to have a broadsword-shaped birthmark. She ran a finger over it, feeling a strange tug in her body. "In high school, I had a friend who had a heart-shaped birthmark. I was so jealous. It was like she was marked by love."

He lifted his head and studied her, a little too fiercely. But then the tension eased from his body, and he reached up to kiss her.

The moment his mouth touched hers, she surrendered herself to it and all other thoughts faded.

Max was breathing heavily again by the time he lifted his head. "I won't let you leave your room if we start again."

His sex-raspy voice made her shiver, and she wanted to ask him if that was a bad thing. "I've got to get to work. My boss is a slave driver."

His eyes narrowed.

She sighed dramatically. "In fact, I wouldn't be surprised if he tied me to my desk."

His big hands glided up her body, down her arms to shackle her wrists behind her. "Something else you like?"

It made her breasts jut out, and she felt his hungry gaze on them. Excitement pooled in her belly, especially as she felt him harden beneath her. She licked her lips. "I don't know. I've never tried."

He rose to lick her lips himself, and with dark passion he said, "Perhaps we should find out."

Chapter Twenty-five

She liked it. A lot.

Carrie grinned as she stretched in bed. She liked it so much she would have liked to do it again. But she had to get to work, so it was just as well that Max left to shower in his room.

She needed to get up and shower, too, but she wanted to revel in the memory of the past twelve hours. And—truthfully—she wasn't ready to wash off the scent and feel of him. She didn't know if she'd ever experience it again.

"No being sad," she ordered herself. Mom always said it was better to have loved and lost than never to have loved at all. Carrie had always scoffed at that, but now she got it. Because if last night was all she'd ever get from Max—well, she'd cherish it forever.

She grabbed her phone and scrolled through her recent calls until she found Gabe's number. Glancing at the bedside clock, she groaned as she saw the time—Gabe would *not* be happy at being awakened so early. She almost disconnected, but the line picked up.

Some rustling and then a disgusted huff. "You realize what time it is?" Gabe said in a sleep-hoarse voice.

She meant to apologize, so she was surprised when she said, "I'm in love" instead.

There was silence and then more rustling. "Okay, I'm up. What did you just say? I swore I heard you say you were in love."

"I am." She curled into the pillow Max used and inhaled his scent. "Max spent the night with me last night."

"And this morning you're in love?" Disbelief colored her every word.

"I know! It's crazy. Who falls in love after one night of incredible, mind-blowing sex?"

"Apparently, you do," Gabe deadpanned.

"And next you're going to ask me if I'm confusing sex and love, and if I'm just blinded by his incredible physique and hot birthmark—"

"Birthmark?"

"—and maybe this is the afterglow of being thoroughly pleasured in more ways than I knew were possible."

"Is it?"

"No." Shaking her head, she rolled onto her back and stared at the ceiling. "I already asked myself that this morning, because who falls in love overnight? Only I don't think it was overnight. I think it accumulated."

"What? Over the week you've known him?"

"Two and a half weeks. God, you're a sarcastic wench in the mornings," Carrie said with a grin. "I bet Rhys loves waking up to that."

"Rhys is long gone before I get out of bed. And we're not talking about me here. We're talking about you." She paused. "Are you sure it's love?"

"Absolutely. Down to the tingles in my fingers and toes."

Gabe sighed. "Okay. I'm happy for you."

"You don't sound happy."

"You can't blame me for being worried. I encouraged you to get freaky with the guy—I didn't mean for you to give him your heart. I feel responsible." She gasped. "Wait a second. Does this mean you're not coming back to me?"

"Of course I'm coming back. My position ends in a little over a week. And I have my career at Cal. I can't just abandon that." She frowned.

"You don't sound sure about that."

"I am." She tried to add extra emphasis, but based on the silence on the other end she didn't succeed. "I can't give up what I've worked so hard for, just for a guy."

"Why do you have to give up anything?"

"He lives in Santa Monica and China."

"If he loves you, maybe he'll move to San Francisco with you."

"I love *him*," Carrie corrected. "He hasn't said anything about love."

Another moment of silence. "I'll kill him."

Carrie laughed. "I love you, you know that, right?"

"Don't think you can distract me, Carrie. I'm serious. If this bastard hurts you, I swear I'll make him regret the day his nuts dropped."

"Duly noted."

"Let me know when I get to break legs," Gabe said through a yawn. "But try not to wake me up next time."

Feeling lighter for chatting, Carrie disconnected and hopped out of bed to the shower. Fifteen minutes later she was clean and dressed and heading down to the library.

There was a distinct frostiness when she walked in—more so than usual. Like every morning, Francesca sat at her usual place. This morning, however, instead of poring over spreadsheets or whatever she usually did, she stared off into space, transferring her chilly gaze to Carrie when she walked in.

Oh, boy. Carrie sighed mentally and pasted a bright smile on her face. "Good morning."

Francesca looked like she wanted to ask what was so good about it, but she just nodded. Briefly. Really it was a jerk of her head more than a nod.

She knew Carrie had slept with Max. Carrie was pretty sure she could bank on that. Francesca ran the household, and someone had to have noticed Max didn't sleep in his room last night and told her. Or maybe someone saw him leave her room, naked, with the only nod to modesty being the clothes he casually carried in front of him.

And given that Francesca had a huge thing for him... Well, the woman had to be hating her now.

Super.

Better to meet this head-on rather than tiptoe around it. Carrie took a deep breath. "I know you're—"

"Don't you think you should get to work?" Francesca arched an eyebrow. "Considering how late you are?"

"That's what I want to talk to you about—"

"I don't believe there's anything to say."

"Yes, there is." She sat down on the loveseat across from her. "I know—"

Francesca visibly bristled, her already ramrod-straight spine becoming even stiffer. "You don't know anything. You think you're so secure in your new *position*"—she spat it like it was a four-letter word—"but he'll get what he wants from you and then you'll be gone."

"I know."

That stalled her. "What?"

Carrie shrugged. "It doesn't take a genius to know that. I wasn't entirely clueless going into this. But this isn't about me."

"It's not?" Francesca asked carefully, suspicion drawing her fine features together.

"Of course not." She leaned forward, willing the other woman to really hear her. "You're beautiful, smart, and have a lot to offer. You have to stop pining away for him and do something that'll make you happy. You've got to let him go."

If she thought Francesca was rigid before, it was nothing compared to how she held herself now. "Are you through?" she asked very precisely.

Carrie slumped in the chair. "I guess I am."

She sat there for several more moments, wondering what her mom would do. Maybe she'd call her later. Maybe she'd talk to Max about his assistant and make him see how cruel he was, fostering her infatuation for him.

On that depressing thought, she got up and went to her corner. Her mind wasn't in her work this morning, though. It wasn't even on her thesis.

One guess what she was thinking about.

Fortunately, Don walked in with the breakfast tray. Francesca acknowledged him with a cool nod before returning to her manic typing. So Carrie made up for her coldness with a bright smile. "Thank you."

Don bowed, a smile lighting his gaze. Then he gestured to the tray. "The master left a note for you."

"Oh." She picked it up and stared at the thick white paper. She waited until he left before she unfolded it. In crisp black letters, it read:

Eat the apple pastry—you can afford it.

Max. She grinned, remembering their workout last night. Picking up the pastry, she took a big bite, closing her eyes and sighing in pleasure.

Indulging helped get her on track with her work. She busted out her laptop and the text before reaching for her dictionary.

Not on the desk. She frowned and looked around for it before she remembered she'd taken it up to her room.

"I'll be right back," she said, getting up.

Francesca looked like she was going to protest, but then a peculiar light dawned in her eyes and she just nodded.

Strange. Carrie shrugged it off and ran up the stairs to her room, throwing the door open. She started when she saw a dark figure by her bed.

The mugger. She reached to throw something at him from the dresser when she saw it was Max.

"Oh, God. You scared me." Putting a hand on her chest, she smiled in relief and closed the door.

He looked delicious in loose cotton pants and a baggy button-down shirt. The open collar revealed his tan skin. His hair was still damp from his shower, and she had the urge to bury her nose in his neck to inhale his fresh scent.

She walked toward him. "What are you doing up here? Hoping for a little midday affection?"

As soon as she said it, she realized he couldn't have known she was coming up. Then she noticed the covers on the bed were flipped up and her suitcase peeked from under the mattress.

The bottom fell out of her stomach as the light went on in her head. "You *are* the one who's been going through my things."

He paused and then nodded.

"The monastery. You remember." She glanced at the luggage. "You know."

He didn't say a word. It didn't escape her notice that he didn't deny anything, either.

All the puzzle pieces fell into place as she stared at his cold face. The job offer, the friendship, the sex—she didn't have to ask to know that it'd all been calculated. She rubbed the spot over her chest where it felt like her heart was shattering into a million pieces.

It took her several tries before she could say, "You knew I had them?"

"Yes."

"Were you the one who made the calls?"

"What calls?" he asked, eyes hardening.

He didn't know about them. She nodded. That was something at least. "Did you set up the pier? The mugging?"

"Mugging?" His gaze shot to her forehead, and he stepped toward her. "Why didn't you tell me you'd been mugged?"

"What difference would it have made? You were only after one thing. You wouldn't care."

"I would. I don't want to see you hurt."

"Too late." Trying to control the rage that surged in her like a vicious whirlpool, she pushed him aside, kneeled on the floor, and yanked the zipper open to her bag.

A cool wave flowed over her when she saw the Book of Water, but the excitement she'd felt before was gone. She'd wanted the thesis so badly, it never occurred to her that she could want anything else like that—least of all a man.

She gathered the scrolls in her arms and tossed them at him. "Take them."

They bounced off his body and hit the floor. He stared at them for a moment before he looked back at her. There was something in his eyes—

No. She wasn't going to be conned into believing him again. Being gullible once was a learning experience. Twice was just plain stupid. She turned her head away, pulling out the journal and shoving it at him so he had to accept it. "You have everything now. Get out."

"Carrie, give me a chance to explain."

She raised her hand. "Let's not do this. I don't need it spelled out for me, and I'm sure you'll be more comfortable if we don't do this. I'll pack my bags and get out of here as soon as possible."

He frowned. "Where are you going?"

Clenching her hands, she willed herself to stay calm. Really, she wanted to hit him until he hurt as much as her heart did. "What does it matter? You have what you want, and I'll be out of your hair."

Still he didn't move.

She snapped. Running forward, she scooped up the scrolls and shoved them into his arms. "Go already! What are you waiting for? Another round in bed? Because I'd sooner cut my heart out and pass it over."

He stared, like he was seeing her for the first time.

She lowered her voice, trying to get a grip. "You know, I was going to return them. I never meant to take them in the first place, it just kind of happened. But I would have handed them over to you if you'd just asked."

Max's brow furrowed. He looked down at the scrolls and then back at her. Something clicked in his head—she could tell by the way his expression cleared.

But she didn't want to know what it was or why. Ordering herself not to cry, she yanked open the dresser drawers and grabbed bundles of clothes to dump into the suitcase. He stayed out of her way, but she could feel his eyes on her the whole time.

Whatever. He could stay and watch. She threw her jeans in, punching them to make them fit. As long as he didn't say anything, because she didn't think she could stand to hear the truth out loud. It was bad enough knowing he'd used her the whole time—that he'd probably planned her seduction from the start—and she fell into it like an eager teenager.

She looked around. Her underwear was left. She scooped it all into her arms, shoved it in the suitcase, and zipped it up. She had soap and a toothbrush in the bathroom, but she couldn't stand being there a second longer. She could just buy new stuff at Walgreen's. It seemed a small enough price to pay, comparatively.

Hefting the luggage, she walked out the door and hurried down the stairs.

Don appeared in the foyer as if by magic. "Can I help you, miss?"

"No. Yes," she amended, setting her bags down. "I'd appreciate it if you could call for a taxi to the airport."

"Of course. Right away." He rushed off, returning a moment later to let her know the cab would arrive shortly.

She was waiting by the door when she remembered her things in the library. She debated leaving them behind—better than facing Francesca—but her laptop was there, as well as her notes. Neither were things she could replace easily.

Leaving her bag there, she strode to the library and pushed open the door. Francesca looked up the moment the door opened.

Carrie went to the desk and quickly gathered her things. "You'll be happy to know I'm leaving."

"Leaving?"

"Oh, come on. You had to be in on it, too. Yeah, that must be why you resented me so much. Not only did you have to deal with him coming on to me, but you had to pretend to like me, didn't you?" The silence was answer enough. She hugged her papers to her chest. "Well, you have him back now. Good luck with that."

Knowing Francesca wouldn't pass up this opportunity to twist the knife in her chest, Carrie hurried out of there. The last thing she needed to see was the cold woman gloating. Cursing not having her messenger bag, she stuffed everything in the suitcase and left the house—and her heart—behind.

Chapter Twenty-six

Max stared down at the text in his hands and then at the rolled parchments on the floor. One of them was the Book of Water—he could feel its pull. He should have been triumphant. His mentor would be appeased, and the world would remain safe.

But the only thought going through his head was that he'd made the biggest mistake of his life, letting her leave.

A noise made him look at the door, hope rising in his chest that Carrie had come back. But only Francesca stood in the doorway.

Her pale eyes took in the scene, and he had the impression she saw more than he'd have liked. He wanted to yell at her to go away, but he had to know. "Is she gone?"

"Yes."

An inexplicable pain stabbed his chest. He kept remembering the shattered look in Carrie's eyes as she shoved the texts at him. A consummate actress would have been able to manufacture that look; but Carrie's body language gave her away. Not even a great actress could fake trembling hands. But then, he'd known she was innocent, hadn't he?

"Sir?" Francesca shifted closer but remained outside the door. "Is there anything I can do?"

He almost laughed at that. He wanted to tell her to bring Carrie back, but he knew she'd never come back. Not if the look in her eyes was any indication. He'd mishandled the situation. He'd completely screwed up.

Becoming aware Francesca waited for a response, Max shook his head. "There's nothing."

She studied him with the all-knowing gaze she'd possessed even as a child. Nodding, she turned to walk away, but then she paused and looked over her shoulder. "If I may say, this is just as well."

He frowned at the unsolicited comment. "Excuse me?"

"She wasn't deserving of you."

Raising his eyebrow, he let cold ire infuse his voice. "I don't believe I requested your opinion."

"No, *sir*"—she inflected just enough condescension that he couldn't miss it—"you didn't. But here it is, nonetheless. Ms. Woods doesn't belong in your world any more than you belonged at the monastery."

It was like déjà vu—Sun Chi's words in a different form. Except she was wrong about Carrie. He remembered the feel of Carrie sleeping in his arms and knew she definitely belonged.

Francesca took a step forward. "You've been acting contrary to yourself. She obviously didn't bring out the best in you. You need more than her."

Anger sparked his chi. "Your professional opinion?"

"No. The opinion of someone who was once your friend." She took a deep breath. "I understand—"

"I don't believe you do." Logically, he couldn't blame her for thinking as she did—not when days ago he would have agreed. But he'd had trouble thinking logically ever since Carrie first batted her big brown eyes at him. "Leave."

Paling, Francesca took a step back. "Sir, I—"

"Now."

She hesitated, swallowing audibly, and then nodded.

He watched her leave, but his mind was on Carrie. He had to fix this with her. After he dealt with the scroll.

Marching to his room, he opened his personal safe and put all the documents inside before calling Sun Chi.

It took several minutes before the monk came to the phone. "Bái Hǔ?"

"I have the Book of Water and the journal, *sifu,* as well as the other texts taken."

"And the woman? Did she read the scroll? The journal?"

"The journal, I don't know. The scroll, yes." Max ran a hand over his neck. "I plan on taking care of her."

"I am happy, Bái Hǔ, that you have accepted your destiny. I feel certain this is the path you must walk. May Guanyin guide your hand," Sun Chi said, ending the call.

He knew what the Keeper expected of him—to silence Carrie.

The phone's casing corrugated under Max's grip, and he tossed it aside. If his mentor knew Max's plans for Carrie, he wouldn't be happy.

But Max knew without a doubt that this was the way. Carrie was his path. He just needed to convince her to let him walk it with her.

Chapter Twenty-seven

When Carrie arrived back in San Francisco, Gabe was waiting for her as she exited airport security. She blinked a couple of times, wondering if she'd willed her friend there.

Gabe beat her to the punch. "I came to pick you up. You sounded so upset when you called, I thought you could use a friend."

She didn't know whether to smile or weep, so she settled on a hug. "You shouldn't have, but I'm glad you did."

"You would have done the same." Gabe patted her shoulder and then pushed her forward. "Come on. Your chariot awaits."

"You don't have a chariot," she pointed out as they went downstairs to the parking elevators. "Did you borrow Rhys's car?"

"No. The wanker bought me wheels. Can you believe it?" Gabe shook her head in disgust, but the look in her eyes was starry infatuation. "And he didn't just buy me any car, he bought me a Lotus. I keep telling him to take it back. I have a bus pass, what do I need a car for?"

Carrie wasn't really up on her car models, but she could have guessed which car belonged to Gabe. It was sleek and sexy, black with shining silver trim. "Your man certainly has good taste."

"That can't be disputed." She bleeped the doors open, took Carrie's bag, and stuck them in the small trunk. "Wait till you see how fast this thing can go."

"Oh, boy. Can't wait."

Gabe flashed her a look as they settled. "I'm going to chalk up the sarcasm to your extremely agitated state and ignore it. Buckle up."

They zoomed through the parking lot, stopping only to pay, and raced up 101 to the city. Carrie sat back and zoned out, letting the purring vibrations of the car lull her. Thankfully, Gabe let her zone out. She wasn't sure she was ready to bare her soul—the hurt was too fresh.

She must have dozed off, because the next thing she knew they were pulling into a parking spot. Small wonder—she'd barely had any sleep last night because of all the—

Don't think about that. She pushed back the memory and focused on the here and now. Which wasn't where she expected. She blinked her eyes. "This isn't the Tenderloin."

"There *is* a distinct lack of crack whores hanging out on the corner, isn't there?" Gabe turned off the car and unsnapped her seat belt. "Come on. Time for therapy."

Therapy? Yawning, she followed Gabe out. They walked for a block before Gabe detoured into a storefront.

Not a storefront, Carrie realized as she obediently

trailed in behind her. A restaurant of sorts, but like out of the Victorian era with its high-backed chairs, mismatched china, and doilies. "Where are we?"

"Lovejoy's." Gabe smiled at the hostess. "We have a reservation for two under Gabe."

The grandmotherly lady smiled in welcome and gestured at a table in the window. "Go ahead and take that one. I'll be right with you."

Carrie sat down and placed the linen napkin in her lap. "What exactly are we doing here?"

"Tea and sympathy," Gabe said as she perused the menu. "I'm exploring my new British side."

"Rhys brought you here?" She looked around, trying to imagine the tall, virile man in this dainty shop. She couldn't picture him here any more than she could picture Max.

Don't think about him.

"Actually, Brian brought me, believe it or not."

"Brian?" Brian, Rhys's majordomo, had been in some kind of special forces. He was scary looking—bald and bulky and tattooed. Carrie was sure he had knives hidden underneath the frilly French maid's apron he always wore.

"He wanted to ask the baker for their scone recipe. He's such a wuss," Gabe said affectionately, setting the menu down. "Shall I order for us?"

"Considering I haven't looked at the menu, sure."

Carrie expected the inquisition to begin as soon as the waitress had taken their order. Surprisingly, Gabe idly chatted about the gallery in New York that was courting her and the new series she'd started painting until they had a pot of tea on the table and their food was delivered.

"Okay," her friend said, pouring tea for her, "you've got tea. My sympathy is a given. Now tell me what happened."

Carrie couldn't help smiling, which was a gift in itself. "I'm not sure there's much to tell. I was a fool who fell for a pretty face."

"Hmm." Eyeing her skeptically, Gabe added a generous spoonful of sugar to her tea and pushed the bowl over. "I think there's more at play than that. Actually, I *know* there's more at play."

"What do you mean?" She stared at the sugar, sighed, and pushed it away. For the sake of her butt, she could take her sympathy bitter.

Gabe shook her head. "You first. I don't want your story colored by what I have to tell you."

"Uh-oh." Carrie cupped her hands around the tea and absorbed the warmth. "That sounds ominous."

"You don't even know."

There was only one thing it could be about. "It has to do with Max, doesn't it?"

Gabe hesitated, then she nodded. "He's not who he appears to be."

Her laugh contained no mirth whatsoever. "That's an understatement if I've ever heard one."

"Okay." She set her cup down with a clatter. "I gave Rhys Max's name so he could do a background check on him—"

Carrie groaned.

"I couldn't help it. I was worried about you." She shrugged. "I didn't count on Rhys knowing who he was."

She stilled. "Rhys knows Max?"

Gabe nodded. "They have history. Bad, World War II

kind of history. They studied, um, kung fu at a monastery together. They became like brothers and stayed close even after they left. Until there was this girl."

Jealousy slithered up her spine. "A girl?"

"Woman. Whatever." Waving her hand dismissively, she picked up a sandwich. "Rhys didn't give me details, but apparently she was seeing Max but came on to Rhys. Max caught them, thought Rhys had betrayed him, and went berserk."

"How awful." But it all clicked into place—the thick wall around him, his isolation, all his distrust. And by stealing, she'd played into that. No wonder he'd done what he'd done. It didn't make it right—he should have been straight with her—but she could understand. A little.

"Rhys thinks Max is using you to get to him." Gabe watched her carefully.

"You can tell Rhys his fears are unfounded."

"But—" Gabe frowned. "When you called sounding so upset I thought you'd found out he'd used you or something."

"He did, just not for the reasons you think."

"Tell me. Start at the beginning."

The beginning was standing outside Gabe's place, listening in on her conversation with Rhys. She couldn't tell her—not unless she wanted to chance losing Gabe's friendship.

So she just said, "He lost something and thought I'd taken it."

"He accused you of stealing from him?" Gabe gawked at her. "What an ignorant bastard. You're the most honest person I know."

She bit her lip, trying to control her blush.

"The bastard," Gabe said again, shaking her head.

Carrie slumped. "That's just it. He's not really a bastard."

"Yeah, he is." She crossed her arms. "You aren't going to become one of those codependent women who keeps going back to a man who's absolute crap for her, are you?"

Carrie frowned, thinking of her mom. "I don't think so."

"Good, because otherwise I'd have to kick your ass." Gabe picked up another sandwich. "So tell me what you mean."

"I'm not excusing him for using me, that was awful." She remembered walking in on him going through her stuff and shuddered. She never wanted to feel like that—like the bottom fell out of her world—ever again.

Was it just that morning? It seemed like so much had happened since. She felt so different somehow.

"But?" Gabe prompted.

She sighed and poured herself some more tea. "But hearing about his past makes me understand why he went about it the way he did."

Her friend watched her thoughtfully as she chewed. When she finished, she asked, "If he came back, would you forgive him?"

"He's not coming back," Carrie said grimly. It was finished. "He found what he wanted. He's probably on a plane back to China by now. I doubt he'll even remember who I am in a few weeks."

"I think you underestimate yourself."

"Yeah, because a corn-fed Iowa girl is so in the same league as a billionaire." Her smile tasted bitter, and she hated feeling that way. She'd give herself today to be sour, and then she was going back to being perky if it killed her.

Gabe watched with her implacable gaze. Then she shrugged and snatched another sandwich off their tower of food. "If he ever shows up, I reserve the right to make my displeasure of how he treated you known. With my fists."

She chuckled. "You're so violent."

"I tell Rhys it's one of my charming traits."

"Does he buy it?"

"Hell, no." She shrugged. "He likes trying to tame me."

"This is like my mom telling me about the vibrator model she enjoys."

Gabe grinned. "Seriously? Which model?"

"Don't know. I tuned out when she mentioned a rotating probe." She made a face. "I don't need details like that. I mean, great that she's dating, but some things I'd rather be blissfully ignorant of."

"What does she say about Max?"

"She doesn't know. I need to call her to let her know I'm back." She sighed, imagining how that conversation would go.

Better than the conversation with Leonora. She groaned and rubbed her eyes. Her advisor was going to be less than thrilled when she found out Carrie lost the source of her findings.

"Come on. You look tired." Gabe tossed her napkin on the table. "Let's get you home."

Gabe insisted on paying and then raced her through the city to the Tenderloin. She pulled over in front of Carrie's apartment building and popped the trunk. "In case you didn't figure it out, I'm not coming up. If I left my car here, it'd be stripped in two seconds flat."

"That's okay." Carrie gave her a hug across the seat. "Thanks for being so great today."

"It's the tea." She patted her shoulder. "Go out there and get your bag before someone nabs it out of the trunk."

"Tell Rhys he has good taste in cars."

Gabe rolled her eyes. "And make his head more swelled than it is? I don't think so."

Laughing, she got out and hauled her bag onto its wheels. Gabe waited until she was in the building, then zipped away. Probably to make sure she wasn't mugged in the five feet from the car to the lobby. The Tenderloin was exciting that way.

By the time she trudged up to the fourth floor, she'd resolved that the next time she traveled she was taking fewer books. She fished her keys out of her bag and reached to unlock the deadbolt.

Except she didn't have to. Her door hung splintered on its hinges, propped open, with crime-scene tape criss-crossed over the doorway.

Carrie stared at the trashed door. Fear chilled her even though she knew whoever had done this had to be long gone. The police had obviously been there and checked everything out.

Frowning, she dragged her bag inside and looked around, her mouth dropping open as she noticed the gutted futon, the ripped-apart books, and torn-up papers. She leaned down to pick up her copy of *Taxation and Governmental Finance in Sixteenth-Century Ming China*. Tears filled her eyes as she stupidly stood there and stared at it.

"Buck up," she told herself. There was nothing that couldn't be fixed or replaced. At least she hadn't been here when it happened.

Taking a deep breath, she called Ross, the building manager, to ask about her door. After a gruff apology for not fixing it sooner, he told her he had a replacement and would be right up to fix it.

As she waited for Ross, all she could do was sit there and stare at the violent chaos around her. She didn't know who'd done this, but they'd done a complete job of it. Nothing had been left unmolested. Even her mugs had been broken. The only saving grace was that her clothes didn't appear ripped up—only thrown around the room.

She'd have to wash everything. Damn it. She hated doing laundry.

Chapter Twenty-eight

Carrie had barely closed (and triple locked) her new front door after Ross left when her cell phone rang. She froze, her breath catching. She pulled out her phone and looked at the caller ID.

Her mom.

Right. She exhaled. Because no one had any reason to terrorize her. Ross told her the break-in had happened a couple weeks ago, right after she left, when she still had the scrolls and journal.

Her relief lasted only a second. If she talked now, her mom would know something was up. If she didn't answer the phone, her mom would worry. And she was just putting off the inevitable.

So she flipped the phone open. "Hey, Mom."

"Honey, are you okay?"

Leave it to her mom to cut to the chase. She swore her mom had some sort of Spidey sense when it came to her. "Why do you bother to ask when you obviously know I'm not?"

"I'm giving you the opportunity to own your issues."

Yeah, but how much of her issues was she willing to own up to right at this moment? She looked around her apartment and decided that not telling her mom about the vandalism was a prudent course of action. No reason to alarm her over something that was a moot point.

Which left her drama with Max. "Well, I got let go from my fellowship and I'm home again."

"What does *let go* mean?" It was clear from her voice that it did not compute. "Max decided he didn't need the work?"

"No, he and I had a disagreement." Sitting on the wooden frame of her futon, she hugged a half-gutted pillow to her chest. "I decided it was best for everyone if I left."

There was a long pause. Finally her mom said, "Honey, did you have sex with him?"

"*Mom.*" She hid her burning face in the pillow for a second.

"After almost thirty years being my daughter, you'd think you'd be used to talking about sex. It's natural, honey. Everyone does it."

"I'm only twenty-eight. And just because everyone does it doesn't meant that I want to think about that. Especially if the *everyone* is my mom."

"We aren't talking about me right now. We're talking about you."

Unfortunately.

"You have to get over this thing you have about intimacy."

"Mom, I don't have any issues regarding intimacy." She thought back to last night and blushed at some of the things she said and did. "None at all."

"Then why did you run?"

Because he'd used her—he'd lied and seduced her to get the documents. Of course, she understood his motivation better now, and she couldn't deny that she'd lied for them, too. But she hadn't set out to purposefully deceive him. And she hadn't ruined him for all other women.

"Carrie? Why did you run?"

She gripped the phone. "I told you, we had a major disagreement about work stuff and it was best for everyone to call it quits."

"You had sex, connected closer than you expected to, got spooked, and ran away before he could hurt you worse," her mom said with all the confidence of Oprah. "Honey, not all men are your father."

That stopped her cold. She hated it when her mom brought him up. "This has nothing to do with him."

"Yes, it does. I know how much you loved your father and how it hurt you when he left."

Carrie clutched the pillow. Of course it hurt—she'd been five. A five-year-old didn't know better.

"I'm not judging him," her mom said. "He obviously wasn't cut out for the responsibility of a wife and child. But you can't judge all men by him. Not all men are going to abandon you like he did."

"Come on, Mom. I don't believe that."

"Don't you?"

"No," she said more hesitantly than she would have liked.

"You didn't run away because you realized you cared too much about your Max?"

Okay, maybe—but she had just cause. "He was never my Max."

"Maybe not, but I had a feeling about him."

"Well, stop having feelings. It's over." Even she heard the sullenness in her tone.

"You're so rigid sometimes. You need to learn to go with the flow. I don't understand how a daughter of mine could be so *repressed*." She said it like it was a curse. "But you know I love you unconditionally, even if you throw away these chances for happiness in pursuit of your career."

Carrie rolled her eyes. "This is the twenty-first century, Mom. Women's careers are important."

"Love is important," her mom replied with fervent belief. "You can have both."

"You didn't." As soon as she said it, she wanted to take it back.

"Is that what this is about?" her mom asked quietly. "You think I made a mistake marrying your father?"

"No, of course not." She just didn't understand how someone could give up her dreams and live an ordinary life the way her mom did. Love led her astray, in Carrie's opinion. "It's just..."

"That I gave up the chance to be a famous doctor just to be an acupuncturist?"

The words hung heavy in the silence. Carrie mentally groaned. "Mom, I didn't mean—"

"I'll have you know that I'm a darned fine healer. I'm still answering my calling, but I enjoy a freedom I wouldn't have had as a doctor." Her mom exhaled deeply and then continued just as passionately. "Honey, life isn't cut-and-dried. Sometimes the road you're on isn't the only one that's right. And certainly no road is worth it without love."

She started to argue that, but then she pictured herself, teaching at Cal, alone except for her research books, and shut her mouth.

"I'm sending you a romance novel I read. Maybe it'll inspire you."

Carrie smiled. "As long as you leave the vibrator out."

"Promise me if your Max comes back to you you'll treat it like a sign and give it a real try. Leave your fears and really give it a go."

"He's not my Max, and he's not coming back."

"Promise," her mom ordered like a drill sergeant.

"I promise," she said with a sigh, only because she was positive he'd already be on a plane bound for China. "Mom, I'm sorry I implied you weren't great."

"I'm not sorry." The sureness in her mom's voice bolstered her. "They were your feelings, and you had the right to express them. They would have festered otherwise."

"I love you, Mom."

"I love you, too, honey. I'll talk to you soon," her mom said before hanging up.

Carrie flipped her phone closed. "That sounded ominous."

She hoped her mom wouldn't be too crushed when Max didn't show up. If he did, it'd be because he decided he needed to off her to keep her quiet.

She snorted and got up. She had to put this place back together. Then she had to figure out how she was going to salvage her thesis.

It took well into the evening to pull her apartment into some semblance of order. By the time she finished, all she wanted was bed, which was fitted with a messily patched futon mattress and clean, just washed sheets.

But first…She pulled her laptop out of her bag. She needed to e-mail Leonora, to let her know she'd returned as well as set up a meeting to let her know that she'd lost her main documentation in linking Yongle to the Scrolls of Destiny.

Reaching into her suitcase, she rifled for her power supply. Her hand brushed something smooth, something that felt remarkably like—

Frowning, she yanked the bag open wider.

Sitting on the bottom right next to a pair of dirty jeans was one innocuous-looking scroll.

Chapter Twenty-nine

Max stood outside Carrie's apartment building, stunned. Horrified. Angry. Slums like this were common all over the world, but he'd never pictured that she'd live in one. Someone all sweetness and light belonged surrounded by lush gardens and chirpy little animals.

Stepping around a man passed out on the street, he went to the door and looked through the directory listing. *C. Woods 413.* He pressed her number into the old intercom.

It took a moment before her voice responded. "Yes?"

"Buzz me up."

Silence.

He knew she recognized his voice, and as soon as he thought it he knew she'd call him arrogant for thinking so. No, without a doubt he knew her dilemma was whether or not to let him back into her life. If she opened the door, it'd be telling.

She had to let him in.

The door buzzed.

Max pushed it open before she changed her mind. The stale stench of urine hit him as soon as he entered the lobby. Jaw clenched, he took the stairs two at a time to the fourth floor.

Her door was ajar, and he was glad to see that she had sense enough to keep the chain hooked. He rapped on the plywood.

Her face popped immediately in the crack. She stared at him for a long, heart-stopping moment. He drank in her beautiful eyes and—God—that lush mouth. The desire to reclaim it overwhelmed him, and he had to clench his hands to keep from shoving his way in and devouring her.

He waited for her to say something. He wasn't sure what he expected. Anger. Coldness. Something, but not the blankness she greeted him with.

She undid the chain and let him in. "Did you come to kill me?"

He recoiled. "Of course not."

"Don't sound so surprised." She shrugged casually, but the way she fingered the edge of her sweater gave away her nervousness. "The most logical reason for you to come here the day after I left is that you realized you need to off me in order to keep the Book of Water a secret."

"Off you?" He shouldn't have been surprised when she stepped back to avoid touching him, but it caused a pang nonetheless. "That's overly mobster, don't you think?"

"Seemed the most logical reason you'd be here." Shrugging again, she closed the door and dead bolted it.

Something in his chest squeezed, watching the slight shake in her hand. "Does it?"

"For all I know, you're the monastery's enforcer. So, yeah. I know about the Book of Water, after all."

"I trust you." He blinked, surprised he said that. More surprised to realize that he meant it.

She shifted uncomfortably and waved to her left. "Have a seat. I was just making myself some tea. Can I get you some?"

He didn't want any damn tea. He wanted her back in his arms. But he nodded politely and, taking off his coat, sat where she indicated.

She disappeared into the nook he supposed was her kitchen, and he took the opportunity to look around. Her apartment was more barren than he'd imagined, and tattered around the edges. He'd expected heaps of stacked books covering every surface, considering the way she'd surrounded herself with them at his house. There were a couple on the table in front of him, but otherwise the space was spartan.

He sat down, staring at the shabby, stitched-together futon like it could tell him what the story was here.

"Here you go. Sorry, my fancy china had a mishap." She thrust a travel mug at him and sat on the other side of the makeshift table. Cradling a plastic cup between her hands, she gazed cautiously at him. "So why are you here?"

"I came for you."

"I thought you said you weren't going to kill me."

"I'd never hurt you." He rubbed a hand over his neck. "I can't believe you'd think that."

She studied him, her gaze strangely guarded. It used to be open. He'd done that to her.

"You want me to finish the translation?" she asked.

"No." He frowned. "Well, yes, if that's what you want. But that's not why I came."

"Maybe you should just come out and say why you're here."

"I want you." When he saw that she waited for more, he punctuated it with, "Period."

He thought he saw relief in her expression, but she lowered her gaze to her cup before he could be sure. When she looked up, there was only determination. "Why?" she demanded. "You want sex?"

"No." He scowled. "Well, yes. But that's not the main reason."

"Then why?" She stood up, her tea sloshing over the side. She hissed, waving her hand. Setting the cup down on the table, she started to pace. "You already said you won't kill me. I can't imagine what other reason you could have."

Panic rose up his throat, such a foreign emotion he almost choked. He could feel himself losing her, but for the first time in his life he couldn't think of how to fix it. He couldn't pull connections, and his powers were useless.

It left truth.

He reached for her burned hand, pressed it between his, and willed the coolness of his metal to soothe her skin. Gazing at her steadily, he urged her to see his honesty. "I regret how I handled you."

She stared at him.

Did she hear him? Was he too late?

But then she exhaled, her shoulders slumping. "I know you do."

He frowned. "You do?"

"You couldn't help yourself."

"I couldn't?" What was this? Reverse psychology?

"Not given your past."

"My past?" he repeated, letting go of her hand.

"With, you know, that woman. And Rhys."

He stiffened. "What do you know about Rhys?"

"Not much, actually. He didn't really pass on much information at all. Except about that woman that set him up." She pursed her lips. "He might have said she was a bitch, but I think I just inferred that on my own."

"You talked with Rhys?" His scar stung, as if his skin was blistering from fire all over again.

"No, I talked to Gabe. Gabe is his girlfriend, remember?" Her brow furrowed, and she placed a hand on his arm. "Are you okay?"

No, he wasn't. Of all the things he'd expected to discuss, Rhys and that night seven years ago wasn't one of them. "I'm fine."

The worried expression on her face didn't dissipate. She gently encouraged him back to the couch, sitting down next to him with her legs curled under her. "Gabe gave me a short synopsis of what happened, and as soon as I heard it I knew you couldn't help distrusting me. You were burned badly."

He ran his hand over the ridges, wanting to laugh at the irony of her words.

Her gaze followed the motion of his hand.

She couldn't know the significance of the scar, but he wanted her to understand. He calmed his energy and said, "When I was seventeen I went to the monastery. One of the monks there had a reputation for knowing the ancient arts, and I wanted to study with him. Rhys had the same idea. We were fast friends. Like brothers."

She nodded but didn't interrupt.

"We lived at the monastery for years before we reen-tered the world. Rhys was always attracted by power. He wanted the affluence I'd always taken for granted. It sometimes came between us." He set the mug down and steepled his hands in front of him. "I knew he'd do what-ever it took to rise to the top, but I never realized how far he'd go."

"How far did he go?" Carrie asked, wide-eyed.

"He used Amanda, the woman you referred to, to try to steal from me. Amanda worked for me as my curator, but we became involved."

Her face paled. "Oh, God."

He nodded, knowing the parallel between her and Amanda wasn't lost on her. "I had something Rhys wanted. He realized Amanda was the way to get it and manipulated her into stealing it from me."

"What—"

He shook his head. He couldn't tell her he was a Guard-ian until he knew where she stood. That would endanger her. "That doesn't matter. What matters is that I caught her and Rhys red-handed, trying to break into my per-sonal safe. Rhys and I fought." He ran a hand over the scar Rhys had left him with. "Amanda got caught in the middle and was wounded. Badly. She died on the way to the hospital."

Carrie gasped.

"Being betrayed by the one person in the world I'd ever trusted, that I loved, cut deep."

"Amanda?" she asked softly.

"Amanda? *No.*" Amanda had just been a pawn. He couldn't even remember what she looked like exactly. "Rhys. He was the brother I'd never had. By virtue of what we were, he understood me better than anyone, and he used that to try to increase his personal power."

"But—" Confusion lined her face. Max knew she was going to defend Rhys's position, just like the Keeper had, and he steeled himself, bothered by it more than he cared to admit.

But she just sat quietly, watching, waiting for him to continue.

"I returned to the monastery. To lick my own wounds." He gazed at her steadily. "Until you came along seven years later."

"And then I stole from you, too. Kind of." She blinked at him, horror lining her features. "Oh, God, I'm so sorry."

"Not just that, but when I discovered you knew Rhys—"

"You assumed I was in cahoots with him," she finished. "In your situation, I would have done the same."

In her place, he doubted he would have been as understanding as she was being now. In fact, her softness and sweetness was the last thing he expected.

But that softness turned stern as she withdrew her hand from him. "That, however, doesn't mean that I'm just going to forgive you for the way you treated me."

"Of course not. Especially after I tell you the next part, but I don't want any further secrets between us."

"Next part?" she asked cautiously.

"I thought you were the key to avenging myself against Rhys."

She nodded sadly, as if it didn't surprise her. But she surprised him by asking, "And what about Francesca?"

He blinked. "Francesca? What about her?"

"Do you have something going on with her?"

"*Francesca?*" He shook his head, completely confused. "She's like a sister to me."

Carrie snorted. "She doesn't think of you as a brother. I'm surprised she didn't throw a party the second I left."

Leaning forward, he gazed straight into her eyes so she could see his sincerity. "I'm not attracted to Francesca in any way."

She glanced at his lips and licked her own. When she spoke, her voice was husky. "She's very beautiful."

"But not my type." He tucked one of her escaped curls behind her ear.

"What's your type?"

"Smart, spirited, soft"—he brushed his fingers down the smooth skin of her cheek—"women from Iowa who speak Chinese and prefer spending their days in dusty libraries rather than salons and designer stores."

She scowled, her lips pouting. "Women?"

"One woman." Unable to resist, he leaned forward and pressed his mouth to hers. His hand went around to the nape of her neck, holding her because he didn't believe she wouldn't move away.

But she didn't try to break his kiss. She also didn't do anything to encourage it. She accepted it, open but with reserve. She did, however, put her hand on his shoulder, her fingers curling around to his back, inches away from his mark.

It tingled, as if it anticipated her touch.

He wanted to crawl over her and make her take him. He wanted to strip her, for her to strip him, and feel their bare skin together. He wanted to feel her surround him— to be engulfed by her love.

Startled, he pulled back. He stared at her, taking in her sinful mouth and her glazed look, and he knew. He wanted her love.

Would she give it?

As if she heard him, she retreated, leaning back against the couch's arm. "It's time for you to go."

He nodded, running a finger along her swollen lower lip. "May I call on you?"

"Can I stop you?"

"No."

She smiled faintly.

He stood and held a hand out for her. She hesitated but accepted his help up, allowing him to hold it until they reached the door.

She withdrew from him and unlocked all the deadbolts.

As if they would keep anyone with malicious intent out. He shook his head. "You shouldn't live here."

After a momentary hesitation, she said, "It's not so bad."

"A man is passed out on the sidewalk, and there was questionable activity down the block."

She shrugged. "The rent is affordable enough that I don't need a roommate. I can put up with the rest."

He started to tell her what he thought about that but stopped when he saw the mulish set to her mouth. Instead he pulled a card out of his pocket. "My number, in case you need me. Use it."

She sighed but took it.

"One more thing." He pulled out the check from his inside jacket pocket and held it out.

"What's this?" she asked as she took that, too.

"Your salary, for the work you did for me."

She just stared at it.

He wanted to kiss her pursed lips, but he knew better than to push her. "Lock up after I leave."

Her frown deepened. "Of course."

Not really feeling reassured, he inclined his head and walked out. He waited outside her door until he heard every lock slide into place and then placed his hands on them, one by one. He drew on *jīn ch'i,* fortifying the metal of each lock until they were strong enough to withstand the common methods of breaking and entering.

Satisfied, he ran down the stairs. Hopefully his car would still be on the street. With its wheels and windows intact.

Ear pressed to the door, Carrie breathed a sigh of relief when she finally heard Max's soft footsteps jog down the stairs. He'd lingered outside her door for an awfully long time. For a second she'd thought he was going to come back.

She was afraid he'd realized she still had one of the scrolls. Actually, when he showed up on her doorstep, she figured that had to be the reason. Never in a million years would she have thought he came just for her.

But he had.

And to deliver her check. Looking at it, she counted all the zeroes again. It seemed wrong to accept it after everything that had transpired between them.

Sticking it in her pocket, she leaned against the wall and closed her eyes. She tried to figure out how she felt. Angry still, of course. Stunned, definitely. Hopeful—how could she not? And scared.

No secrets, he'd said. God—she still had one of the scrolls.

Not *the* scroll, but like that was going to make a difference to him when he found out which one she had. She went to her underwear drawer and extracted it. Sitting on her bed, she untied the leather thong and rolled the long parchment open to reveal five columns of neat handwriting.

She ran a finger over the crisp, clerical calligraphy at the very top. *Guardians of the Scrolls of Destiny.* Underneath the header, at the top of each column, was a label: Earth, Fire, Metal, Water, Wood.

It was a family tree of sorts. Actually, a genealogy of the five families over several centuries. Carrie glanced over the listed names, all the way down the columns to the last lines entered under Earth, Fire, and Metal.

Gabrielle Sansouci Chin. Rhys Llewellyn. And Maximillian Prescott.

When she'd discovered this scroll, she'd been totally stunned to read their names. This time, the shock was only slightly less. She still had difficulty believing it.

Gabe never said anything to her, and they were best friends. Carrie had been hurt about that at first, but she realized Gabe couldn't tell her she was a Guardian—she had to hide her scroll from the world.

But it all made sense. She'd felt some sort of force field around Gabe once. At the time she'd convinced herself she'd imagined it, but she hadn't been crazy.

She read the names again. Ironic that she was surrounded by them.

And too bad she couldn't ask them to help her with her dissertation. She was dying to ask about the scrolls and if what the myths said was true. That would have added such great dimension to her thesis. Combined with what she'd studied from the Book of Water and Wei Lin's journal, it'd give her enough to make her thesis defendable.

"Max is going to be so pissed I have this," she muttered, rolling up the scroll and putting it away. Because she was lying to him—willfully and in full knowing this time.

As she saw it, she had a choice to make. Keep the scroll and use it to forward her career, or give it back and keep Max.

Her mom would have smacked her upside the head and told her to be smart. But was choosing Max smart? Yeah, she understood where he was coming from, but that didn't mean anything. He might want her, but he'd been living with his ghosts for a long time. Could he really give them up? Would he really stick with her?

Could she give up *her* ghosts enough to really trust him?

Chapter Thirty

Carrie stood outside Leonora's office. The last time she'd been in this spot, she'd been offered the fellowship with Max. Look how well that turned out.

"Get a grip," she muttered to herself, smoothing the front of her shirt. This would go okay. It had to go okay.

But Leonora wasn't going to be happy when she told her she was altering her thesis. Again. But she couldn't very well publish her findings without proof, and she wouldn't have proof when she returned the genealogy to Max.

As her nerves jangled, she heard a very distant whisper from somewhere behind her.

As turbulent as the sea is, there is always a space of stillness and calm, even if one has to plunge to great depths to find it. Such is life. Delve deep within.

Frowning, Carrie looked over her shoulder even though

she knew she wouldn't find anyone. She recognized the passage—she'd read it last week. And the voice was familiar to her, too, as faint as it was.

"Freaky." She hugged herself, wondering if this was normal. But even as she thought it, she knew it was in no way normal to hear the voice of a scroll in her head. Although the advice was good. What did she have to lose?

Closing her eyes, she pictured a turbulent sea, the exact match for her emotional state, and imagined herself diving in. At first she was bashed in the waves, battered and bruised. But she let the tide take her down deeper into the still darkness underneath. All her worries faded as she drifted in the surprising warmth, and she relaxed, cocooned and safe.

When she opened her eyes, that feeling of still peace remained. She exhaled, thankful but worried. No wonder Wei Lin had hidden the scrolls from the general populace. She'd barely read one and she was *this* affected. Imagine if she'd really studied it.

She wondered how Gabe managed it. No wonder she acted odd sometimes.

Something tickled her face. She reached up to brush her cheek. Her finger came away wet.

Curious, she touched the drop to her tongue. Salty. Like the sea.

No. She shook her head. That was impossible—it was just a tear.

Shaking off sudden goose bumps, she focused on the matter at hand, knocked on Leonora's door, and walked in. "Hi, Leonora."

Leonora and Trevor looked up, their conversation stopping abruptly.

"Oh." Carrie frowned. What was he doing in here? "I thought my appointment was now."

"It is," Leonora said.

She waited for Trevor to move or Leonora to invite her to sit down, but the only thing that greeted her was awkwardness. She took a step back. "Sorry if I interrupted. I'll wait outside."

"Stay. Trevor was about to leave." Her advisor gave him a pointed look.

Trevor's face flushed a dark red. He looked like he wanted to argue, but he just stormed out with a dirty look at her.

"Will he be okay?" Carrie asked, watching him leave. She had the distinct impression she shouldn't turn her back on him.

Leonora waved her hand. "He believed the position was guaranteed to be his. He didn't like hearing that you were currently being favored by the board."

Carrie sank into the chair he vacated, her usual seat across from the hanging swords. "I am?"

"Of course." Leonora tapped her pen against her desk in rapid staccato. "Your claim has the department in a fervor. To have such a discovery about the Scrolls of Destiny linked to Berkeley's History Department would garner the attention we need for extra funding. It'll be quite the feather in our cap."

"Oh." She bit her lip. "About my thesis—"

"The department is so impressed and excited that they're discussing offering you a tenured position."

Carrie almost fell out of her chair. "Excuse me? I think I heard you say—"

"Yes, a tenured position." A ghost of a smile hovered around Leonora's mouth. "It's quite the offer. I didn't achieve tenure for eight years."

"Wow." She slumped against the seat back. The still pond of her mind erupted into a muddy whirlpool, her thoughts chaotic.

Tenure. Within her reach. She'd not only work for a top university but get to stay in the Bay Area. And she'd make a living doing what she was passionate about.

Except she'd have to betray two people she loved.

"This is an excellent opportunity for you, Carrie," her advisor said solemnly. "I'm sure I don't have to outline what this means."

"No," she said faintly. "Not at all."

"Well, then." Leonora continued the manic tapping of the pen. "Tell me about your progress with your thesis. The board would like to see a draft soon. With so much at stake, I'd like to make sure your proof is valid and that it substantiates your claims sufficiently, as well, so we should arrange to go over it."

She thought about the scroll she'd tucked in her dresser at home. She'd planned on surrendering it to Max.

But that was before tenure. It sounded like she could pretty much write her own ticket if she produced her thesis—with the proof to support it.

It'd mean outing Max and Gabe. Maybe not directly, because she could cross-reference the Guardians Wei Lin gathered to help bring peace to Yongle's kingdom with other historical documents that listed the key players. She bet she could find references of the Guardians of that time, proving there was reason to believe the scrolls were more than myth. But she'd have to show the genealogy to support her claim, and she wasn't sure she could keep people from checking out the current Guardians.

Which meant she could kiss anything with Max goodbye.

But tenure...

"Carrie?" Leonora frowned at her. "You seem distressed. Perhaps we should have started the conversation with the reason you've returned from your fellowship a week early."

She winced. "Ma—Mr. Prescott and I had some differences over the way the work was handled, and I decided it best if I tendered my resignation."

Leonora dropped her pen and sat up so straight she looked inches taller. "What sort of differences?"

"Ones that have been resolved." She toyed with the zipper on her bag. "He asked me to continue working for him, but I haven't given him any answer."

"He's a very influential man. To have his name on your résumé would be quite a coup."

"Yeah." But at what price? And if she continued working for him, she'd have to give back the scroll. She couldn't willingly deceive him. "I'm not sure. I think you were right. I had a hard time managing to find time to do my own work."

"In any case, consider it." The pen tapping resumed. "And your research?"

"I, uh, don't have any of it with me." She waited for a bolt of lightning to strike her. It didn't happen, but that didn't mean she relaxed any. "I didn't expect you to have time to go over it today."

"When can you bring it to me? I really should go over your documentation to make sure your dissertation is the strongest it can be."

"I'd feel better pulling my thoughts together a little more first."

Leonora's lips pursed enough to let Carrie know she was displeased. But she said, "That's fine. It's your paper, after all. You know what's at stake."

Did she ever. She had to consciously relax her grip on the bag. "Thanks for being understanding, Leonora. I promise I'll get the thesis into shape so we can go over it."

"Of course. Let me know if you need assistance." Leonora turned to her computer and began typing rapid-fire.

Recognizing she was dismissed, Carrie tiptoed out. She closed the door behind her with a soft click and walked down the hall. She was so engrossed in her thoughts that she didn't notice Trevor until he was right in front of her.

"Geez." She jumped back, hugging her new bag in front of her. "Trevor. You need to attach bells to your shoes or something."

"Carrie," he said in his slightly nasal, disapproving voice. "I didn't know you were back."

He didn't sound too thrilled about it. She guessed she couldn't blame him. "I just returned a few days ago."

"Earlier than expected, isn't that so?"

She frowned. News got around the department quickly. "A little early," she answered lightly, edging away.

"Bái Hǔ must have realized he hired the wrong historian."

Don't lower yourself to his level. The jerk. But she had to bite down on her lip to follow her own advice.

Trevor looked her up and down, his lip curling with distaste. "And I'm sure he realized quickly that you weren't useful for anything else. Leonora and the board will realize you don't have much to offer, too."

"Well, it's been nice talking with you," she said, knowing he wouldn't pick up on the sarcasm in her voice. "But I've got to go—"

"You won't get it, you know." He stepped forward, hands clenched at his sides.

Okay, now she was getting freaked out. The look in his eyes was just a little too psycho. She took a step back. "Won't get what?"

"The position is mine. I'm not going to let you take what I've worked so hard to achieve." He took another step forward.

She backed up again. *Trevor*. It never occurred to her that he could have anything to do with what had happened over the past weeks. Foolish on her part, because he had a lot to gain with her out of the picture.

Touching behind her, she felt the wall inches away. She had nowhere to retreat to. She casually looked down the hall, hoping someone would show up, but it was a Friday afternoon. Translation: the hall was deserted.

He wagged a finger in her face. "You think you can sashay in here with your perky cheerleader attitude and win everyone over into thinking that you're something, but we both know what you are."

She didn't sashay. And she'd never been a cheerleader. "What am I?"

He leaned over her and hissed. "A slut who'll sleep for what she wants."

Whoa. She pressed flat against the wall. Blown away by his crazy enmity, she blinked, not knowing what to say.

Not that he gave her a chance to say anything. His long, Paganini finger poked at her nose. "If you think you've won, you should think again. I'm not going to let you take this from me. We both know I'm more deserving. The board will see it. I'll make them see it."

He spun on his heels and lurched off. At the end of the hall, he turned around and shot her one last venom-filled glare that chilled her to the core.

Chapter Thirty-one

Carrie sagged against the wall, a hand over her pounding heart. What the heck was *that?* She'd known he was off, but she never figured he was psycho. That little soliloquy of his was crazy.

Was he the one who'd terrorized her? He could have easily gotten her address from any number of people at the university, crank calls could be made from anywhere, and Santa Monica wasn't far—it was an easy day trip flying. She needed to check to see if he'd taken any time off while she was gone, and if the days corresponded with the mugging or pier accident.

After his performance today, she couldn't delude herself into thinking she was safe. If Trevor was the culprit, he'd come after her again—she had no doubt.

One thing she knew for sure: she shouldn't hang out here. Rushing out of the building, she stepped out of the oppressive space and took a deep breath of tangy marine air, instantly feeling better. She breathed it in again and let it wash her clean from inside out.

Needing to be off the campus, she walked briskly to BART, avoiding the wooded path she normally walked. Just in case.

The trip back into the city was slow. Checking the time, she decided to take BART straight to the bar. Hopefully Gabe would be there. She needed to run what happened by someone. And tomorrow she was totally finding a self-defense class to take. She was done feeling defenseless.

Only when she got to the Pour House, it was Vivian on duty.

Disappointed, she turned around to leave and bounced straight off a hard body. "*Oof.*"

"Easy." Large, blunt hands steadied her.

She looked up into the all-seeing gaze of Inspector Rick Ramirez. She practically wilted in relief, seeing his familiar face.

His expression never changed, but a subtle frown clouded his dark eyes. "You okay, Carrie? You look disturbed."

"I'm fine, Inspector." Better than fine now. You couldn't get safer than with a cop.

"Rick." He flashed a brief, crooked smile, accenting the smoldering Latino thing he had going on. "I'm off duty."

It wasn't unusual for him to hang out at the bar, because of Gabe—well, really because of her twisted brother Paul, who had disappeared after murdering her ex-boyfriend. Carrie knew Ramirez was waiting for Paul to contact Gabe, but she thought the cop had a small thing for her friend, too. "Gabe's not here tonight."

He glanced at the bar. "So I see. Care to join me?"

"Oh." She blinked. "Sure."

He placed his hand on the small of her back and guided her to two empty seats at the bar counter. She slid onto the left one and dropped her bag on the floor in front of her feet.

She watched Rick ease onto the other stool, taking his suit coat off and folding it neatly on his lap. Loosening his tie so it hung loosely around his neck, he unbuttoned his shirt and exhaled.

"Long day?" she asked.

"Started at four this morning with a double homicide." He gestured to Vivian.

Carrie ignored the daggers Vivian mentally threw at her and squeezed his arm. "Are you okay?"

"I should be used to it."

Despite his schooled expression, she could tell he wasn't. She squeezed his arm again. "Well, that puts my day into perspective."

He angled toward her, but before he could say anything Vivian was there leaning over the counter to show off her ample (and fake) cleavage. "Hello, Inspector."

Carrie rolled her eyes. In all the months since Rick started coming here, he hadn't given Vivian any indication that he was the least bit interested. Vivian was amazingly blind. And determined, given the way she was showing off her assets.

"A shot of Patrón and—" He lifted his eyebrow at her.

She didn't normally drink—ironic since she was a bartender—but today warranted something strong. "Me, too."

Vivian leveled her a hostile look and ambled off to pour their shots.

That was sashaying. Carrie wasn't sure she could get her hips to move that way.

Shoving one shot at her, Vivian handed the other to Rick with a batting of her eyelashes. When he took the drink, she let her fingers linger on his hand. Carrie didn't bother to hide her grin as Rick placidly withdrew Vivian's claw from his person and turned to her. "A toast before you tell me about your day?"

With another glare, Vivian huffed and walked off to help another customer.

Carrie lifted her shot glass. "To driving Vivian off."

His smile grew slow and sly. "I can drink to that."

She took a sip, tried not to shudder, and set down her glass. She noticed him watching her with humor and she shrugged. "I'm not a big drinker. The most I ever have is a beer, and that leaves me reeling."

"Then whatever happened today must have been something."

"On the scale of things, it wasn't anything compared to your day." When he just continued to steadily watch her, she shrugged. "I had this strange confrontation with a rival at school. It spooked me a little."

"What happened?"

"It wasn't a big deal." Unless he was tied to everything else. Then Trevor was totally dangerous.

Rick continued to stare at her with his no-nonsense cop's gaze.

"Next you'll be shining the bright lamp in my face." She sighed. "I was leaving my advisor's office, and Trevor cornered me to voice his unhappiness with the way the board is favoring me instead of him. We're both up for the same job."

He stilled. "What did he do?"

"Why do you think he did anything?" she asked to stall,

taking another sip of tequila. Rick went on predator mode as quickly as Max. Maybe it was a guy thing. Though she couldn't think of any other guy like that. Except Rhys.

"Cop instincts." Rick angled himself to completely face her and looked her over.

"He didn't touch me," she assured him quickly. "He just went postal for a minute and it freaked me out. I've never seen him lose it that way. It's probably just stress."

"That doesn't excuse his actions. That's like saying the man who murdered the two people this morning was justified because his heart was broken at finding his girl-friend cheating on him."

"So you're saying going postal isn't socially acceptable?"

"Don't take your safety lightly," he said, as serious as a heart attack.

She sighed. "I wish someone would teach me kung fu. You wouldn't give me a couple pointers, would you?"

"No, I wouldn't."

She waited for him to expound, but he just sipped at his drink. She huffed in (mostly) mock exasperation. "Why not?"

"Because most people who study martial arts know enough to be dangerous."

"I won't hurt anyone."

He shook his head. "You'd be a danger to yourself. You'd feel like you knew enough to handle yourself in any situation and take unnecessary chances. The best defense is to run."

She thought back on how Trevor cornered her and frowned. "What if you get caught and can't run?"

"You shouldn't get caught. That's where awareness comes into play."

"I still think it'd be cool to be able to kick someone's butt."

He flashed one of his rare grins.

Toying with her glass, she tipped her head and studied him. "You know, you're really too hot to be unattached." Even the little bit of gray at his temples was sexy.

The amusement left his face. He lifted his glass to his lips. "How do you know I'm unattached?"

She shrugged. "Gut feeling. And you come in here all the time to see Gabe."

"I come in here hoping to get a lead on her brother, who's wanted for questioning in two murders."

"I thought he was sighted in South America."

"I've got the feeling he'll be back."

"Hmm." Actually, she did, too. But she didn't really believe that was the only reason he hung out at the bar all the time. "I just hope you aren't waiting for Gabe, because she and Rhys were meant to be together. And Rhys will never let her go. That man adores the ground she walks on."

Rick grunted and downed the rest of his drink.

Smiling, she pointed at Vivian with her chin. "I bet I could set you up with her, though."

"Thanks, but I'll pass."

"You sure?" Carrie leaned in and nudged his shoulder. "I hear she's pretty affectionate."

"I don't want her talons anywhere near me. I prefer natural women." He raised his eyebrows. "You think I'm hot?"

"I did two weeks ago." She frowned at her glass. It seemed she preferred cool Vikings these days.

"Met Mr. Right?" he asked with unerring intuition.

"I'm not sure I'd call him Mr. Right. I'm not sure I'd call him, period."

"Sounds like the man has some groveling to do."

"Would you grovel?"

"If I loved her, I'd do anything to keep her." He shrugged. "My job is a negative. The hours are long and erratic, and it's dangerous. Most women can't handle that."

"If she loved you, she would."

"That's a lot of love."

"But worth it, I bet." Carrie pushed the shot glass away. "I should get home. I've got an exciting night of working on my thesis ahead of me."

"Come on. I'll give you a ride."

"You don't have to do that." She hopped off the stool and tripped on one of the legs.

He had the grace not to say anything, but he did arch his eyebrow. Taking her by the elbow, he urged her toward the door. "No trouble. Unless you live in Berkeley or something."

"I'm not worth a trip across the bridge?"

He tugged on her ponytail but answered in all seriousness. "You're worth it. Let's go."

"Oh." She turned around to grab her bag. "Ready."

As they walked to his car together, it struck her how it felt comfortable to be with him—but not exciting. Not like Max. She frowned.

"I know the car isn't much, but it's not that bad," he said as he opened the door for her.

She smiled her thanks as he closed the door. She waited until he settled in the driver's seat to say, "I didn't frown at your car. I was just thinking."

"Looked painful."

Seriously. "I live on O'Farrell, close to Polk."

He turned and stared at her. "You're kidding me."

"I'm not some cream puff who needs to be sheltered. And my neighborhood isn't *that* bad."

"Not if you're looking to score."

This time of night, it took only ten minutes to get home. Double-parking in front of her building, Rick turned the car off and joined her in looking out the window.

His mouth was set in a firm, disapproving line. "I can't believe you live here."

"Yeah, it's pretty lush," she said in an overly perky tone. She held her hand out to him. "Thanks for the ride. Next time, drinks are on me."

Instead of replying, he got out of the car.

Before she could ask him what he was doing, he'd already shut the door and locked it. Confused, she followed him out. "What are you doing?"

He took her arm. "I'm walking you to your door."

"You don't have to." She tested his grip and found it unshakable. "I do this every night on my own. I'm sure I can do it tonight, too."

"You were spooked earlier. I'll make sure your apartment is secure and then be on my way." His tone was firm.

Still, it was ridiculous. She was a grown woman, for goodness' sake. "It's up three flights of stairs."

"Are you telling me you think I'm out of shape?"

She shot a pointed gaze at his middle, which lacked any hint of fat. "If the donut fits..."

The corner of his mouth quirked—just the barest hint of amusement. He pushed her forward. "Open the door before someone thinks I'm your pimp."

"I used to have such a peaceful life, but suddenly it's filled with overbearing men." She pulled out her key and opened the security gate. Rick, of course had gone into cop mode and wasn't paying attention to her. Like someone was going to jump out at them. But he had her best interests at heart, so she humored him by following behind.

She couldn't help stomping a little, though. And she had to ask, "Aren't you going to unholster your gun?"

Ignoring her, he glanced back at her flatly and then picked up the pace so she almost had to run after him to keep up. By the time they reached her floor, she was huffing and puffing. He looked like he'd gone for a stroll in the park.

"I take back any disparaging remarks I made about the condition of your health," she said, panting, as they rounded the corner. "In fact, I bet you run marathons."

So intent on keeping up, she didn't notice when he suddenly stopped and she ran smack into his back.

"Hey." She looked around him to see what the deal was. "Why'd you stop?"

Then she saw why. Down the hall was her new door, and under it smoke billowed out in thick puffs.

Chapter Thirty-two

"Oh, my God." Carrie darted around Rick. All her stuff was in there. Her books and schoolwork. *The scroll.*

"Carrie, *no*." Rick grabbed her by the arm and pulled her to a stop. With his free had, he pulled out his cell phone. "I'll call 911 and get the fire department out."

"It'll be too late." She yanked free and ran down the hall. Behind her, she heard him curse and then issue terse orders for a fire crew as he treaded after her.

She checked the doorknob. Unlocked. *Hot.* Hissing, she pulled back and shook her hand, then used her sweatshirt to open it.

The heat hit her, and the heavy smoke made her eyes burn. She looked around, dazed. She thought it'd be a little fire that she could pour some water on to put out. This was an inferno. Orange flames licked over everything like a scene out of hell.

"Damn it, Carrie." Rick pulled her back. "The fire department is on the way. We need to evacuate and wait for them."

"It'll be too late." She tugged them both forward. "I need to get the scroll. It's just across the room."

"A room that's in flames," he yelled over the blaze's crackle.

"I need to get it." She broke free and was able to take one step before she was pushed to the floor.

A jacket dropped over her head. She lifted the end to find Rick's face right in front of her. "It's just over there, in my dresser."

His glare singed her more than the flames. He pointed a finger. "If you want to do this, you follow me. We're going in and out fast. We need to get the building cleared. Why the hell isn't the fire alarm ringing?"

"Someone disconnected the fire alarms after Mrs. Warren moved in down the hall. She set them off every morning when she burned her toast," she added inanely.

"Come on." He crawled ahead of her, agile and quick. She felt awkward, but she needed that scroll, so she made sure she kept up.

The smoke was thick, even on the floor. By the time they reached the dresser, they were both coughing.

Hurry, she urged herself. She lifted the coat and gasped when she saw her dresser burning.

The genealogy. She reached for the drawer—

"*Carrie.*" Rick captured her hand. "It's too late. We need to go."

Sirens wailed outside. Wait for them? No—they were close, but not close enough.

The disembodied voice she associated with the Book of Water whispered in her mind:

*All things are created. Wood feeds fire. Fire creates
earth. Earth bears metal. Metal carries water. Water
nourishes wood.*

*All things are destroyed. Wood parts earth. Earth
absorbs water. Water quenches fire. Fire melts metal.
Metal hews wood.*

Water. If she could douse the flames even a little, she
could retrieve the scroll.

She shook her head. No way would she be able to cart
water from the kitchen or the bathroom back and forth
through the blaze. But at Leonora's office, she swore she
felt condensation on her face after she envisioned the water
soothing her. Was that what the voice was trying to tell her?

Not that a drop of water was going to help.

Try.

She closed her eyes, found her inner sea, and dove
in. The sizzling around her made it difficult to concentrate, and the waves in her mind fought her. She started
struggling against them.

No—a tsunami. Hope leapt in her chest, and she
encouraged the waves bigger. They broke over her head,
one by one, each one swelling larger.

"What are you doing?" Rick's hand gripped her arm—
tight—and he lifted her up.

"Hey!" Her eyes flew open and she began to cough
again. "I almost had the tsunami thing going."

"Jesus, Carrie." He set her down behind him. He
picked up a sweater that wasn't burning from the floor and
wrapped it around his hand. "Which drawer?"

"That one."

Taking hold of the scorched handle, he yanked the drawer all the way out. It clattered onto the floor, breaking apart, her underwear falling in little puffs on the floor.

"It's not here," Ramirez said, kicking aside the smoldering bits of fabric.

"Because I hid it behind the drawer." She grabbed the sweater from him, wrapped her arm, and reached into the burning opening.

There. She snatched it out, beating at the flames singeing the edges of the parchment.

"Come on." Rick pushed her forward. "Move."

Hacking, her lungs burning, she stumbled ahead of him. She dodged a sudden burst of sparks and hoped her head wasn't on fire.

They dashed out into the hall. Other tenants ran panicked and screaming, calming mildly when Rick took over and herded them down the stairs.

The firemen met them on the second floor.

"Fourth floor," Rick yelled hoarsely. "Apartment 413."

They nodded and hustled past. Clutching the scroll, Carrie followed Rick out of the building.

The first breath of fresh air stung. Gawkers lined the sidewalks, watching the flames licking her apartment window.

Her apartment.

Gasping, Rick steered her toward a waiting ambulance beyond the firemen and their equipment. An EMT waved them to sit inside and held out an oxygen mask to her. "Breathe into this. You, too, Inspector."

She knew better than to argue. Rick, too. They let the fireman check them as the fire was quickly brought under control. Rick went over to talk to the captain, leaving her with the medic.

"Except for being a little crispy at the edges, you look okay." The EMT smiled at her. "But I'd encourage you and the inspector to go to the hospital for a more complete exam."

"I just want a glass of cool water and a bed," she croaked.

"Hope you have another bed somewhere. You won't be going up there again for a while."

She looked at the building and felt a heavy weight settle on her shoulders.

Rick came back and kneeled in front of her. "You okay?"

"Would you be okay?"

"I'd be madder than hell."

"That pretty much sums it up." She frowned when she saw the fatigue lining his face. "I should be asking you if you're okay. You've been up almost twenty-four hours straight. You don't need to deal with this. You should go home and get some sleep."

"After we take care of you."

"I'm—"

"You can't stay here," he said over her. "Fortunately the fire was minor and easy to contain, but they're examining your apartment for signs of arson."

"Arson?" She blinked, the pit of her stomach twisting.

"Even if they were to leave, your apartment is uninhabitable. The smoke alone would be bad enough, but you no longer have a bed, either. Is there someplace you can go for the night?"

Truthfully, she didn't want to go back in there, anyway. "I don't know."

"No family in the city?"

"My mom is in Iowa."

"Iowa. Why doesn't that surprise me?" A smile hovered at the edge of his mouth. "Is there a hotel you prefer?"

"No, but I'm not staying in a hotel." With her savings cleaned out from the trip to China, she didn't think she could even afford the crappy hotels around her neighborhood—not even one of the scary ones that rented by the half hour. Unless she cashed Max's check, and she couldn't bring herself to do that. It seemed wrong, not only because she hadn't finished the work, but also because she'd slept with him. No, the check would stay tucked away in her bag.

Rick studied her. To her relief, he didn't question or press her. Instead he just said, "Any friends you can stay with?"

She stifled the image of her staying with Max—in his bed—as soon as it popped up. She was in no mental space to deal with that.

Gabe, but Rhys had recently convinced her to move in with him. Rhys's house had plenty of room (for her and half a dozen of her close friends), but she didn't want to inconvenience them.

"How about Gabe?" he said as if he could read her mind.

She shook her head. "It's two in the morning. She'll be asleep."

"Then you'll come home with me." He stood up and held out his hand.

"No." She hid her hands behind her back. "That'll put you out, and you've already gone above and beyond."

"You can't stay here. You'll either call Gabe or come home with me. Decide."

God save her from bossy men. She pulled her cell phone out of her bag.

Gabe answered on the third ring. "Yeah?" she rasped sleepily.

"I woke you up." She groaned. "I knew this was a bad idea."

"Carrie?" Her friend's voice was suddenly more alert. "What's wrong with your voice?"

"Smoke."

"You've been smoking?"

"No. Listen, there was a fire in my building, and I need a place to crash until I can get my apartment cleaned up."

"Of course you can crash here. We have plenty of room. But are you okay?"

"Yeah." She hugged her new messenger bag close, and it occurred to her it was all she had in the world.

"Should I come pick you up?"

"No, I'll take a cab."

"I'll drop you off," Rick corrected.

She rolled her eyes but didn't have it in her to argue. "Rick will drop me off."

"Rick? You mean Ramirez? Did someone die?"

"No." Though someone could have died—namely her. "Rick was dropping me off and stayed to help with the fire."

"You're hanging out with *Ramirez?*" A long second of silence. "We've got to have a talk about your taste in men."

Men were the least of her worries at the moment. "We'll be over there in minutes."

"Okay, and then you have to tell me what's going on."

"See you soon." She hung up and faced Rick. "I'm more than capable of taking a cab."

"I know you are." He steered her toward his car with a light hand. "But it's no trouble. It's on my way home."

"You live in Sea Cliff?" She frowned at him as he opened the door for her. Sea Cliff was the ritziest neighborhood in the city. She couldn't picture a cop living there. Not unless Rick had a huge trust fund he never talked about.

"Actually, I live in the Mission," he admitted when he got in his side.

"That's nowhere near Sea Cliff. They're at opposite ends of the city."

He turned the key in the ignition. "Tonight I happen to be driving through Sea Cliff first."

His set expression made arguing seem pointless. She secured her seat belt, unsure whether she should feel flattered that he cared enough to see her safely to Gabe's or annoyed because he was treating her like a kid.

"It's probably best to be flattered," she decided aloud as he pulled away from the curb.

He frowned at her in question but didn't say anything.

Just as well. She hunkered low in her seat. "You're lucky your car was still here."

"They wouldn't touch a cop car."

"How would they know it's a cop car? There are no markings."

He just raised an eyebrow and zoomed off toward Rhys's house.

She gave him the address and closed her eyes. Next thing she knew, he was shaking her awake.

Stretching her arms, she looked around. "We here?"

"Yeah. Looks like they're waiting."

Sure enough, all the lights were on. The front door opened and Gabe's silhouette hovered in the doorway.

"Better go before she comes out here and accuses me of holding you against your will," he said.

She squeezed his arm. "You're a great guy. Some woman is going to be so lucky to have you."

"When you meet her, probably best if you tell her to run."

"Straight into your arms." Leaning over, she kissed his cheek and then dashed out of the car with her bag.

Gabe held the door wide open for her to enter. "Holy shit. I don't know if I should be concerned over how you look or the fact that you just kissed Ramirez."

"I told you there was a fire. And stop about Rick." She poked her friend. "He's a nice guy."

Gabe snorted.

"He can't help it if he's hung up on you."

"He's not hung up on me. He's hung up on my brother." She closed the door. "Good thing I love Rhys. I'd hate to deal with all that incoherent male posturing."

"What incoherent male posturing is this?" a British voice asked.

They both turned to find Rhys leaning against the archway of the foyer. He wore a pair of silk pajama bottoms. His chest was bare, and on his left pec was a dark birthmark in the shape of a broadsword.

Just like Max's.

Rhys strode to Gabe and dropped a kiss on her forehead, but the whole time he studied Carrie. "You look like a chimney sweep, darling. Gabe said there was a fire, but she didn't say you'd rolled around in the ashes."

"It was in my apartment." Carrie shook her head as

they both tensed in concern. "I'm fine. I just lost all my stuff."

"She looks absolutely knackered, love," Rhys said, stroking his hand down Gabe's hair. "Why don't you show her to her room before she falls over? We'll discuss everything else in the morning."

"You heard him." Gabe took her arm and led her up the wide staircase. "Let's get you to bed so I can go back to bed."

Carrie looked behind them. "Isn't Rhys coming up, too?"

"He's taking care of a couple things." Before Carrie could question what that meant, Gabe threw open a door and switched the light on. "Your new digs. Hope they measure up."

Carrie took in the sleek lines of the modern furniture, the soothing pale colors, and the fluffy comforter on the bed and wanted to burst into tears of relief. It made her feel clean, and after what she'd gone through at her apartment, that was something. She set her bag down next to the bedside table. "I should take a shower so I don't get ashes on the sheets."

"Through there." Gabe pointed at a closed door to the left. "Hand me your clothes and I'll get them cleaned."

Tiredly, she struggled out of her clothes, gave them to Gabe, and took a long, hot shower.

When she came out in a towel, Gabe was sitting on her bed, holding a large T-shirt. "In case you want something to sleep in."

"Thank you." Taking the shirt gratefully, Carrie slipped it over her head. It fell almost to her knees. She tugged the towel off and gave it to Gabe, who held her hand out for it.

"Come on." Her friend took her arm and led her to the edge of the bed, gently pushing her down to sit after she pulled back the covers. "Lie down. Sleep as long as you need. You're safe here."

Sighing, she snuggled under as Gabe tucked the comforter around her. "Thanks, Mom."

"You think *I'm* maternal." Her friend chuckled. "Just wait until you see Rhys and Brian in action. I swear they should have been mother hens instead of manly men. Go to sleep. I'll see you when you wake up."

She nodded, closing her eyes. The door clicked softly shut, and oblivion followed moments after.

Chapter Thirty-three

Carrie woke up late the next morning. If eleven thirty-five could still be called morning.

"Barely," she croaked as she got out of bed. Her throat still felt scratchy, but her voice sounded marginally better than last night.

Last night. It came back to her in a rush—the thick smoke, the violent flames. She'd been lucky.

Someone had set that fire specifically. They'd meant to hurt her.

Problem was, she didn't know what to do about it. And the only bargaining chip she had was the identity of three people she loved.

Someone had set her cleaned clothing on the chair in the corner. She wrinkled her nose at the subtle scent of smoke as she got dressed. If a washing hadn't cleaned the smoke out of these clothes, all the stuff in her apartment was garbage.

After she washed her face and pulled her hair into a ponytail, she worked her way downstairs. At some point she had to figure out what to do about the tenure. Thank goodness she'd taken her laptop with her. Otherwise her thesis would have gone up in flames with the rest of her things.

She had a shift this evening at the Pour House on top of everything.

Sigh.

Wondering if any bus lines came out to Sea Cliff, she walked into the kitchen. No one around, she drifted out into the hall.

She heard a thump and some heavy breathing coming from the back of the house. Gabe and Rhys making out? Driven by curiosity, she went to investigate.

It was just Rhys working out in a room that looked much like Max's rec room. The only difference was that one wall was covered in an assortment of weapons.

Rhys was topless again—or still—and was doing some sort of exercise that looked very much like what Max had been practicing on the beach. Except he used his hands instead of a sword.

He must have felt her presence, because he stopped and turned to face her, picking up a towel to wipe sweat from his face. "You're up. Sleep well, darling?"

"Like the dead." She smiled at him, hoping her weariness wouldn't show. She'd been plagued by dreams where she was sinking in water and unable to surface. What she'd give to have the old water/sex dreams with Max back.

Rhys surveyed her with his all-seeing gaze—so much like the way Max always studied her. A small pang of longing shot through her heart.

He walked to her, and even that predator grace of his reminded her of Max. She shook her head. Pathetic. But the similarities were uncanny, down to the birthmark they shared.

Birthmark. Frowning, she remembered the passage in Wei Lin's journal where he described marking the Guardians. She'd thought he meant it figuratively, but maybe it was literal. Two genetically disparate people having the same birthmark was improbable.

Did Gabe have one, too? Carrie wished she could ask, but she couldn't without giving away what she knew. And without alerting them that she had the list of Guardians.

Rhys cocked an eyebrow. "You all right, darling?"

"Yeah." She nodded, feeling far from it. She had the find of the ages, and she couldn't share it with anyone. Plus, it seemed her life was in danger because of it. "Thank you for taking me in. I hate imposing on you like this."

He arched his brow, taking a swig from a water bottle. "There's no imposition between friends."

"Still." One of the swords on the wall caught her eye. She went over to it. It looked so similar to—

"We need to discuss what happened and our course of action," Rhys said, disrupting her chain of thought.

"I really appreciate you giving me shelter for the night, but there's nothing to discuss." She turned to face him. "My place caught fire. I'm going to get it cleaned up and call it that."

"And if you get hurt the next time?" He slipped a shirt over his head and came to stand next to her.

"There won't be a next time. It was probably faulty wiring," she said, hopefully with enough surety so that he'd believe the lie. Because if she admitted that someone had been threatening her, she'd also have to admit why, and that could cost her Rhys and Gabe's friendship, not to mention put them in danger, too. Carrie couldn't have that. "The building is old and probably not up to code. A fire was bound to happen."

Rhys's stare told her he didn't buy that for one minute.

"I keep telling you, you shouldn't feel obligated to take care of me."

"It's what one does for someone one is particularly fond of," he said mildly.

"Are you fond of me?"

"You're ours now, darling." He tugged her ponytail.

Her nose tingled with tears. "That's one of the nicest things anyone's ever said to me."

Rhys smiled. Then he tossed his sweaty towel in a bin and said, "I took the liberty of making some calls."

She groaned.

"It appears there was a gas leak. The leak was caused by someone cutting a gas line," Rhys said gently. "A repairman had been there recently, so it could have been him. However, no fingerprints were left. It seems bizarre that a repairman would bother to wipe his prints."

She made a noncommittal noise even though she couldn't help agreeing.

Rhys reached up, drawing a finger along the sword on the wall. "Gabe says you've developed a relationship with Max."

Looking at the sword, she suddenly knew why it seemed familiar—it was just like the one Max had. "You can't think he's behind this."

"Can't I?" he asked in a deceptively reasonable tone.

"Of course not. He has no reason." Except that he had a history of going through her things. And it was possible he'd found out she still had one of the scrolls. She bit her lip.

Facing her, he rubbed a finger over the ridge of the scar that bisected the corner of his mouth. "It seems that maybe you're having doubts yourself."

"It just seems that, even if he had motives, he wouldn't have to resort to this kind of extreme."

"This kind of extreme is precisely what he'd enjoy." Rhys leaned on his elbows, his gaze intense. "Seven years ago Max vowed he'd do anything to exact revenge from me, and I can't help but think he's using you to get to me."

Yeah, he would have—at one time. Max admitted as much himself. But she couldn't even consider the possibility—deep down, she knew he wouldn't hurt her. "He didn't set the fire."

"You don't know what he's capable of."

Oh, she thought she had a pretty good idea. "Did you really plot with Max's girlfriend to betray him?"

Rhys stilled, motionless like a cautious predator. "Why do you ask?"

"Max told me what happened."

"*Max* told you?" Shock and disbelief warred on his face. "What precisely did he say?"

"That you turned on him and corrupted the woman he was dating. That you seduced her into stealing something from him."

He smiled, a cold and humorless twist of his lips. "Difficult to corrupt what's already rotten. Amanda had nefarious designs on him. Max had unwisely told her things about himself that he should have kept secret."

That he was a Guardian? Carrie couldn't picture him revealing that—unless he'd cared about the woman, but she couldn't make herself believe that he had. The few times Max had mentioned the past, he'd been more focused on Rhys's betrayal than anything else.

Which meant the woman must have used sex to pry the information out of him, and that pissed Carrie off big-time.

"And she pit us against each other," Rhys continued. "I imagine she thought she could carry out her schemes while we fought each other. It worked, too well. Max swore one day he'd make me regret what happened. Harming you would do that."

"It's not Max." She shook her head. "He could have taken care of me anytime while I lived with him. He had ample opportunity. Or he could have tortured me to death and left my body to rot when he came to visit me a couple days ago."

Rhys's face went cold. "He's here? In San Francisco?"

"Yeah." She frowned at the menace in his voice. "It's still a free city, right?"

"Shite." Rhys strode to the room's entrance and hit a button on a panel she hadn't seen. There was a crackle, and then he said, "Brian, in the workout room please."

Brian entered the room almost in seconds. "You called, boss?"

Rhys simply said, "Max Prescott is in town."

The natural smile faded from the man's face.

"We'll need to make arrangements. Gabe—"

Brian held a hand up. "No worries there."

"We'll have to arrange something for Clothilde, as well. And Carrie, of course."

"Why me of course?" she asked, her gaze ping-ponging between the two men. She didn't get why she'd be classified with Clothilde La Rochelle, either. Madame La Rochelle was Gabe's mentor.

Rhys continued as if she wasn't there. "I'll hire someone unobtrusive for Clothilde, but Carrie—"

"I'll take care of it," Brian said.

"Take care of what?" she asked louder.

He had the nerve to reach out and pat her head. "Don't worry yourself about it."

Her eyes narrowed. "Why do I have the feeling I'm not going to like what you have planned?"

"Just a little extra protection, sweetheart." Brian turned to his boss. "Will that be all?"

"For now." He nodded. "Thanks."

"I don't get it," Carrie said, watching Brian leave. She turned to Rhys. "Why the crazy reaction to Max? You guys obviously have history together. Good as well as bad. Look at that sword."

His eyes went to it before he studied her. Finally he said, "How do you mean?"

"Max said you guys were like brothers. That sort of bond doesn't just fade away. Even your swords match."

Rhys looked at it. She didn't think he was going to say anything, but then in a low voice he admitted, "Max made that for me."

"No way." She blinked at the sword. Stunning. An artist had crafted it, and it was hard picturing Max as that person, for some reason. "Seriously?"

"Max has an affinity for metalwork."

Guardian of the Book of Metal. She wondered what other skills he kept hidden, and if he'd ever tell her. She pursed her lips, studying the sword.

Rhys took her elbow. "Let's find you some breakfast."

Brian was on the phone in the kitchen when they walked in. He nodded at Rhys, communicating more than she understood. Part of which must have included food for her, because Brian set a skillet on the stove without hanging up.

"What am I missing?" Gabe said as she breezed in. Socking Brian in the arm, she went to stand next to Rhys. He slid his arm around her waist, so possessively Carrie would have sighed if she weren't so befuddled.

Rhys snaked his hand into Gabe's long, loose hair and tugged her head back for a searing kiss.

Carrie knew she should have turned her head to give them privacy, but Brian stared, a goofy, proud grin on his face, so she decided she'd stare, too. Hard to turn away from that much passion.

She thought of Max for the millionth time that morning, and her heart constricted.

When they pulled apart, Gabe still had her hand over Rhys's heart, and he looked like he wanted to toss her onto the counter and have his way with her.

Gabe smiled at her and then turned back to Rhys. "What are you plotting now? I hope it's helping Carrie get her apartment together and not acquiring another company."

He stroked her back until she was almost purring. "Carrie is going to be staying here with us."

"Cool," Gabe said at the same moment Carrie exclaimed, "No way."

They all turned to look at her.

"Rhys thinks Max was responsible for the fire, and now he wants to put me under lock and key," Carrie explained, knowing her friend would understand how distasteful that was and back her up.

Gabe nodded. "He reacts that way when one of his little chicks is threatened."

"So you agree with me that it's completely ludicrous?"

"No, actually I think his plan is a good one. Only until we figure out what's going on."

She threw her hands up. "This is ridiculous. Max isn't going to hurt me."

"Not physically, maybe, but what's to say this isn't one of his games?" Gabe arched her eyebrows. "You yourself told me how he played you before."

Rhys stilled. "What did he do?"

She shot her friend an exasperated look. "Did you have to mention that?"

"You've got to lay the facts out."

Carrie shook her head, refusing the tea Brian held out to her. "You guys, I really appreciate your concern, but if you're making a big deal out of it because of Max, that's just wrong. And you're not taking into account that I'm a grown woman."

"So what you're saying is you want us to butt out," Gabe summarized succinctly.

"Pretty much."

Her friend studied her for a long, silent minute and then tapped Rhys. "You heard the woman. You need to back off."

"Gabrielle—"

"No." She put a finger over his lips. "This is her decision, and as much as we don't agree with it, we have to respect it."

Brian crossed his arms. "That sucks."

Carrie got up and patted his massive arm. "I promise I'll let you guys dictate every step I take if anything else happens. But I really think this was random," she lied, thinking of Trevor.

"You promised, though," Gabe said. "We all heard."

"No kidding. I'm not going to go back on my word."
She just had to figure out who it was without putting her
loved ones in danger. "Not that I'm ungrateful or anything, but would it be okay if I head out now? I need to see
how much was damaged and what can be salvaged."

Gabe snapped her fingers. "I'll help."

"You—"

"Don't even think of protesting, babe. I'm going to
help, and you'll thank me for it."

"And you're eating breakfast before you go." Brian's
body language was like a challenge.

"Okay. You guys win." She sat down on a counter stool.
"You're a tough crowd."

"Only because we love you," Rhys said, tugging on her
ponytail again.

She rolled her eyes, but underneath she glowed with
warmth. Which, under the circumstances, was pretty
amazing.

Chapter Thirty-four

Her apartment was uninhabitable.

Carrie's heart sank the moment she walked in. Her kitchen was a husk, and her bathroom only slightly better off. Most of her possessions were reduced to ashes. Her books and papers—incinerated. The only thing intact was her new door, and even that had streaks of black on it.

She kicked up some soot on her way to the closet. The few pieces of salvageable clothing reeked of smoke so badly that no amount of washing would ever remove the smell.

"Demoralizing," she mumbled, dropping a singed sweater she'd loved on the floor with the rest of the debris.

"It's not so bad." As Gabe swung open a cabinet door in the kitchen, it broke off in her hand. Shrugging, she propped it on the floor. "This place needed a remodel anyway. It was a dump."

"Thanks," Carrie said dryly, turning around.

Her friend joined her in the middle of the studio,

bending to pick up what was left of a book spine. "*The Rise and Fall of Imperial China*. Sounds riveting. Not."

"Thank God I had my laptop and most of my notes with me." Carrie bit her lip, overwhelmed by the damage. In the light of day, it looked devastating. "What am I going to do? It'll take weeks to get the apartment habitable. Not that it makes any difference, because I doubt Ross will let me continue to live here with everything that's happened."

"Just because of the fire?"

And the break-in. She was a liability, even for a run-down apartment complex in the Tenderloin. Except Gabe didn't know about the previous incidents, and she wanted to keep it that way.

Someone knocked on the door, saving her from replying.

Gabe's brow furrowed. "You expecting someone?"

"Maybe it's Rhys?"

"He had a meeting this afternoon."

"Maybe he sent Brian." Carrie brushed her hands on her jeans and went to open the door.

Max filled the doorway, his face as stern and beautiful as ever. "Hello, Carrie."

Shock froze her vocal cords.

Something crackled in the air, and Gabe gasped. Her friend blinked once, and then her nose twitched like she scented something bad. Then she hissed, "You bastard."

Carrie knew if she wasn't blocking the doorway her friend would have launched herself at Max. She sighed, dreading this encounter. "Gabe, I don't think you've actually met Maximillian Prescott. Max, this is Gabrielle Sansouci."

Max's expression chilled dangerously. Carrie groaned, but before she could tell them to knock it off, Max stepped into her apartment, brushing Gabe's arm.

"Bastard," Gabe spat again.

Oh, God. If she didn't do something, Carrie had a feeling they were going to have a showdown. And she didn't much look forward to picking up their broken pieces when they were done.

Stepping between them, she pushed them apart. "Stop it, guys."

Max frowned at her. "What's wrong with your voice?"

"As if you don't know." Gabe glared at him. "And if you came to finish where you left off, I can tell you, this"—she waved at the blackened mess—"is the last bit of havoc you wreak in Carrie's life."

Carrie watched him look around them. His face became stonier as he took in the charred remains of the apartment. She put a hand on his arm, hoping to stem the impending eruption. "It's not as bad as it looks."

"No, it was worse." Gabe's gaze shot daggers at him. "She arrived here in the middle of a burning inferno."

Carrie sighed. "That's not helping, Gabe."

"You came home to a fire?" He turned his icy attention back to Gabe. "Who's to say Rhys didn't do this?"

Gabe swelled with anger. "You *bastard*. He'd *never* hurt her. Unlike some people I've heard of."

"Stop," Carrie commanded. "Really. The culprit here is a gas leak."

"A gas leak someone manufactured." Gabe glared at him. "Carrie wants to believe this was random, but none of the rest of us buy it. Not even the police."

"Neither do I." The way he looked at Carrie, she could tell

he was remembering the pier. Surprisingly, Max directed his next question at Gabe. "The police were here?"

"As luck would have it, a homicide inspector was with Carrie when she arrived home."

Max turned his flinty gaze on Carrie. She read the jealously there but didn't bother to justify herself. If he really did trust her, he'd have to prove it. "A fire was bound to happen here. This building is rundown even by Tenderloin standards. I doubt it's up to code in anything."

"I beg to disagree," a gravelly voice sounded from behind Max.

Carrie groaned. *Rick.* Just the sort of help she didn't need. She dropped her head in her hands.

"This should be interesting," Gabe murmured.

She lifted her head and looked at her friend incredulously.

Gabe shrugged, her mouth quirking in amusement for the first time since Max arrived. "It's the simple things that make life fun."

"This is not going to be fun," Carrie whispered, watching the way Max and Rick checked each other out.

"I don't believe we've met." Max's cool voice was everything but polite as he held his hand out. "Maximillian Prescott. A *friend* of Carrie's."

She groaned again, feeling her cheeks flame at the way he said it. Like they had some kind of lurid thing going on. Which was hardly the case.

Rick took Max's hand, studying him in his intense way. Finally, he nodded. "Inspector Ramirez, homicide detail. Also a friend of Carrie's."

"Okay, back off, guys." She stepped between them and pushed them apart, a hand on each of their chests.

Max pressed his hand over hers and stepped back so she couldn't reach Rick. She glanced at Rick, whose expression was tinged with amusement. She frowned at him, annoyed that he was feeding into Max's territorial jealousy.

Max turned her to face him. "Tell me what happened."

She looked into his eyes, surprised at the depth of concern there. She'd expected to see the usual slate wall, impenetrable and veiled. Before, he'd shown true emotion only while they made love—blazing hot and seething emotion.

Don't think about that, she commanded herself, feeling her face burn.

He cocked his eyebrow, which made her flush even more.

Gabe cleared her throat. "Seems crowded suddenly. Think I'll wait outside."

"You don't have to wait." Carrie smiled reassuringly. "Really."

"Okay, but call me if you need anything." Gabe stepped up to her and awkwardly patted her shoulder. "Brian gave you a key to the house, right?"

"Yeah." Carrie hugged her with her free arm. "Thanks for everything."

"This made it all worthwhile." She flashed a cocky grin and turned to Max. "One false move and I'll pull your gonads out through your mouth."

His eyes narrowed. "I'll keep that in mind."

"Good." She turned to Rick, her expression going cautious. "Any word, Ramirez?"

"I was about to ask you the same."

"If you're waiting for my brother to contact me, you're

never going to catch him. I'm outta here." Gabe pushed past the inspector and strode down the hall.

Carrie watched the way Rick stared after her friend, with two parts suspicion and one interest. Not that she could blame him—Gabe was stunning.

Max must have noticed where Rick's curiosity lay, because his grip on her became slightly less possessive. Ever so slightly.

Rick turned back to them. "I just came to see how you're doing, Carrie. It doesn't look as bad as I thought it'd be."

"How bad was it?" The chill anger in Max's voice made her shudder.

"Just smoky." She patted his arm reassuringly.

Rick's lips twitched with humor. "I talked to the arson task force and they have no leads. I'm glad you'll be staying with Ms. Sansouci. It'll be safer for you there until we figure out if this was a random act or targeted."

"I haven't figured out where I'll be yet. I don't want to impose on them."

Max stepped forward. "I'll make sure she's taken care of. Thank you for your concern, Inspector."

Rick obviously reappraised Max. He must have decided Max was okay, because he nodded and handed over a card. "Let me know if there's anything I can do."

"Of course." Max pocketed the card. "I'm sure we'll be in touch."

Rick nodded again and left, too.

Leaving her alone with Max.

Chapter Thirty-five

Carrie looked up at Max, and her heart suddenly began to beat triple time.

Without a word, he closed the door and walked her backward so her spine pressed against it while all of him pressed against her.

"Why didn't you call me last night?" he asked softly, holding her hips.

"I didn't—" She swallowed a moan as he began to nibble his way up her neck.

"You didn't what?" he whispered against her skin. "You didn't think of me?"

"You're kidding, right?" She laughed shakily. "I think of you all the time."

His hands skimmed up her sides to rest just below her breasts. "Didn't it occur to you I'd be angry that someone did this to you? Someone tried to hurt you again. I need to help you, if only for my own sake."

It hadn't occurred to her, actually. She closed her eyes,

trying to find that still pond of calmness, but it was impossible with him right there.

His mouth hovered over hers so when he spoke, she not only heard the words but felt them, too. "Carrie, why didn't you call me?"

"The truth?" she asked, opening her eyes.

"No more deceptions between us."

She mentally grimaced. He didn't know she still had a scroll with her. "I wasn't sure."

"About?"

"You don't figure into my plans." She put her hand on his shoulder, to hold him back. Or to steady herself—she wasn't entirely sure which. "I wasn't looking for you."

"I wasn't looking for you, either." Freeing her hair from her ponytail, he speared his fingers into her hair and tipped her head back.

She curled her hand around his shoulder, to that broadsword-shaped birthmark on his back. Like before, it gave her a zap that she felt straight to her heart. "Then why are you here?"

"Because it's where I belong." He stared straight into her soul. "I meant it when I said I want you."

A thrill shot through her, but reality tempered it. "You may feel that way now, but what if you change your mind? Time changes things."

His thumb caressed her jaw. "Time won't change the way I feel about you. I tried to fight it, I tried to deny it, but I'm still here."

"You say that now, but—"

"I don't know what you're afraid of, but I know you're brave enough to fight your fear and take a chance with me." He lifted her chin and forced her to meet his solemn gaze. "I'm not going to leave you. I would go insane without you. You're all I think about. I haven't been able to stop thinking about you since the first time I saw you."

"Because you were supposed to follow me to get back the texts," she said, fighting the hope clawing her chest.

"Because you're unforgettable." He kissed the corner of her eye. "Because I love your mind and how you aren't afraid to show your passion." His lips trailed over her cheekbone. "Because you're so sexy but don't realize it." He lowered his mouth to hers. "Because you were destined to be mine."

His lips claimed hers, gentle and reverent. His hands roamed, snaking under her shirt, holding and touching her as if he needed reassurance that she was whole and healthy.

She sank into his embrace. He felt right—like she was finally home, safe and sound and beyond any of the troubles that plagued her. Anything seemed possible.

But then she remembered that last scroll, tucked away in her bag, and she cringed with guilt. They weren't supposed to have lies between them, but here she was keeping secrets. What would he say if he knew she still had a scroll? One that named him as a Guardian.

He'd change his mind about wanting her. He'd walk away from her, once and for all.

Hands on his biceps, she pushed herself away. Keeping her eyes lowered, she slipped out of his arms. "Now isn't a good time. I have to get to work."

His confusion was tangible. She could feel him studying her, trying to figure out what was going on. Feeling like a coward, she tried not to notice the awkward silence as she straightened her clothes.

Hair. Focus on your hair. She gathered her curls in a haphazard ponytail, looking around for her elastic.

"Here." Max took it out of his pocket and held it out to her.

"Thanks." She subdued her locks, watching him rake his own hair back. "I—"

Max enfolded her in his arms, pressing a gentle kiss on top of her head. "I'll pick you up after your shift tonight and bring you home."

"That's not necessary. I can stay at Gabe's again."

"You'll stay with me. Until we figure out who's behind the attacks." He held her close, his grip firm without being restrictive. "You know that the fire wasn't an accident. Not with the way the dock was tampered. And you said you were mugged."

"But—"

"Were you supposed to meet anyone when you were in Santa Monica?" he asked, interrupting her. "Tell me the truth, regardless of what it is."

His seriousness puzzled her. "Who would I meet? I didn't know anyone in LA except you and your employees. Why do you ask?"

He searched her eyes. "I found someone crawling up the side of the house to your balcony."

Her blood chilled. "What?"

"I chased away someone trying to get to your room. Twice."

Oh, God. She would have doubled over if he hadn't been holding her. "I didn't believe him when he called."

"Who?" Max's grip tightened, his voice low and insistent.

"I don't know. His voice was masked by an electronic

voice changer. He didn't say anything, he just threatened me. He said he knew I had what didn't belong to me and that I needed to give it up."

By the way his eyes went cold, she could tell Max knew what *it* was. "Who else knew you had the Book of Water?" he asked.

"No one. I didn't tell anyone." She winced. "But my thesis wasn't a secret. The whole Asian History Department at Cal probably heard I'd made a discovery to tie the Yongle Emperor to the Scrolls of Destiny."

Carrie tried to read what he was thinking as he studied her, but his gaze was impenetrable and distant. Finally, he said, "What else has happened?"

"Don't freak out."

He went still and predatory, every bit the white tiger. "What happened?"

Sigh. "My apartment had been ransacked while I was away."

"That settles it. You're staying with me." He kissed her, slow and soft, belying the anger she felt seething under the surface. He let her go and turned to leave. "I'll see you at closing."

She watched, a little dumbfounded and a lot confused. There was one more thing she hadn't told him.

It was all for her thesis, she reminded herself. She couldn't give up everything she worked for. She just couldn't.

But could she for Max?

Without thought, she did what she always did when she was unsure about something. She called her mom.

The phone rang four times before her mom picked up, sounding breathless. "Hello?"

"Did I catch you at a bad time, Mom?"

"Honey, of course not. I was just doing the homework for a Tantra class I'm taking."

"Perfect timing, then," she said in a mix of amusement and sarcasm.

"You should try it. You lie down naked and—"

"Mom, how do you know if the person you've fallen in love with is worth the risk?" she blurted, picking up her now ashy bag and clutching it to her chest.

"Carrie," her mom said in her soft, unconditionally loving voice, "you of all people could never fall in love with someone who wasn't worth it."

She bit her lip. Was Max worth the risk?

Yes. The answer reverberated inside her, strong and clear.

"Honey? You still there?"

"Yeah." She sighed. "I guess I know the answer to that question."

"You don't sound happy."

"It complicates things, and I'm just not sure how much I'm willing to give up."

"Carrie, you shouldn't have to give up anything for love. Compromise, yes. Give up, no."

Really? She thought of her mom's life and wondered how she could believe that.

"It was a compromise, honey, not a sacrifice," her mom said with her motherly sixth sense. "I never saw moving to Iowa as giving anything up. It didn't work out the way I would have liked, that's true. But it revealed new paths to me that I never would have found. I can't regret any of it, not when I'm so happy now."

"But—"

"No buts. I wouldn't change *anything*. I got to have you, and that's been the greatest joy of my life. No regrets, honey. But that doesn't mean my choices would be right for you. Whatever you do, you should do with the same conviction and passion that you've shown your career. Otherwise, no, it's not worth it."

Tears stung her eyes, and she had to swallow a couple times before she could speak. "But how do you know it's the right choice? How do you know it'll last?"

"Carrie, nothing lasts. It could all end tomorrow. It's how happy you are in this moment that counts. Grab your nuts and take the plunge, honey. If you're thinking about it, he's worth the risk. I didn't raise you to be a coward. Or clueless."

She laughed through her tears. "I love you, Mom."

"Love you too, honey." There was a pause. "How's the condom supply? Should I send more?"

Chapter Thirty-six

Carrie decided to give back the scroll. Tonight—when she saw Max.

Wiping the counter after a customer who just left, she glanced at the time. Ten after midnight. He was due at one, when she closed.

Just thinking about seeing him made her stomach churn with anxiety. The *what ifs* kept running through her mind, the biggest one being what if he walked away and she was left with nothing—no love and no career.

No, she wouldn't think about that. She dropped an empty beer bottle into the recycling bin and began cleaning up the well area. She'd just have to believe it would all work out. The alternative wasn't worth dwelling on.

The slightly queasy feeling stayed with her, though. If she didn't know better, she'd think it was foreboding.

Half an hour later, the last of the customers left. Because it was slow she let Manuel, the busboy, head home, too.

But as soon as he left, Carrie wished she'd asked him

to stay. She looked around the bar, shuddering at the stark emptiness. It was creepy.

"Get a grip," she told herself as she stocked the refrigerator. What she was feeling was just nerves about Max, because she wasn't only surrendering the genealogy, she was surrendering her heart.

Her gut twisted with gigantic butterflies.

Plus, she wasn't sure how he was going to take it. So it was natural that she'd be jittery.

As she stood up, she was hit by another wave of uneasiness—like someone was watching her. She looked around, expecting to find another customer lurking in a dark corner.

No one.

"This is ridiculous." Shaking her head, she ducked under the bar. She'd just lock up. Johnny wouldn't mind, and by closing early, she'd be ready to go when Max arrived, too.

She heaved a sigh of relief the moment she twisted the front door's lock shut. Silly, but small wonder she'd feel that way, given the past few weeks.

Since she'd spent most of the evening prepping the bar area for the next day, it took her only about half an hour to finish up. She glanced at the clock and fished out her cell phone from her bag under the register.

Max answered on the first ring. "Carrie?"

Crazy how just one word from him set her heart racing. "Hey. I closed early. I just have to take out the trash and I'm done for the night."

"I'm five minutes away. Wait for me and I'll take care of the trash for you."

She tried to picture Maximillian Prescott—the legendary

Bái Hǔ—taking out the garbage. The picture wouldn't gel. "It's just a couple of bags and some recycling."

"Which means it'll be no problem for me to help you with it," he replied with cool reason. "Wait for me."

She rolled her eyes. "See you soon."

Closing her phone and dropping it on her bag, she studied the trash. She never said she'd wait for him, and the sooner she was done, the sooner they could have their chat. Now that she'd decided to give him the scroll, she wanted it out of her hands.

Picking up the two bags of recycling, she walked through the bar, down the hallway, and out the back door.

The Dumpster was about ten feet away from the door, flush against the stuccoed outer wall. She paused in the doorway and checked out the alley. She took the trash out every night she worked, and usually it was no big deal.

Tonight, something was wrong. Eerie. Even the air felt too still. But when she looked up and down the alley she didn't see anything.

There was nowhere for a person to hide, except maybe on the other side of the Dumpster. "You're letting your imagination carry you away," she reassured herself.

Taking a deep breath, she stepped away from the door. She jumped as the door clanged shut, hurrying to the recycling bin to dispose of her loads.

She practically ran back to the back door. Throwing it open, she went in, locking it behind her for the first time ever. She laughed shakily. Geez, she was paranoid.

She grabbed the other bags of garbage and took them out. The same feeling of impending doom hit her the second she opened the door again, but she told herself she was being overly sensitive. Squaring her shoulders, she hefted the bags outside. She set a bag down against the metal bin and stretched on her toes to push the lid up.

As she was dropping the first bag in, she felt something shift behind her. Cool air brushed the nape of her neck. Fear froze her to that spot, her breath caught in her chest.

Turn around.

Before she could move, someone pushed her into the Dumpster.

Her hands came up to keep her from hitting the metal barrier with full force. Her palms stung at impact and she cried out.

Her attacker grabbed her ponytail and pulled her head back.

Oh, God—he was going to ram her head into the Dumpster. She'd pass out and be at his mercy. Her heart pounding, she reached behind her, trying to scratch him.

He shoved her, pinning her to the awful-smelling bin with a hand at her head and a forearm across her shoulder blades. "Where is it?" a robotic voice asked.

It was him. Anger burned away the fear in her system, and a burst of adrenaline made her bold enough to play the dumb blonde. "There's money in the register. Take it all."

He slammed her into the metal. "You know what I want."

Ow. She winced in pain. "Refresh my memory."

Her attacker shoved her again and then punched her in the kidney. "Refreshed enough?"

She gasped as the pain shot through her. It would have been so satisfying to Jackie Chan this guy across the alley. "My wallet is inside. If you—"

Grabbing her shoulder, he dragged her around to face

him. Her back arched involuntarily as it hit something protruding on the Dumpster. She hissed, except it was cut off by the arm that lodged itself across her neck.

"I want to know where to find the Scrolls of Destiny."

She shook her head. "The scrolls are myth—"

A fist punched her in her gut, making her jerk forward. Only the arm barring her throat caught her. "You found proof of their existence. I want it."

Gagging from the pressure, she choked out, "I don't have—"

He jabbed her side.

Searing pain shot up her body. She sagged against him, gasping for breath, for relief. Then she drew her knee up to nail him in the groin.

He blocked her effortlessly, growled, and wedged his forearm tighter into her neck.

Great—she'd pissed him off.

"You'll regret that." The thug's arm cocked back, aimed at her face.

"It's inside," she croaked.

The leather-covered fist hovered, but then it grasped her wrist and yanked her around. He twisted her arm behind her and pushed her toward the door. "Show me."

She tried to think of a way out, but pain muddled her thoughts.

Max. Maybe he would arrive in time to help her.

But as she stumbled down the dark hall ahead of her attacker, she realized she'd locked the front door. Max wouldn't be able to get in.

She was on her own.

Chapter Thirty-seven

The door was locked.

Max tried it again. It wasn't closing time yet—why was it locked?

Pressing his hand to the deadbolt, he reached out with his chi and unlocked it. The click was soft, barely audible. He started to let himself in, but as he held the handle in his hand he sensed something wrong. Very wrong.

He paused, alert, *jīn ch'i* focused and ready. He didn't hear anything, but he knew Carrie's stillness. This stillness was unnatural.

Using the darkness of the entrance as cover, he stepped inside, careful to close the door noiselessly. He stayed in the shadows, dispersing his energy and becoming one with them as he looked around the corner.

A slim person in black from head to toe stood behind the counter, rummaging through a bag. It very obviously wasn't Carrie. Max narrowed his eyes, recognizing him. The prowler from his house.

Carrie. An unfamiliar feeling caused his mark to prickle. Fear—for her safety.

Surveying the room, he found her on her knees in front of the counter, one hand on the floor and the other holding her head. Blood seeped through her fingers, dripping on the ground, the iron in it pulling him.

Anger seized him. *Jīn ch'i* pulsed, rising to the surface, ready to attack. He started forward, needing to go to her.

But, hands clenched, he pulled himself back. *Assess the situation first.*

His gaze narrowed on the person behind the counter. The bastard was in for a world of hurt. Max just needed to leave him lucid enough to find out why Carrie had been targeted and if anyone else was involved. After that, all bets were off.

The man growled, an electronically masked sound of anger and frustration, and ducked from behind the bar.

Headed straight for Carrie.

Rage unlike anything Max had ever felt before slashed through him—worse than even that day when he discovered Rhys had betrayed him. Knowing better than to fight in anger, he focused it into *jīn ch'i,* until it was honed and ready.

He stepped out from the shadows.

The bastard didn't see him. Intent on Carrie, he headed straight to her, shaking the bag in his hand. "Where is it?"

When Carrie shook her head, he moved to kick her in the head.

"*No.*" Stepping out from the shadows, Max gathered *jīn ch'i* and slashed at her attacker. He watched in satisfaction as blood welled in the slice-like gash at the man's thigh.

Dropping the bag, the attacker stumbled and grabbed the wound. The bag dropped on the floor wide open, and a scroll rolled out next to it.

A scroll? Max frowned. He thought he had all of them.

They both dove for it, but the intruder had the advantage of being closer. Scooping it up, he turned to escape. And halted.

Because Max stood between him and the exit. Max grinned, cold and mean. He wasn't going to let the bastard get away a third time.

Gathering his chi, he aimed at the arm this time. He flung his hand out, throwing a razor-sharp blade of energy.

The bastard grabbed the cut but didn't drop the scroll. Head low and determined, he rushed at Max.

Max waited until the last possible moment to step aside and punch. It impacted harder than he expected, sinking into softness.

He frowned. *It's a woman.*

Distracted by the realization, he didn't see the round-house kick until it was about to connect to his ribs, and then it was too late to do anything but flex his side. Still, it hit solid and hurt like a bitch. He hissed through his teeth.

She stepped in, arm cocked for a second strike. He blocked the chop to his throat and grabbed her.

Her boot heel ground into his foot.

"Shit." The move surprised him into letting her go.

Not waiting, she whirled and ran through the bar and the hallway.

The back door. He began to follow—

Carrie moaned.

He froze, torn between going after her attacker to get answers and tending to her. But in the clarity of the moment, his heart told him where he needed to be.

Turning, he knelt on the floor next to her. All the blood made him pause. Logically, he knew head wounds bled— he'd been cut enough times in sparring practice to know that firsthand. But seeing Carrie bleed scared him to his core.

Very gently, he cradled her in his lap and pushed her hand away to take a look. A lump rose around the cut, and the beginning of a nasty bruise already tainted her fair skin. Blood dripped down the side of her face.

It drove him insane. If he'd had his sword, he would have cut down her attacker, woman or not.

Carrie moaned again, and he ran the backs of his knuckles across her cheek. "Carrie, open your eyes for me."

Her lashes fluttered. It looked like it took effort, but she opened her eyes. Pain twisted her expression, and she lifted her hand to her head.

He caught it and held it in his. "Don't touch. It's going to hurt."

"It already hurts," she said, a little slurry. She struggled to sit up. "How did you get in?"

"Wait." Holding her still, he placed his hand over the cut. *Jīn ch'i* flared, and he began to breathe in tandem to its pulsing. Focusing his chi in his hand, he let it flow into her.

"Feels tingly." Carrie sighed, nuzzling his hand.

The iron in her blood responded to him, and he focused on binding the metallic particles. Slowly, the flow of blood stopped under the clot he created at the surface of the wound. Once he was satisfied it would hold, he changed how he channeled his chi, making the palm of his hand cold like the flat of a sword at rest. Gently so he wouldn't jar her, he rested his hand right over the lump.

He tried not to notice how it looked like it'd grown bigger.

She sighed and her eyes fluttered shut. "Nice."

"Stay awake."

"Not going to fall asleep. Just enjoying the coolness." She rubbed her head against his palm.

"You'll hurt yourself if you press too hard."

Her smile was faint, but it reassured him unlike anything. "You won't let me."

True. Never again. His arm tightened around her. He had to force himself to keep his hand light on her forehead.

As if she read his mind, she set her hand on top of his and pressed. "No, that feels good."

He grunted, not entirely convinced of that.

"In fact, I'd say you're my hero. You not only kicked some bad-guy bootie, but you've done something to make my head feel better."

"What happened?"

"This?" She touched the back of his hand. "He knocked my head against the Dumpster."

He gritted his teeth as a wave of rage swept through him. If that bastard were still here, he'd kick her ass all over again. "I thought you gave me all the scrolls from the monastery."

Carrie froze, then pushed his hand away and kneeled in front of him. "I thought so, too. But then I got back home and there was one lodged deep in my bag. I didn't keep it on purpose, I swear. I was going to return it to you tonight."

He waited for the usual feeling of betrayal, but all he felt was anger and concern—anger that anyone had dared to hurt her and concern over what the attacker may have gotten.

Carrie tugged at his shirt. "Are you angry with me?"

"No."

"You are," she said miserably.

Yeah, because she'd foolishly placed her life in danger. At least it hadn't been the Book of Water. That was in one of his safes. "What did the scroll contain? Do you know?"

"Um." She bit her lip, wincing. "The list of all the Guardians through history. To now. Including you, Gabe, and Rhys."

Damn. That was as bad as one of the Scrolls of Destiny being taken. "Do you know who she was?"

"Who?"

"The woman who attacked you."

Carrie gaped. "It was a *woman?*"

"Yes." He brushed a tendril of hair away from her face, the better to see how her wound looked. It hadn't gotten worse, but it was still livid. "You didn't know."

"I assumed it was a man." Her hand caught his. "I'm so sorry. I know I blew this. But I'll find out who it was and get it ba—"

"*No.*" He took her by the back of her neck, lowering his face so she could see how serious he was. "You will not try to find out anything. You'll leave this to me."

Worry lined her beautiful features. She stared into his eyes for a long, silent moment, and then she shook her head. "I can't do that. This was my fault, and if you got hurt trying to fix something I did, I'd never forgive myself."

"Get hurt?" The idea was ridiculous. She was the one who could get hurt—who already got hurt. He glanced at the lump on her head and rage suffused him all over again. "You won't go anywhere near this person."

"But—"

"Enough." He began gathering her things, putting them back in her bag.

"What are you doing?"

"Taking you home. My home."

"In Santa Monica?"

"My home here." He held out her bag. "And there will be no debate about it."

She accepted it, looking like she wanted to argue. But then her expression cleared and she just studied him, a faint frown to her mouth. She nodded and stood up. "Okay."

His eyes narrowed suspiciously. "Just like that you're agreeing?"

"Yeah. For you." She slung the bag over her shoulder. "But don't think I won't make you agree to some concessions of my own."

His suspicion grew. "Like?"

"Later. For now, just take me home."

He kissed her temple and, supporting her by the elbow, escorted her to his car. At home he could protect her and keep her safe until he figured out how to rectify this situation. For his own sake.

Chapter Thirty-eight

Her head throbbed, and she felt like she'd taken on all of Emperor Qinshihuang's warriors. Despite it all, sitting in Max's car, Carrie felt oddly at peace.

She glanced at Max's profile, his features stern and focused on getting them to wherever it was he lived. "I didn't know you had a home in San Francisco."

"I didn't. I recently bought it."

When he'd been keeping tabs on her, or after when he wanted to spend time with her? She closed her eyes, wanting to ask. Only she wasn't sure the answer mattered anymore.

The smooth purr of the car stopped, and she opened her eyes. A garage. A pretty sizable garage for the city, but there were only two other cars in it. She knew nothing about cars, but she could tell they were both as expensive as the one she was currently in.

Max leaned toward her. "You awake?"

"Mm." She stretched as she unbuckled her seat belt.

"Stay."

She would have rolled her eyes if it didn't hurt so much. But she knew he meant well. And, actually, she wasn't sure her legs would carry her.

He hopped out of the car and came around to her side. With tender care, he helped her from the seat and guided her through the garage and into a long, industrial-looking hallway. He stopped in front of the elevator and pressed the up button.

She rested her head on his chest. His heart beat under her cheek, at a reassuring tempo that echoed inside her. "You're not going to turn out to be a mad scientist taking me to his laboratory to commit strange experiments, are you?"

He glanced down at her, an eyebrow cocked.

"Of course, if the experiments are sexual in nature, I may be amenable."

"Not sure you're up for it."

Given the way her head was starting to hurt, he was probably right. "I'll lie there, and you can take charge."

His only response was a quick glance at her before the elevator arrived.

She looked around as much as she could without jarring her head. "This looks like a freight elevator."

"It was. It's an old warehouse that's been renovated."

Renovated nicely, by the look of things, because she doubted the elevator was the original. Too modern and sleek-looking. "Ever watch *Fatal Attraction*?"

"Did you hit your head harder than I thought?" he asked as they reached their floor. He led her to an oversized door, unlocked it, and disabled the alarm before ushering her inside.

The dimly lit space looked cavernous. The wall on

the far side was floor-to-ceiling windows that showed an impressive bit of San Francisco's skyline. Even though there was such little light, she could see the outline of support beams in the middle of a large, open room with minimalist furniture, just like he'd had in Santa Monica.

Max guided her past the living area, past a kitchen area that gleamed even in the darkness, to a spiral metal staircase. When they reached the top, she saw this was the source of the lighting downstairs—the glow from the lamp by the bed. The enormous bed with pristine white covers.

Max motioned for her to sit on the bed and then strode to an opening in the wall to the right. A light came on seconds later, followed shortly by a rush of water.

The bathroom. Cool how it didn't have a door, but you'd have to be intimate with whomever you lived with. If you lived with anyone.

Not wanting to think about that, she looked around the room. It was a loft within a loft—the railing at the end of the room seemed to overlook the downstairs.

Max came back and kneeled at her side. "Up for a bath?"

"A bath." Just the thought of it was soothing, enough for her to drag her carcass up off the bed.

The bathroom was austere, just like she expected, all shiny metal with white accents and fluffy towels. Only instead of looking barren, it was refreshing. Of course, the sound of the running water could have had something to do with it.

She caught a glimpse of herself in the mirror and winced. No wonder he'd acted freaked out—the lump on her head looked bad. At least it throbbed only dully now, thanks to whatever it was he did to her.

He tested the water in the tub, one of those huge, two-person baths with jets. Apparently satisfied, he stuck his hands in his pockets. "Will you be okay on your own?"

"On my own?" She looked at the tub and then back at him. "You're leaving me here?"

He frowned with concern. "Can't you undress by yourself?"

Hands on her hips, she shook her head, which she regretted because the motion made her dizzy. "No, I can't."

"Does your head hurt?" He stepped closer to her and put his hand against the lump on her head.

Coolness hit her at once, and she moaned with how it eased the pain. "How do you do that? It's like you radiate cold. Is it a Guardian thing?"

He stared at her blankly. She didn't think he was going to answer, and that sent a spiral of disappointment through her. But then he said, "We'll talk about that tomorrow. Right now you need a bath, some aspirin, and bed."

She thought of the bed out there and pursed her lips. "You're joining me, right?"

"In the bath?"

The shocked expression on his face made her grin. "Sure, there, too." She lifted her arms. "Undress me. I'm helpless and hurt."

His eyes narrowed. She knew he didn't believe her. Of course, her grin might have been a giveaway. But he stepped forward and took the hem of her shirt.

She held her breath, lost in his not-so-cool gaze and the pulse of his body right in front of her. His fingers brushed her sides, and she gasped at the current that shot through her. He dragged the shirt over her head, slowly so his fingers never lost contact with her skin.

Her nipples pebbled. She glanced down and saw how they poked from her bra. She mentally patted her back for choosing to wear one of the sexy bras her mom sent her. If you have only one bra left in the world, better for it to be black lace than white cotton.

Her breasts tightened under his steady gaze. Without a word, he unsnapped the bra, eased it off her, and tossed it aside. His hands drifted to the waist of her jeans and plucked open the top button. Unzipping them, he pushed them down and waited for her to step out of them. She held his shoulders and lifted each leg one at a time, trying not to notice how his mouth was level with ground zero.

"Get in," he said, his voice raspy.

At least she wasn't the only one affected here. She sank her body into the tub slowly, sighing as the heat overtook her. The water lapped at her, soothing waves of comfort that took away some of her residual headache. "Are you joining me?"

"You were hurt."

She rolled her eyes, grimacing with a small twinge of pain.

Muttering under his breath, he stormed out of the room. She was too complacent to get up to see what the deal was. Not that she had to worry—he strode back in with a glass of water.

"Take this." He motioned to her to hold out her hand. When she did, he dropped four pills in her palm. "Ibuprofen," he said before she could ask, holding out the water. "Take all four. Your head hurts more than you're admitting."

"And then will you get in?" She watched him as she popped the pills and took a swallow of water.

His hands clenched, like he was holding himself back. "Drink all the water."

She sighed in disappointment. He was going to resist, drat him. "What if I need my back washed?" she asked pathetically, handing back the glass.

She expected him to just grunt and walk out. He surprised her when he set the glass on the counter and yanked his shirt over his head.

Chapter Thirty-nine

Conflicted.

Max undid his pants, his gaze never leaving Carrie. He wanted to dive into the tub—into her. His hands shook he wanted it so badly.

She held her arms out. "Come hold me."

He needed to, if only to reassure himself that she was okay. He glanced at the knot on her forehead and felt his chi roil with anger. She still looked pale, and no matter what she said, he knew she wasn't one hundred percent.

Dropping his pants, he quickly got out of his underwear and faced her. "Move forward."

She shifted, and the water sloshed as he climbed in. He sat behind her, and she leaned back against his chest.

Without thought, his arms went around her waist. He gritted his teeth, hyper-aware of his cock pressing so urgently into her back. "Relax," he said, more to himself than to her.

"I'm not used to this," she said after a moment of silence.

He nuzzled her hair, nodding. He wasn't, either. But

he deliberately misunderstood her. "Of course you aren't. Most people wouldn't have been able to deal with what you have and not fall apart."

To distract her before she could reply, he began to massage her shoulders. He felt her tension just under the surface and, with a breath of *jīn ch'i*, cooled her inflamed muscles. A small relief, but he was happy to give it.

"Don't stop that. Ever. It's too good." Carrie nestled into him and looked over her shoulder at him with her big, innocent eyes. "Okay?"

He nodded, reaching for a bar of soap. "Lean forward."

"If it means more, who am I to argue?" She rested her chest against her knees and dropped her head forward.

He lathered his hands until they were good and slippery, studying the elegant curve of her back before running his hands down it.

She groaned. "You could make a fortune as a massage therapist."

"I already have a fortune."

"It was a figure of speech. I meant you could have anything you wanted."

He wanted only her.

Focusing on her and not on the incessant throbbing of his dick, he coaxed her body into letting go of its tension, working his thumbs in slow circles.

"I'm a sucker for a good massage," she said softly. "It's my mom's fault. I used to have trouble going to sleep when I was a kid. She'd give me warm milk and then lie down with me and rub my back until I went to sleep."

"Were you too active to sleep?"

"No, too scared."

"Scared of what?"

"Were you scared of anything as a kid?"

"No." He worked his fingers down her lower back, right at the top of her butt. "What were you afraid of?"

"You were probably a badass even as a toddler. Your first toy was probably a sword."

"Stop changing the subject and tell me what scared you." She seemed so indomitable, it was hard to imagine anything frightening her. "It wasn't the dark."

"Why are you so sure of that?"

"Intuition." He rubbed his hands up and down her back, gently, trying to reassure her. "Tell me."

Trust me.

Max didn't think she was going to tell him, but finally she sighed. "I was afraid my mom would leave while I was asleep and I'd be alone."

He stopped, caught off guard by her admission, but then resumed kneading. "Why would you be afraid of such a thing?"

"Because I went to sleep one night and when I woke up, my dad was gone."

"Gone?" He frowned at the idea of anyone even thinking of abandoning her. He felt a surprising urge to find the man and beat some sense into him.

"Looking back, it was a good thing," she continued. "My mom's wonderful. She's been happier since he left."

"Why did he leave?"

"According to my mom, he decided he didn't want to be a husband and a dad. In my five-year-old mind, I was afraid my mom would leave, too." She peeked back at him, patting his thigh as if she could hear his angry thoughts. "It's in the past. I've moved on."

"Have you?"

"I—" She shrugged.

Holding her by the shoulders, he leaned her back so she rested against him again and reached for the soap. "I'm not your father, Carrie. I won't leave you. You can see for yourself, after everything, I'm still here," he whispered, relathering his hands.

He lowered his sudsy hands to her neck and massaged the soap into her skin. He worked his way down to her breasts, doing slow spirals around them without touching the peaks.

She arched her back. "You're doing this on purpose. I know you are."

"What?" he whispered into her ear.

"Making me desperate for you."

"Are you?"

"Desperate?" She half laughed, half groaned.

He thumbed her nipples, slowly and softly at first but quickly increasing the speed and intensity until she moaned nonstop.

Just below the surface, he could see the triangle of hair between her legs. He couldn't help himself. He trailed his right hand down into the water. "Open."

She did, quickly and without question.

This time, he didn't tease—he needed to feel her softness. So he dipped his fingers into her warmth.

Crying out, she hooked her legs over his knees so they opened wider, inviting his touch.

Max increased the pressure, rubbing her faster and harder until she strained against him. With each wiggle of her body, his own throbbed in response. He clenched his jaw, trying not to imagine slipping into her from behind but failing miserably.

"Max." Her head thrown back on his shoulder, she gripped his forearms.

He kissed the side of her neck. "Next time it'll be my tongue playing with you like this."

She shot off like a rocket, calling out his name and rocking uncontrollably against his hand. Relentless, he kept at her until he was sure she had nothing left to give.

Slumping against him, she turned her head and pressed a kiss to his chest. She lay there as he quickly finished washing her body. He pulled the plug, scooped her in his arms, and carried her to the shower.

Lifting her head, she frowned at the glass cubes that formed the stall. "We aren't clean enough?"

"Just to rinse and warm you. Can you stand?"

"Yeah."

He watched her carefully as he set her down. "How's your head?"

"Fine." She rubbed his chest reassuringly. "I'm just rocky from being pleasured."

Cocking an eyebrow, he turned on the shower. "Pleasured?"

"I call it like I feel it. God, the water is nice," she said as she stepped in.

He angled all four shower heads so they focused on her.

She surprised him when she ran a hand up the extremely hard length of him. "I didn't reciprocate."

His entire body jerked at her touch, but he pried her hand from him and kissed it. "Later."

"Why not now?" Pursing her lips, she stared at his hard-on. "It seems a shame to let it go to waste."

"Later," he said again, lowering his mouth to hers as he turned off the water.

She stood quietly while he patted her dry. A statement to how tired she was, he thought. He quickly rubbed the moisture off himself and picked her up again.

She snuggled against him. "This could become a habit."

A habit he wouldn't mind—he liked her in his arms. He took her into his bedroom and laid her down on the big bed. She scooted so he could get the covers out from under her and tucked beneath her chin. He dropped a long, slow kiss on her lips and turned.

"Will you hold me?"

He paused, looking at her from over his shoulder.

"Just till I fall asleep?"

He couldn't resist the plea in her eyes. He nodded. "Yes."

Moving over to the middle, Carrie turned on her side so her back faced him. He crawled under the comforter and slipped his arms around her and pulled her into his chest.

She snuggled closer.

A lump formed in his throat. Clearing it, he asked, "Want me to rub your back?"

She wiggled against his still-raging erection. "Maybe we should—"

"Shh." He caressed her hair back from her face. "I'm fine. Sleep now."

He held her like that, stroking her hair. He told himself he'd stop once she fell asleep, but even then he couldn't bring himself to leave her. In his arms, she was safe.

His arms tightened, thinking of the danger she'd been in. He should have protected her better—especially after the fire. Insupportable. And as he gently kissed her temple, he vowed it would never happen again.

Chapter Forty

Mmm…" Carrie stretched her legs, folding her arms underneath her pillow. Her sheets felt more luxurious than they usually did. Maybe she used more fabric softener in the last load.

Yawning, she opened her eyes to a pristine view of the bay.

View of the bay?

She bolted upright, realized she was naked, and pulled the covers up to her chin. She flashed on the evening after that disastrous chem midterm in college and how she went on a bender and ended up in Kevin Chesapeake's dorm room.

But then she felt the lump on her head, remembered the previous night, and exhaled in relief.

"Good morning."

She turned her head so quickly it throbbed in protest. Max stood at the top of the spiral stairs, glowering. Before she could say anything, he turned and descended the stairs.

"Do I look that bad?" She wouldn't doubt it if she did. She felt like her head had been caught in a turbine.

Maybe if she had some coffee, she'd feel more human. She looked around the room—which was more impressive in daylight, by the way—for her clothes. No sign of them. She glanced at what she supposed was a closet to the right and wondered if it'd be weird to wear some of Max's clothes.

She rolled her eyes. A little late for that kind of modesty.

"Take this."

With a small yelp, she jerked around to find Max next to her. "I didn't hear you come up."

He said nothing, his implacable stare steady, his hands outstretched with a glass of water and what she assumed was more ibuprofen.

Given how achy her head felt, she accepted his offering without question. She downed the entire glass of water before he could tell her to and handed it back. "Do you think I could have a coffee chaser?"

He reached out and brushed her hair back, examining her head. "You don't want to sleep longer?"

"I'll only feel more groggy."

"Then you should have something to eat, too. Do you feel up to coming downstairs?"

"Yeah, but—" She looked around, holding the sheet close to her chest. "Do you know where my clothes are?"

"I threw them away."

She blinked. "Excuse me?"

"They had bloodstains on them." He crossed the room to the closet, opened the door, and pulled something white out of it. "I've asked Francesca to pick up some clothes for you. Wear this in the meantime."

She took the silky shirt from him. "Yours?"

He arched his eyebrow. "Who else would it belong to?"

"Right." She rubbed her fingers on the fabric, knowing it was going to feel like heaven against her skin. "Um, did you throw away my underwear, too?"

"It'll all be replaced," was all he said before leaving and going back downstairs.

"That didn't answer my question," she called after him. Lounging around in just his shirt—no panties—seemed so Sharon Stone. She held the shirt up to the sunlight. At least it wasn't see-through.

She pushed the covers aside and eased her legs over the side. Slipping the shirt over her head, she rolled the long sleeves so they didn't dangle half a foot past her fingertips.

"Bathroom." She stood up cautiously and headed over to wash her face. She was surprised that it was tidy in there—no evidence of last night's bath. Carrie washed her face and brushed her teeth with a new toothbrush she found in a cabinet. After a futile attempt to calm her curls, she gave up and followed the scent of coffee downstairs.

Last night she hadn't appreciated how large the downstairs area was. Huge. And not just because it was sparsely furnished.

Max waited for her in the open kitchen. It was modern and sleek, with shining chrome and polished wood like the rest of the loft. He leaned against the countertop, holding out a mug to her.

The aroma hit her, and she practically lunged for it. Her first sip was heaven. She inhaled its smell, conscious of the way he watched her, and looked at him from over the rim. "You sweetened it for me."

"You prefer it that way." He turned around. "Sit. I'll bring you some food."

"Do you need help?"

"No. Sit."

"We've got to do something about your bossiness." But, cradling her cup, she pulled out a chair from the table in the nook and eased herself into it. "Though truthfully I don't mind having a hot guy serve me."

Shooting her a narrow glance, he reached for a pan hanging from over the stove.

"I'm kind of curious about what you'll feed me. Who knew you'd have skills beyond swordplay?"

A grunt.

She smiled as she took another sip. A few minutes later he set a plate in front of her. Pancakes with a pat of butter and fresh fruit. He set down a small pitcher of what smelled like maple syrup. Her stomach growled eagerly at the aroma. "This isn't the gourmet meal of Fruity Pebbles I expected."

He crossed his arms and leaned against the counter. "Eat."

"Yes, sir." She didn't think about the carbs or how tight her jeans were going to be as she dug in, it was so delicious. Though she had the sneaking suspicion it tasted even better because he'd made it for her.

While she ate, she was conscious of him watching her. She wanted to tell him to sit down and join her, but she was too busy eating.

Max didn't say anything until she was done. "More?"

She actually considered it for a minute before she shook her head and rose to wash her plate. "Did you make the pancakes from scratch?"

He lifted his eyebrow. "Hard to believe?"

"Kind of."

"Let your mind rest—it's one of the few things I can cook." He stepped in and took the plate from her. "I'll do that."

"If you pull out an apron to wear, you'll totally shatter my tough-guy image of you." Staying next to him, she watched his hands. They were as efficiently adept with the dishes as they were with her body last night.

She cleared her throat. "So when do you think Francesca will arrive with clothes?"

"Why?"

"I can't go out wearing this." She gestured to his too-big shirt.

He grabbed a towel and faced her head-on as he dried his hands. "You aren't going anywhere."

"I think I misheard you." She put her hands on her hips, realized that hiked the shirt up precariously close to her privates, and fisted her hands straight at her sides. "I'm sure you couldn't have been ordering me around."

"I'm not ordering. I'm telling you how it's going to be."

She sputtered for several seconds before she shook off her shock. "Who are you to tell me what to do?"

He stepped forward, towering over her, his face stony in his anger. "I'm the man who saved your impertinent hide last night. In case you forgot, someone is out for you. You had your head bashed in, and the night before, your house was set on fire. I won't let you give this bastard another opportunity to strike at you."

Yeah, but she had to get that genealogy back before someone used it against Max. Not that she knew where to start, but anything was better than sitting around waiting for the next bad thing to happen.

Trevor. Her cheeks flushed as she thought of his confrontation. He was enough of a creep to attack her. It didn't explain the woman last night. Maybe he hired someone?

Maybe she was wrong and it wasn't Trevor. A woman who could fight, scale a wall, and knew where Carrie could be found at all times?

Francesca.

Carrie gasped. She'd wondered about Francesca, but she'd gotten obsessed with Max. And then her suspicions transferred to Trevor.

Max looked at her. "What is it?"

As if she could tell him. The woman was his assistant—someone he grew up with. Carrie had to make sure she had real proof before she accused her. To distract Max, she patted his chest. "I'll take precautions."

"Too risky. I won't allow it."

"What do you mean, you won't allow it?"

"Just what I said."

She threw her hands in the air and stalked upstairs, mumbling to herself. "High-handed, arrogant, obstinate, caring jerk."

She needed something to wear. She couldn't go shopping like this.

And she couldn't wait. She wanted to rule Trevor out, just in case, before dealing with Francesca. She couldn't bear the thought that Max—or Gabe and Rhys—could be outed because of her. Or worse—hunted.

In the meantime, she'd have to make do with Max's clothes and then hit the Gap when it opened. She went to his closet and sifted through the clothing.

"What are you doing?"

She looked over her shoulder. Max stood, arms crossed, legs braced, looking like an irritated warrior. She tried not to notice how hot he was in his loose cotton pants and flowy shirt, but she failed. Scowling, she said, "Do you have another pair of pants like that?"

He slowly approached the closet. "Why?"

Her heart beat nervously at the look in his eyes. She backed up until a wall of clothing stopped her. "What are you doing?"

"Keeping you from putting yourself in danger."

His growly voice made her shiver—and not in a bad way. But she lifted her chin and said in her best professorial voice, "How exactly will you accomplish that?"

He stopped in front of her, bracketing her in his arms. "Watch me."

Chapter Forty-one

Carrie's heart pounded—in excitement, damn him. "This isn't a good idea."

He swooped her into his arms, took her to the bed, and set her down, blanketing her head to toe with his hard body. "It's an excellent idea."

One part of him was harder than the rest. She wiggled, trying to break his hold but the only thing she succeeded in doing was fitting that part of him right up against her. "I'm annoyed with you."

"I know." His teeth grazed the skin bared by the open collar of her shirt.

"Really annoyed." She arched her neck, spearing her fingers through his hair. "You're being heavy-handed."

"I have to," he murmured against her neck.

Carrie tugged his head back so his eyes met hers. "No, you don't. You could trust me to know what I need."

His jaw tightened, and she could see his struggle to try to give her that. But finally he shook his head. "I can't accept that."

She heaved a sigh and let him go. "Why not?"

"Because I care. About you."

"That's nice and all, but—"

He leaned down so his stormy eyes filled her entire field of vision. "I care about you."

"You *care* about me?" Anger filled her chest until she couldn't feel the hurt his words caused.

"Yes." His expression became wary. "Do you mind?"

"Yes, I mind." She tried to wiggle away from him but he held her in place. "Let me go."

"Not until you tell me what's going through your head."

"That's *it?*" Laying limp in defeat, she glared up at him. "You jerk. Everything that's happened between us, and you *care?* Next you'll tell me how you hold me in great esteem."

"I do."

Another bit of her heart broke. "*Jerk*. I thought you wanted me."

"I *do*."

Something in his voice broke through to her. She frowned, not trusting what she heard. "What does that mean?"

"It means I won't see you hurt." His features went all fierce. "I'll do whatever I have to do to see you safe. You are mine, Carrie."

"But what does that mean? Do you love—"

Someone cleared her throat from behind them.

Max rolled off the bed and stood ready. Wide-eyed, Carrie leaned up on her elbows. Rhys stood at the foot of the stairs, Gabe peeking from behind him.

Carrie frowned. "What are you guys doing here?"

"We were summoned, and when no one answered the door we let ourselves in." Gabe smirked. "But I think the real question is, what are *you* guys doing here? And can we watch?"

Summoned? Carrie looked at Max, hoping he'd get the mental message that she had nothing to do with this. He just stared straight ahead, glowering at Rhys, looking like he was ready to lunge at any second.

But that just made Max's next statement all the more puzzling. "They're here because I called them."

Chapter Forty-two

Max never imagined he'd end up in the kitchen, making coffee with Rhys's woman, while Rhys and Carrie adjourned to the living room.

He glanced at them, sitting too close together, and clenched his fists to keep from pounding the counter. Or Rhys, for that matter.

He'd called Rhys to warn him off from trying to harm Carrie again. But Rhys denied the attacks—vehemently— and insisted on helping locate whoever had targeted Carrie.

Given his lack of leads, he'd accepted Rhys's help. Reluctantly. After much swearing on both their parts. The union might have been necessary, but Max didn't have to like it.

Coming to stand next to him at the counter, Gabe set the cups she'd gotten out of the cupboard on the tray he'd found. "Remember how I told you I'd pull your gonads through your throat?"

What the hell was she getting at? He glanced at her, annoyed, and realized he'd never really looked at her. He could see she'd be considered striking with her long dark hair and vivid blue eyes. She wasn't nearly as beautiful as Carrie, but that was Rhys's loss.

She poked a finger in his face. "I wasn't kidding. If you're messing with Carrie, I'm going to unleash a world of hurt on your ass."

Crossing his arms, he glared at her. "And if I find out you and Rhys are behind this, after all—"

"Me and Rhys?" Her voice raised, her eyes narrowing. "What do we have to do with anything?"

He stepped close, pitching his voice low and threatening. "I know Rhys. I know he'll do anything for power. Including hurting a friend."

She glanced at his neck before looking him in the eyes and shaking her head. "That was the old Rhys. The new Rhys is different."

She sounded so confident, he almost believed her. Almost. "And you?"

"Me? What about me?"

"The person who attacked Carrie last night was a woman."

Gabe blinked a couple times. As comprehension dawned on her face, her cheeks flushed and anger lit her eyes. "You can't seriously think—"

"I do."

"Bastard," she hissed. "She's my best friend."

"Everything okay in there?" Carrie called from the other room.

They both looked up to find Rhys and Carrie staring at them.

"Fine." Gabe banged the sugar bowl onto the tray and glared at him, daring him to contradict her.

As if he'd give her the satisfaction. Setting the carafe on the tray, he picked it up and carried it to the living room, Gabe following on his heels.

He put the tray on the table and poured a cup for Carrie. As he turned to hand it to her, he noticed Rhys holding her hand.

His chest swelled with fury. "Move."

Rhys calmly held out her hand for him to take and got up to join Gabe where she sat.

Still holding her hand, Max claimed the spot Rhys vacated.

Carrie looked at him, worry etched on her face. Biting her lip, she turned to the other couple. "I've put you all in danger."

"It seems you're the one being attacked, darling," Rhys said evenly.

Max's body stiffened at the endearment, but she snuggled into his side and he found himself soothed.

"Hey," Gabe called out. "Stop playing footsie and tell us what's going on."

He had no idea how Rhys put up with her. If it were up to him, he'd duct tape her mouth shut. In fact, he was sure he had a roll in a toolbox somewhere.

Carrie squeezed his hand as if she knew the direction of his thoughts. "Gabe, you know the time I met you at your house before we went to the Asian Art Museum? I arrived early and heard you and Rhys talking. I heard him mention Wei Lin."

Gabe set down her cup. "And that meant something to you?"

"Yeah, it spurred me to go to the monastery in China to

research Wei Lin and try to prove that there was a historical basis for the Scrolls of Destiny."

The stunned silence was so thick he could have cut it with his sword.

Carrie sighed. "Long story short, I thought if I could find proof that they actually existed and tie it into my existing research, I'd be a shoo-in for the job at Cal. I never thought I'd actually find anything. But then next thing I know, I'm smuggling ancient Chinese documents into this country—"

Gabe groaned. Max noted Rhys's expression didn't change, but he could see his former friend processing the information.

"I know," Carrie wailed. "What was I thinking? I wasn't thinking. When I found Wei Lin's journal, all rational thought escaped me. I never would have taken them if I knew one of the scrolls was the Book of Water."

Rhys's gaze darted to Max, looking for confirmation. Max nodded once.

"You took a scroll?" Gabe reeled back. "Oh, shit."

"I didn't mean to. I only meant to read Wei Lin's journal. And I was going to return them. Really." Carrie toyed with her cup handle. "I'm sorry if you feel I betrayed you. I hope I can make it up to you."

"You put yourself in danger for a freaking term paper?" Gabe shook her head. "You could have been arrested. Or worse. Like having your apartment set on fire."

"The documents weren't in your apartment when the fire happened, were they?" Rhys asked.

"I'd given them back to Max. Except one." Carrie's knuckles were white, she gripped her coffee cup so tightly. "The one that listed all the Guardians."

"So you know?" Gabe asked cautiously.

"Yeah. If it were any other circumstance, I'd want to know everything about being a Guardian, like what you can do and what it feels like. If you can fly." The excited light faded from her face. "Although I'm afraid I'll get firsthand knowledge of your powers when I tell you the genealogy—the scroll that lists all of you as Guardians—is what was taken."

Silence fell, heavy and loaded. Rhys glanced at him, and he knew the same thing was going through his mind. They had to recover the text and eliminate the threat.

Carrie turned to him. "I was going to give it back to you. I swear. Last night. Only I got attacked—"

"And she took it," Max finished for her.

"Yeah." Carrie worried her lip as she studied her friend. Finally she said, "You aren't angry with me?"

Gabe snorted. "Of course I'm angry with you."

"I'm so sorry—"

"Not about the scroll, babe. That you put yourself in danger over something so meaningless. I used to think you were so levelheaded. Who knew you had such a melodramatic streak in you?" She shook her head. "Yeah, I'm still going to talk to you. You're my best friend."

Carrie hopped up and gave Gabe an awkward hug that landed her in a pile on top of both her and Rhys. "I love you so much. I'm so sorry I screwed up, but I promise I'm going to make it right."

"You're not doing anything," Max said tightly, wanting to rip Rhys's hand off Carrie, even if it was just on her arm.

Brow furrowed, she glanced at him. Some sort of understanding lit her face, and she pushed herself off them and came back to him.

Damn if that didn't melt what was left of the hard shell around his heart.

"As much as it pains me, I have to agree with Max," Rhys said mildly.

"They're right, babe. You aren't equipped to deal with this."

"I can—"

"No," Gabe and Max vetoed together.

"Darling, I'm going to have to agree on this." Rhys set his coffee cup on the table. "We have connections you don't. I'm sure we can get this matter resolved in no time. Without any further danger to you." His gaze hardened as he looked at Max. "Isn't that so, Max?"

Max clenched his jaw so hard he felt his bones creak. But he had to protect his scroll and Carrie. He gave one jerky nod.

Carrie huffed, frowning at them. "I don't see how you guys could be privy to any more information than me. It's not like the person who took the genealogy is going to sell it."

"Maybe, maybe not." Rhys stroked his scar.

The same way he always touched his scar. Max ran a hand over the burn mark Rhys gave him, not sure he liked the similarity.

"It could be that the person took it to auction it to the highest bidder," Rhys continued.

"I don't know that I agree." Carrie pursed her lips. "Everything just seemed so, I don't know, *personal*. The threats made it sound like I'd done something to thwart him, which is why I thought it might be Trevor."

Max stiffened. "Who the hell is Trevor?"

"A colleague." She grabbed his arm. "Are you absolutely sure it was a woman last night?"

"Yes." His eyes narrowed. "Who's Trevor, and why haven't you mentioned him?"

"I mentioned him, just to Ramirez. But if the perp was a woman, it couldn't have been Trevor. Unless he hired someone to attack me." She frowned.

"Give me his name anyway." Rhys pulled out a PDA and began tapping. "It won't hurt to officially cross him off the list, and it's a place to start."

Max noted the name mentally as Carrie gave it to Rhys. He'd do his own checking.

"If we're looking for a woman, I have a suspect." Carrie stared at him oddly.

"Who?"

"Francesca."

"Francesca?" He shook his head. "She has nothing to do with this."

"Of course not. Silly me."

He frowned at the heavy sarcasm in her voice.

"Never mind." She rubbed her head, looking wrung out. "I'm so sorry, guys. I'll ask around—"

"No," Max and Gabe said simultaneously again.

Gabe frowned at him before turning to Carrie. "Let us handle this. We have an advantage because the baddie won't expect us on his or her ass, and we have our powers to back us up. Not to mention that you'll be chilly going out like that."

Flushing, Carrie shot him an accusing glare as she tugged down the edge of the shirt. "Max threw my only clothes away."

"Uh-huh." Gabe winked. "You want me to bring you some clothes, or are you happy as you are?"

"I've arranged for new clothing," Max said coolly. He'd take care of his woman.

Rhys helped Gabe to her feet. "I'll let you know as soon as I have information."

With another glare at Max, Carrie escorted Rhys and Gabe to the door. He followed behind like a lackey.

The women hugged, whispering things he couldn't catch. And then Rhys faced him.

He felt the air around them shimmer, full of memories of the past—good and bad. He remembered the way he'd thought of Rhys as his brother, and how Rhys had lied to him. As if to protect him, *jīn ch'i* rose inside him.

He hadn't loved Amanda, he'd always known that. What he felt for her was nothing compared to what he felt for Carrie.

But Rhys . . . His jaw clenched. He could deal with Rhys in this situation. Forgiving was going to take work.

"She staged that day, you know," Rhys said. "She wanted to pit us against each other. I hadn't realized what she was up to until you arrived."

He hated admitting it, but Rhys's words rang true. A truth he'd suspected deep down but hadn't wanted to accept before.

"I may have been tempted by what Amanda offered, but I would never have carried through with it. It would have meant destroying you, and I'd never harm someone I loved." Rhys and Gabe exchanged a look before he continued. "I'm not sorry she came to the end she did. She made her own fate. I am sorry, however, that it drove a stake in our relationship. I'm willing to let the past rest between us if you are."

Was he? Could he?

Rhys led his woman out, the door closing softly behind them.

"If you can forgive me, Max, I don't see how you can't forgive Rhys." Carrie shook her head and stepped around him.

He grabbed her arm. "Where are you going?"

She eased out of his grip. "To take a shower while I wait for clothes."

He watched her walk to the kitchen. She couldn't go anywhere without clothes—it should have been reassuring. And her words rang true. If only he didn't feel like she was up to something.

Chapter Forty-three

Carrie stomped into the living room, each step magnifying her frustration. If there was one thing she'd learned in all of this, it was that she hated feeling defenseless. Thinking you were capable, and then not being able to do a damn thing to help yourself, was the worst feeling in the world. And they wouldn't *let* her do anything. Nor would they listen to her.

They meaning Max.

"Where are you going?"

"To the kitchen." She didn't bother to look over her shoulder at him as she gathered the coffee cups. "I might as well clean up. That shouldn't prove to be too challenging or unsafe for me, should it?"

"You can't fault us for wanting to protect you."

"I can when it takes away my power." She picked up the tray and headed into the kitchen. She set the tray down with a clatter and began rinsing the cups.

Max came to stand next to her. "It's not our intent to take away your power."

She wanted to kick him. "But that's what you're doing nevertheless. You're patting me on the head and telling me to wait in my room like a good girl. Maybe I have something to contribute. And, really, this is my mess. I should have to clean it up."

"You don't know anything more than we do."

She knew the culprit had to be Francesca. Only Max hadn't reacted well to her accusing someone he grew up with. Someone who worked with him—closely. But Francesca had motive and opportunity, not to mention the skills. Plus, she hated Carrie and had never made a secret of it.

She'd considered giving Rhys Francesca's name, too, but Max would have hated that. So she thought she'd look into it herself, only here she was, in Max's steel-enforced fortress, a damsel in distress.

Carrie snorted and dumped all the spoons in the sink. "I *hate* feeling defenseless."

Slipping his arms around her waist, Max turned her around and tangled his hand into her hair. Before she could do anything, he situated himself between her legs.

He tipped her head back. His eyes blazed something sharp, and he lowered them until they were all she could see. "I won't see you hurt."

"I won't see you hurt, either," she replied just as fiercely.

His hands tightened, pulling her against him. His mouth came down on hers, avid and hungry.

It sparked the hunger in her, too. Moaning, she locked her legs behind him to make sure he wouldn't move away. His hands slipped under her butt, scooped her up, and set her on the cold marble countertop.

Panting, trying to catch her breath, she nibbled the taut column of his neck. "I've never had kitchen sex before."

"Good." He gripped the collar of her shirt and tore it open like it was paper instead of silk.

She blinked down at her suddenly naked body. "That was your shirt."

"Looks better this way." He ran his hands down her neck, her breasts, her belly, to her thighs. He spread her legs so her heels unlocked and she was bared to him. But apparently not bare enough, because he bracketed her with his hands and thumbed her open.

Electricity shot through her body. Leaning back on her hands, she watched him watch her. "Tell me this isn't going to be a long, drawn-out foreplay session."

"I want to taste you."

"I want you first."

His blunt, thick finger ran over her. "Let me."

She shivered, from his touch as well as the desire in his voice. She could imagine his tongue gently swirling around her. But she wanted him with her—she wanted to feel him in her—so she sat up, undid his drawstring, and pushed his clothing down far enough to free his erection.

Before he could protest, she brushed her fingers over its head and rubbed in the wetness she found there. Then she gripped it and tugged. "Come here."

Surprisingly—or maybe not—he didn't put up a fight. He stepped in closer until his hardness nestled right where she wanted it. She wiggled herself against him, watching the way his expression darkened with need. For her.

"I like it," she whispered.

"Like." His short laugh was incredulous. He grasped

her hips and thrust himself against her. "*Like* doesn't begin to do justice to this."

She bent forward to lick his nipples, one and then the other. "It seemed an adequate enough word at the time."

"I want to be in you now," he commanded.

"You realize you're bossing me around again, don't you?"

His gaze narrowed. Without warning, he captured her nipple between his lips. He lapped at it once, a long, slow flick of his tongue, before ruthlessly sucking it until she writhed on the counter.

Letting it go with a wet *pop*, he lifted his head. "I seem to remember you saying you didn't mind me taking control in the bedroom."

"This is the kitchen," she managed to say between pants.

He scooped her up, tossed her over his shoulder, kicked his pants off the rest of the way, and strode out of the kitchen.

"Hey!" She tried to squirm off but he had a firm hold of her. "What are you doing?"

"Taking you to my bedroom."

"You're such a control freak." She smacked his butt. "Next you'll pull out handcuffs."

He looked over his shoulder at her. "Don't tempt me."

She blinked at the erotic purr of his voice, picturing him cuffing her to his huge bed. She knew exactly how he'd look at her, how he'd prowl up the foot of the bed until he was poised over her, not touching and letting her anticipate every wicked thing he'd do to her.

A fresh stab of excitement coursed through her, and this time she caressed his muscular butt. "Hurry."

He jogged up the stairs, strode to the bed, and tossed her onto it. Before she got a chance to catch her breath, he sheathed himself in a condom and joined her, sliding inside her as he covered her.

Her body arched of its own accord. "Finally."

Taking both her wrists in one hand, he stretched her arms over her head, using his free hand to palm her breasts. He captured her lips in a voracious, all-encompassing kiss.

It shot from the top of her head to the tip of her toes, lighting everything in between. Intense, full of passion, potent. But soft and loving at the same time.

Because his soul was in it.

She opened herself to him and took all of him in—the dark and the light, the sharp and the soft, the hurt and the love. The energy swirled around her, through her, binding her to him in such an intimate way that for a moment having him inside her seemed incidental.

But then he thrust, and she thought she had to be delusional to even think that. Crying, she locked her legs around his back.

He sucked her lower lip, holding her firmly in place, as his free hand slithered between their bodies. She opened her legs, silently begging him to touch her there because she couldn't make her mouth form the words.

"Do you feel me?" Max whispered. "Do you feel how much I want you? All of you."

She could only nod as he rubbed her softly—the way she liked it.

"You're *mine*." He kissed her again, and the same riotous feelings rushed through her. "You can't doubt that anymore."

She moaned in assent. The room started spinning, and even with her eyes closed she felt like she was spiraling out of control. The only thing she felt was his hardness in her, his fingers playing her, and the tug of his lips on hers.

It all converged—strong and relentless—and she gasped. Her thighs gripped his waist, and she arched up. Her cries mingled with his guttural groans as he came, too.

He slowed and then stopped, blanketing her, his heart thundering against hers. She held him there, not wanting the intimate connection they'd finally created to be broken.

He let go of her wrists and, running his hands down her body, rolled off her and gathered her to his chest. He closed his eyes. "I love you."

The bottom fell out of her stomach. "*What?*"

"I love you," he said again, as if it was the most common thing. He rubbed her back drowsily. "Sleep now."

"*Sleep?*" She propped up on her elbow, gaping at him. "You're kidding, right?"

He wasn't. He was out like a light, breathing rhythmically. He looked so boyish and dear, she couldn't get pissed. Instead, she rested her head on his chest and watched him. Curling her hand around his shoulder, she inexplicably felt the heat from his mark and, at peace, she closed her eyes and dozed off, too.

Chapter Forty-four

Startled awake, Carrie lifted her head from where she'd been nestled on Max's shoulder.

Someone was coming up the stairs.

Footsteps on the metal stairs. Clacking.

Heels. *A woman.*

Her heart gripped. She remembered her attack at the bar—the fear and feeling of helplessness—and she reached to shake Max awake.

She froze as Francesca's immaculate red head cleared the top step.

What was *she* doing here? Angry—for being afraid as well as the intrusion, Carrie sat up, clutching the sheet to her chin.

Francesca walked into the room, stopping abruptly when she saw Carrie in bed. Her gaze fell to Max, still sleeping and obviously naked, and she stiffened. She glared coldly at Carrie before turning and going back downstairs.

This was her chance to confront Francesca. Carrie

hopped out of bed and looked around for her shirt. Remembering Max had torn it off her, she hurried into the bathroom to grab a towel.

Francesca had her hand on the latch to the front door when Carrie skidded to a halt in the foyer. "*Wait.*"

She didn't think Francesca would actually listen to her, but she stopped, her back still turned to her.

Carrie took a moment to catch her breath and then said, "Why did you do it?"

"Bring you clothes?" She gestured to the left. "Because Max requested it."

The über-coolness of the woman's tone pissed her off. "I know you have issues with me, and I understand why, but there was no need to steal the scroll from me."

"What?" Francesca whirled around, her brow furrowed.

"The jig is up." She tucked the towel tighter around her body. "You don't have to pretend. I know it was you. I understand why you did it."

"I have no idea what you're talking about," she replied archly.

"I'm not asking you to return it for my sake but for Max's. If the scroll gets out, his life will never be the same. In a bad way. You can't want that. You love him."

Francesca's face paled. She opened her mouth, but no sound came out until the third try. "What?"

"You love him." A person had to be pretty dense not to notice, but she didn't think it'd be nice to point that out.

"I—" She fingered the pearls around her neck. "I don't know what gave you that idea."

Maybe the protectiveness? The absolute attention to his every need? The mooning looks? Carrie just said, "Woman's intuition. Which is why I understand why you don't appreciate me in the picture. I'm just asking you not to hurt Max out of spite for me."

"I'd never hurt him. Which is more than I can say for you."

Carrie blinked. "Excuse me?"

"All you've brought him since he's known you is trouble. However, regardless of what I think of you—"

"Gee, thanks," she said, rolling her eyes.

"—that doesn't mean I'd steal anything from you."

"Of course you took it. It had to be you. The attacks, the prowler Max saw climbing up to my balcony? I saw the way you beat up the punching bag and your skills climbing that silk."

"Why would I climb the wall when I had access to your room from inside?"

Good question. "Because you wanted to throw us off?"

Francesca just stared at her with the composure of the innocent.

And her gut told her it wasn't faked. "You really didn't take it?"

"Of course not." The woman's spine straightened with all the indignation in her being. "I'm no thief."

Well, damn. She'd been so sure of her hypothesis. But at least she didn't have to prove to Max that Francesca was the baddie.

Then it was Trevor. Or someone else, but Trevor seemed most likely.

"You don't deserve him." Francesca looked down her regal nose at Carrie as she opened the door. "He needs someone who helps him and understands his needs. Someone who doesn't care more for herself and her own career than him. Someone who'll sacrifice everything for him."

Like me was implied, and Carrie heard it loud and clear. Francesca shot her another venomous glare as she left. Carrie figured she probably should have set the woman straight, but she didn't have time. She had to fix this mess she'd made. If Francesca didn't do it, Trevor was the top suspect again.

If Trevor had taken the list of Guardians, he was probably already blurting out all the Guardians' identities to get himself the attention he always craved. She had to stop him.

Hopefully, she wasn't too late.

Grabbing the bag of clothes Francesca brought, she rifled through it until she found a pair of dark jeans and a black shirt. Underwear—she grabbed some random panties and the first bra she came across. Quickly, she got dressed and put on the socks and shoes she found at the bottom of the bag. She wrote Max a note to let him know where she was going, grabbed her wallet, and headed out the door.

Forty-five minutes later, after a brisk walk to the Embarcadero BART station, she was on a train headed for Berkeley. Hopefully Trevor wouldn't be around so she could snoop in his office.

She walked out of the Berkeley BART station, up Center Street, and through the campus. Her heart thumping with nerves, she kept her head down, afraid anyone would be able to see she was about to break into someone's office by looking at her face.

She rubbed her sweaty palms on her thighs and told herself to calm down. If she acted suspiciously, she'd attract more attention. As she walked, she practiced saying, *I'm looking for some papers I was supposed to pick up from Trevor. He said they'd be right here,* just in case someone caught her going through his stuff.

She made it to Dwinelle Hall without incident. She walked through the maze of hallways, down to the bowels where the faculty offices were.

Thursday afternoons were pretty dead—most professors didn't have to be on campus Fridays, so things shut down early. Fortunately. She didn't want to chance someone discovering her, but the emptiness was creepy. Her shoes squeaked as she walked down the hallway, and the sound set her on edge.

She got to Trevor's office and tried the door. Locked. She hadn't considered that. No one ever locked their office doors.

Maybe it meant he had something in there. Only how was she going to get in to check?

She snapped her fingers. Janitor. Turning around, she headed for the custodial closet, hoping someone would be there—preferably someone she knew.

Luck was on her side, because as she rounded the corner she ran into one of the janitors. She smiled, big and relieved. "Hey Bob."

"Professor Woods." He doffed his hat at her. "You're here later than normal."

"I had to pick something up from Trevor Wiggins's office, only his door is locked." She tried to look innocent, which meant she opened her eyes wide. "Is there any chance I can get let in there?"

"Don't see why not." He left his cart and began to shuffle toward Trevor's office. "You know, I picked up that book you mentioned to me. *The Man Who Loved China.*"

"Have you started reading it?" she asked, walking faster in hopes that he'd pick up his pace.

Only he ambled as slowly as ever. "I'm just on the third chapter, but it's real interesting."

"I thought you'd like it." *Almost there.* She craned her neck, seeing the door and feeling a wave of relief.

"I like how the author makes history come alive." He pulled out his key ring and began searching for the right one.

Come on. She looked behind her to make sure they were still alone. "Uh-huh."

"Anyway, if you come across any other books like that, let me know." Bob tried a key, but it didn't turn. "Wrong one."

"Do you need help?"

Bob didn't notice the impatience in her voice. He shook his head and kept sifting through his keys. "I think it's this one."

Carrie held her breath as he tried another one. *Please work. Please open.*

It did.

"See. Just lock it up when you're done, honey." Bob beamed at her and waddled back toward his cart, whistling merrily.

She looked around. Seeing no one, she slipped inside, locked the door, and surveyed the room. "Where to start?"

The desk, of course.

It was piled high with papers waiting to be graded and other random bits of minutiae. It took her precisely one minute to decide there could be an elephant on Trevor's desk and it'd be impossible to find, there was so much stuff.

She lifted an ungraded paper dated from last term.

Shaking her head, she set it aside, wondering what kind of grade the kid ended up getting.

The top of the desk yielded nothing, so she started going through the drawers. Still nothing. She even thought to check for hidden compartments—Trevor seemed the type to go for that kind of thing.

Sitting back on her heels, she looked around the room. It'd take forever if she went through all the bookshelves, and the books on them. Dejection wilted her.

But she couldn't just give up. She started to get to her feet when a piece of paper in the trash next to her caught her eye. Leonora's handwriting. She reached past an old coffee cup and a banana peel to pick it out.

"Strange." Leonora usually e-mailed anything she needed to say. It was a big joke with all the doctoral students, that Leonora's e-mails were even more to the point than she was in person. Carrie shook off a random bit of garbage stuck to it and read the note.

Trevor,

> *I'm holding a small press conference to release information on some research I've been doing on the Scrolls of Destiny. Attend. Also, I believe it's safe to say the tenured position will be yours.*

Leonora

"*What?*" Carrie read through the note again. And again. But even the third time through, she couldn't believe her eyes.

The position was *Trevor's?* She dropped down abruptly into the chair. How could that be? Had he told Leonora about the scroll he'd stolen?

And what bit of research? She crumpled the note and tossed it back in the trash. Why hadn't Leonora said anything to her? She knew Carrie was working with that myth. Unless—

"No." Carrie shook her head, but the suspicion took hold and wouldn't let go.

She stood up shakily and marched out of Trevor's office, down the hall to Leonora's.

The office was dark, but Leonora didn't always turn the lights on. Without knocking, Carrie twisted the knob and opened the door.

No one was there. She drooped, at a loss. Her stomach churned with betrayal. Now she knew an iota of what Max probably felt. She'd rested her dreams on someone who deceived her, too.

But she wasn't going to roll over and take this. First, she'd recover the scroll. If Leonora stole it, she could appeal to the board and maybe get the decision to give Trevor the tenure repealed.

With renewed purpose, she strode to the desk. The woman was so tidy, it was immediately obvious it wasn't on the desktop.

"The drawer." Carrie snapped her fingers, knowing without a doubt that it was in there. She opened it and—

The scroll lay right in the middle, as if waiting for her. She picked it up, closing her eyes in relief.

"I should have known you would turn up."

Gasping, Carrie jerked back and looked up. "Leonora."

Her advisor walked into the office, locking the door behind her. "You always showed tenacious spirit. I should have known you wouldn't give up. But, as the proverb says, there is no never-ending banquet under the sun."

Leonora reached to her left and took one of the swords off the wall. "Your banquet is about to end here, Carrie."

Chapter Forty-five

Her thesis advisor. The proof was in front of her, and still Carrie couldn't believe it. She blinked. "You're going to take me out with a *sword?*"

Leonora held the steel in her hands level, her face calm. Determined. The steady light in her eyes said she hadn't even lost it—she was doing this fully compos mentis. That chilled Carrie to the bone.

Think. Trying to breathe past the thundering of her heart, she bit her lip and tried to come up with a plan to escape. It was kind of hard, seeing as how Leonora was guarding the only exit route with a three-foot blade.

Get her talking. Until she could come up with a way to get out, she'd be okay if she kept Leonora talking. "I mean, I guess it makes sense. You *are* an expert on ancient weapons, after all. You probably know how to use them, huh?" she asked, hoping she was wrong.

"You could say that." The woman twirled the sword on either side of her body, a deadly figure eight that had Carrie taking a step back.

Okay, she was in trouble. She moved the chair in front of her—the more barriers between them, the better. "Nice. I always wanted to learn how to fight with a sword."

"Unfortunate that you'll never learn now." Leonora took a step forward, the blade wavering with purpose, like a snake about to strike. "You should have seized the day."

"Uh, yeah." Carrie felt the bookshelf behind her. Out of room. "You know, you don't need to do this."

"Oh, I do." Holding the sword straight out in front of her, she moved around the visitors' chair. "You don't know how badly I have to do this."

"Uh—" She stumbled over the trash can but quickly righted herself. "I don't understand why that is."

Leonora advanced again, head lowered, gaze intent. "Oh, I'm happy to tell you."

She edged around the side of the desk to put space between them, relieved to get her talking. The woman wasn't normally chatty, but maybe she felt so wronged she'd go on for a while.

One could hope. It'd give her the opportunity to find her cell phone and call Max.

"Do you know what it's like to be me?"

Carrie shook her head absently, patting her bag with her free hand. "I've imagined it."

"A highly romanticized version, I'm sure. Nothing like the reality."

"You're a successful woman who heads a history department for a major university." Where was the freaking phone? "The reality can't be that bad, can it?"

Leonora brought the blade down in a slicing motion, and the air hissed. "You know nothing about me."

"No, I guess I don't." Okay, Leonora was crazier than

she'd originally thought. Calling Max wasn't going to help—he'd never get there in time.

"Do you know how long I've been here?" her advisor said. "Do you know how hard I've worked to get to where I am? I've fought for everything I've accomplished."

Carrie pictured a trail of people killed by sword, lying in her wake, and shuddered. She had to save herself. She glanced left. If she could reach the door, maybe she could get away. Or make enough noise to attract Bob.

She edged to the left. "You totally deserve it, too."

"Of course I do. I'm the most qualified."

"Uh, I'm not as smart as you, so you're going to have to explain what this has to do with taking me out."

"The Scrolls of Destiny." Her voice was a dark hiss. "All these years I've been searching for them. Imagine my surprise when a young upstart student of mine discovered them first. Imagine my dismay." She spun the sword, neatly decapitating a figurine on the bookshelf.

Swallowing a yelp, Carrie jumped to the side, her spine colliding with the shelf. With her free hand, she steadied herself.

"Imagine my *anger*." Leonora advanced around the desk, slow and menacing, her concentration as sharp as the tip of her blade.

Carrie glanced down at the figurine. Hope flared in her chest. If she could knock Leonora out, she'd be able to run. Keeping an eye on Leonora, her fingers groped for it blindly.

Got it. She hid it behind her back and edged closer to the door.

Her psycho advisor didn't notice anything in her ranting. "All these years I did research, I searched, I talked to

people. But nothing. And then someone like you comes
along and finds evidence of the scrolls on her first try.
Not even evidence like I originally thought, but who the
Guardians are."

"Just lucky, I guess." She watched the sword aim at her
and gulped.

"It was wrong. *I* deserved to make the find. Who are
you, anyway? A hick from the Midwest? This is my heri-
tage. Tales about the scrolls were my bedtime stories as a
child. I've spent my life learning about them. *I* deserved
to be the one to make the discovery." Her gaze narrowed
and she aimed the sword at Carrie's chest. "Which is what
will happen, after I claim the scrolls for myself."

Another three feet and the doorknob would be in her
reach. She sidestepped casually so she wouldn't be obvious about what she was doing. "I can appreciate that,
Leonora, but after thinking about it all, I don't think it'd
be a good idea to let the general populace know that the
Scrolls of Destiny exist."

Leonora glared. "Did I ask you what you thought?"

"You know the myth," she continued, ignoring the
question. "There was a reason the scrolls were given
Guardians to keep them safe from the average Joe. If word
gets out that they exist, think of what people would do to
get that much power in their control."

"That's not my problem."

"Of course it is," Carrie said reasonably. "You wouldn't
go down in history as the person who found something
really cool. You'd be the typhoid Mary who brought an
era of chaos and violence down on the human race."

"But I'd still have the power, wouldn't I?" She lunged,
making a sweeping slice in the space between them.

The blade whizzed toward Carrie, so close she smelled its metallic tang. Choking on a scream, she flattened herself against the wall behind her.

Leonora smirked and made another threatening jab.

Okay, toying with her was just unnecessary. Eyes narrowed, Carrie adjusted her grip on the figurine.

The door burst open before she made her move. She felt the *whoosh* of air as it slammed into the wall next to her.

She and Leonora both paused in their macabre dance to look. Carrie heaved a sigh of relief. "Max."

Leonora howled like a banshee and expertly spun the sword overhead as she rushed forward.

"*Max!*" Carrie shrieked. Oh, God—it was going to cut straight into his chest.

Only as the blade came down, the air around it shimmered. She felt a curious surge of familiar energy and watched incredulously as the sword rippled and bent, as if warping away from him.

Still, a thin line of blood seeped through a cut in Max's shirt.

Oh—now she was pissed. "*Leonora.*"

As her former advisor turned, Carrie threw the decapitated statue. It hit Leonora's shoulder, and the woman cried out, her arm dropping.

But she didn't let go of the sword.

Leonora raised her head, her eyes blazing with cold fury. "You'll regret that."

No doubt about it, especially when Leonora raised her arm and stepped forward. She did a figure eight with the sword and, with a battle cry, rushed forward—toward Carrie this time.

She fully expected to be run through—Max wouldn't

be able to reach her in time. But she wasn't going to stand there placidly and let it happen.

Carrie took a book from the shelf behind her and threw it. It caught her advisor off guard, interrupting her attack. So Carrie grabbed one after another, chucking them as fast as she could.

"Bitch." Leonora blocked them with the blade.

Carrie didn't care—out of the corner of her eyes she could see Max reach for one of the other swords on the wall. *Good,* Carrie thought as she threw the last book in her reach.

"Out of options?" Leonora raised the sword over her head and brought it down in a circular swoop.

With a growl, Max pushed her aside and blocked the strike. Carrie flinched at the clang as the swords collided.

Max thrust forward, pressing Leonora against her desk. Carrie knew he was trying to get the action away from her, but concern for him made her take a step forward.

Leonora yelled, a deep-rooted, savage cry, and twirled her sword in a dizzying series of blows—all aimed at Max's head. He parried calmly, his eyes on his opponent the whole time. Then he went on the offense and charged her.

Leonora stumbled, but she recovered instantly and did a fancy block-twist thing that disarmed Max. They all watched the sword arc in the air, clattering to one side of the room.

The wrong side of the room.

No. Carrie tried to figure out how she could get it back in his hands, but she didn't see a way that wouldn't put her in danger, and that would have distracted Max worse than anything.

With a sinister smile, Leonora raised her sword. Letting loose her battle cry again, she advanced.

"*No.*" Carrie lunged forward.

Max stood still, cool as usual. As Leonora's blade descended, his leg arced up, kicking her arm. A sharp crack sounded, followed by the clatter of her sword falling to the ground.

Panting, Leonora gripped her limp wrist in front of her.

Like a broken wrist was going to stop her. Carrie turned to warn Max, but his utter tranquil concentration made her pull short.

Then Leonora gasped. Retched. Clawed at her chest. Her face distorted, flushing beet red. She choked—once, twice—scrabbling to the ground. Her limbs stuck straight out, unbending, like a stiff rag doll. Her mouth twisted in a horrible parody of a smile as she tried to talk.

Carrie kneeled next to her former advisor despite her lurching stomach. "What?"

Her words were a faint hiss through frozen lips. "It should have been my discovery."

Leonora exhaled one last torturous gasp, her eyes open, her features contorted and body rigid.

Carrie gagged.

Max lifted her and wrapped his arms around her, turning her around.

"Wait." She tried to look around his body, back at her former advisor. "I don't understand. She looks ghastly... Like a statue. What did you do?"

"I bound the iron in her body to a solid state," Max said, like it was no big deal, as he led her outside the office.

"Why'd you wait so long?" she asked, her voice shrill

with shock even to her own ears. "You could have pulled that Guardian card when you walked in."

"I needed a moment to gather my chi and wanted you out of danger first." He kissed the top of her head, his hands roaming over her body. "Are you okay?"

She realized he was checking her for injury, and her heart turned over. "You should be yelling at me for coming here and putting myself and you in danger."

"I was going to get to that later." He lifted her chin. "First—"

His mouth came down on hers, a hint of desperation and fear in his kiss. But that burned in their desire and became a passion and something more. Something like—

"Wait." She pushed him back. "I need to say something."

He shook his head. "Later. First we need to take care of what happened here."

Carrie looked back through the doorway, feeling the blood drain from her head again as she caught a glimpse of Leonora's stiffened legs. "Right."

Max propped her against the wall. "Wait here."

She did as he said—for about two seconds. That was how long it took her to tuck the genealogy into her bag. Then, because she couldn't stand not knowing what he was doing, she peeked inside, careful to keep her gaze averted from Leonora's body.

He was wiping down the sword he used, holding it with his jacket to keep from touching the parts he cleaned. She must have made a noise, because he lifted his head and scowled. "I thought I told you to stay outside."

"I told you I had problems with orders outside the bedroom." She watched as he replaced the sword on the wall. "What's the plan?"

"We're going to call the police and tell them we found her like this."

"Will that work?"

He arched his brow. "I'm filthy rich. Of course it'll work."

"Because I'll take the blame. I don't want you to get in trouble for the mess I created."

His expression softened. "I appreciate that. But for now I'd like you to stay outside, out of my way."

Nodding, she went out to the hall, sank down against the wall, and wondered if Rhys knew any good criminal lawyers.

Chapter Forty-six

It happened pretty much how Max had said.

He called Rick, who called a connection at the Berkeley police department. The police came and closed off the crime scene.

They were, of course, completely mystified by the cause of death. It astonished them so completely, they barely questioned why the office was in shambles. They'd never seen a woman stiffened because her blood had solidified. Not shocking, really. Carrie doubted Max went around and petrified many people.

Rick's homicide detective friend took their statements, believing Max when he said they came to pick up a text she needed and found Leonora dead. Because the cause of death seemed to be a medical problem, they took Max's word at face value. They didn't even seem to notice the slash on his chest.

It was a relief. And Carrie was even more relieved when they were allowed to leave.

They drove back to the city in silence. Night had fallen,

and she was glad for it. It felt a little concealing, a little safe. Or maybe she just felt safe because she was with Max.

She stared at his profile. She had things to tell him. He'd stopped her before, but once they were at his place she wouldn't let him distract her. "We're going to your place, aren't we?"

"Yes." He glanced at her.

"Okay. Good." She relaxed and then tensed up again as she tried to figure out how to tell him she loved him—that she wanted to take the risk. Her stomach churned, and she closed her eyes and tried not to dwell on it.

They arrived at his place all too soon. Without a word, they got out and took the elevator to his loft.

She stood across from him, hands clenched inside her jacket pockets. Soon she'd get her feelings out in the open and everything would be okay, even if he decided she was more trouble than she was worth.

Only on Max's doorstep, there was one hunky Brit and a manically pacing artist-slash-bartender.

Gabe whirled the second she heard the elevator doors open. "What the hell took you guys so long to get back? Did they detain you?" She rushed forward to Carrie and grabbed her arms. "Are you okay?"

"You guys can stop asking me if I'm okay." But she smiled to soften her words, and she hugged Gabe tightly. "In case I haven't said so, I love you."

Gabe frowned and looked over her head to Max. "Is she okay?"

Carrie rolled her eyes. "I'm fine. Just worn."

"What are you doing here?" Max asked them, though his attention was on Rhys.

"We wanted to make sure Carrie was all right." Rhys pushed off the wall and stood straight. "But now that we see she is—"

"I'm not leaving until I know what happened." Hands on her hips, Gabe glared at all of them.

The elevator doors opened again, and they all turned as Rick strode out. He stopped short when he saw everyone standing in the hall. His face set, angrier than she'd ever seen him, he zeroed in on her with his hard cop's gaze. "What the hell happened tonight?"

"That's what I want to know," Gabe chimed in.

Sigh. Looking imploringly at Max, she said, "Maybe we can take this inside."

He didn't look happy, but he let everyone in.

Before the inquisition started, she smiled at Max. "I'd love some tea. Maybe you could make some for all of us?"

He grumbled in dissent as he stalked off to do it. She watched the play of his body. The cut on his chest—she bit her lip as she remembered that. No telling where that sword had been. She'd have to make sure she took care of that later.

A hand wrapped around her forearm. "Darling, you look like you could use a seat."

Nodding, she let Rhys guide her to the couch. "Thanks."

"What happened?" Rick asked tightly.

She schooled her face and hoped she looked innocent. "Officially, we went to campus because I needed to pick something up. Unfortunately, we found Leonora, my thesis advisor, dead on the floor in her office, apparently because of some blood-related problem. We called the police, of course, and had to wait for them to take our statements."

Silence reigned. She heard Max slamming things around and could feel his impatience to be back out there.

Finally, Rick said, "And unofficially?"

She blinked. "What makes you think there's anything unofficial?"

He looked around the room. "Because I'm not sure anything here is what meets the eye."

Smart man. But it was hardly her place to reveal other people's secrets to him, as much as she hated leaving him in the dark, because she knew he'd stew until he learned the truth. He was just that sort of person. "That's really what happened. I went to get a scroll I'd misplaced"—she shot a look at Gabe and Rhys—"and found Leonora. I was told she had some condition where the blood just solidified in her veins. Her office was trashed, but otherwise there didn't seem to be any sign of foul play."

"Interesting," Gabe said dryly.

"I know." Carrie tucked her feet under her, huddling for warmth. "They think maybe she suffered an attack and then messed up the room, trying to make noise to attract help."

Rhys glanced at Max as he walked in with a tray. They exchanged a long look, and she could tell they communicated something in some way. She didn't know whether that pleased or annoyed her.

"She suffered an attack."

She looked at Rick. "That's what it looked like. Don't you believe me?"

"Yes." He answered so quickly she knew he meant it. "But I know without a doubt that there are things you aren't telling me."

Gabe arched her brows. "Isn't Berkeley out of your jurisdiction, Detective?"

"Inspector," he corrected with a flat look.

"Whatever." Gabe waved her hand. "At least you didn't bother to deny that you're sticking your nose into stuff that's none of your business."

"Guys." Carrie shook her head, holding her tea close. "Can we hold off on the animosity just for one night?"

Gabe snorted. "I may have to leave."

"Good idea." Max stood to one side, glaring. "Everyone out."

"Eloquent." Gabe set her untouched teacup down and held out a hand to Rhys. "Let's blow this popsicle stand."

Nodding, he walked over to Carrie and squeezed her shoulder, ignoring Max's death stare. "A bit foolish, darling, but I'm glad it worked out."

"Me, too. I'm so relieved I managed to resc"—she glanced at Rick—"uh, find the scroll I'd misplaced."

"Harm to you would have been a greater tragedy." He slipped an arm around Gabe and walked her past Max, to whom he nodded. "We'll talk, I'm sure."

Max just grunted in his usual way. If she weren't so exhausted, she would have smiled.

Then he turned to Rick. "Are you still here for a reason?"

Rick stopped watching Gabe leave to measure up Max. After a moment of tense silence, he faced her. "I'm guessing I no longer have to worry about your safety."

She wasn't sure whether he meant that the threat to her was gone or if he was talking about Max. She figured she'd assume the latter. "I think that's fair to say."

"Good." He gave Max another long look before walking out.

"Thank goodness they're gone." She huddled into the couch some more, cuddling her lukewarm tea.

"Are you cold?" Before she could answer, he went to a closet she hadn't noticed and came back with a throw blanket. Very carefully, he tucked it around her legs.

She frowned at it. She would have rather had his body heat for warmth. "Aren't you going to sit down?"

He did—two feet away from her. What was that about? Stifling her exasperation, she tried again. "I have something to say."

He hesitated and then nodded. "Go ahead."

She heard her mom tell her to stop being afraid. She bit her lip and let it out before she lost her nerve. "I love you. I'm not saying it to pressure you into anything. I just—I just realized maybe there's room for more than one passion in my life. I don't have to give myself up to love you."

He stared at her steadily.

God, this was hard. But she lifted her chin and continued. Even if he walked away, she wanted to know she was brave enough—loving enough—to try.

Easier said than done. She took a deep breath. "So I love you. With all my heart. I probably always will—"

"Probably?" His brow furrowed.

"Well, not probably. Most definitely. I've never loved anyone enough to jump in front of a sword for him." She pursed her lips. "Not that I've had to jump in front of many swords before."

His lips twitched. "I should hope not."

"And like I said, I'm not saying this with an agenda. I just thought you should know." She bit her lip again and looked at him. He still gazed back at her, but she couldn't read anything in his face. Had he changed his mind?

It didn't matter. What mattered was that she took the risk. And she admitted to herself that she loved him.

"Are you finished?" he finally asked.

She thought about it a moment and then nodded. "Yeah."

"Good." He closed the distance between them, kneeling next to her as he took her cup and set it on the table. Tangling his hand in her hair, he tugged her hair back and brought his mouth down on hers.

This time, from the moment their lips touched, she felt him—all of him—open and giving, surging heat and strength and metallic tang between them. He breathed into her.

Tingly. And brimming with more than she'd ever imagined possible.

"Wait." She pushed him back again. "What does this mean?"

He brushed the hair back from her face and held her still, like he was afraid she'd try to run away. "It means I love you."

She gasped. "Still? After everything I've put you through?"

Humor lit his usually solemn eyes. "I do."

"But—" She shook her head. "I thought—When I said all that and you didn't react—I just thought—"

He drew a finger across her lips. Blinking at the electric feel of his touch, she closed her mouth. Then she let her tongue peek to lick the tip.

The humor faded, leaving a need that made her weak in the knees. He sat on his haunches. "How could I not love you? You're everything good and pure in the world."

"Are you forgetting that I stole? From a *monastery?* And almost got you killed?"

"I didn't say you were perfect." Pushing her blanket aside, he pulled her on top of him as he reclined onto his back. "I meant that you're honest in your feelings, and when you falter you own up to your mistakes. I love that about you."

"Oh. That's kind of nice." She rotated her hips against his, feeling his growing excitement. "Wait. Shouldn't we take care of your cut?"

"What cut?" he murmured against her lips.

"Oh. Well, then." She reached for his waistband, trying to pop the stubborn button. "If only there weren't so many layers between us."

She thought he'd take the hint and start to undress her, but he laid back, his gaze concentrated on her shirt.

Slash.

Gasping, she looked down to see a long rip dividing her top, right down the middle. She blinked at him.

Another ripping sound and her bra hung loose, slit right at the center between the cups.

"That's"—Carrie swallowed, majorly turned on—"interesting."

"I use my powers for good." He brushed aside the remnants of her clothing, his hands grazing the tips of her breasts. "Remember that."

She laughed. "I'll try, but I may need lots of reminders."

"I think that can be arranged." Max slid his hand in her hair and brought her mouth down to his. His kiss was a loving whisper against her lips. "Starting now."

Epilogue

Carrie frowned at the ends of the bow tie, dangling from the collar of Max's tuxedo shirt. "Don't they make these things pretied with clips anymore?"

Sliding his hands around her waist, Max walked her backwards toward the bed. "We could forget dinner and start our honeymoon early."

"No, we can't." She pushed him back and attacked the stupid bow tie again, muttering. "Francesca can probably do this perfectly."

He leaned down to nibble her lips. "There are a lot of things you do better than Francesca ever could."

"You better not be speaking from firsthand knowledge."

He smiled the way he always did when she got jealous—a little surprised and a lot amused. "The only thing my hand knows is your body."

She hid her own smile by biting her lip. She loved it when he said things like that. She loved the way he worshipped her body—every chance he got.

Adjusting the bow tie one more time, she tipped her head and looked at it. "I think it's crooked."

"I could go without," he offered, easing a finger inside his collar. "I never liked these things. Feels like a noose."

Standing on her tiptoes, she kissed him softly. "I appreciate the sacrifice you're making for our wedding reception."

He grunted.

Grinning, she slipped past him and walked to the closet. The surliness was pretense. Mostly. Underneath, he was just as excited to celebrate their marriage as she was. He'd complained at having to wait six months to get married, and since their private ceremony earlier at City Hall, he'd barely left her side. Maybe making him wait six months was overkill, but she'd wanted to deal with everything before embarking on this adventure with him.

Life sometimes turned out so differently than expected. Hers didn't go in the direction she'd wanted it to, but it all worked out, just like her mom said it would. She left Berkeley, of course—with her PhD in hand, only because Max insisted she complete the process.

And then he not only gave her his love, but he gave her a dream job, too: curating his awesome collection. Her first official job was to arrange for it to be shown at the Asian Art Museum—some of the pieces seen by the public for the first time ever. The gala opening last week had been a smash.

"Do you need help getting dressed?" he asked, coming to stand behind her. Close.

"Like you'd help me put my clothes on." She'd bought a dress several weeks ago. But when she'd tried it on yesterday, it'd been a little tight around the waist. Maybe she could still squeeze into it.

"I'm good with zippers. And bra clasps." He nuzzled the nape of her neck, leaving a trail of love bites that gave her goose bumps—the good kind.

Laughing, she turned and pushed him away. "Out. I need to get dressed."

Grumbling, he left her—reluctantly. She stared after him, knowing she had a goofy grin on her face, before returning to the wardrobe dilemma. She slipped out of her robe, stepped into her dress, and zipped it as far as she could reach. Tight, but not seam-poppingly so.

"Honey?" her mom called. "Can I come up?"

"Of course."

Max had flown her mom out three times in the past six months. This time, he brought her mom to attend not only the opening night of their collection, but their wedding, too. She and Francesca—sigh—had been the witnesses at the legal ceremony earlier.

"Honey, I have a present for you," her mom said as she cleared the top of the stairs.

"Mom, you didn't have to get me anything." Carrie took the small gift bag and rifled through the tissue paper. She felt something silky at the bottom and pulled it out. The moment she saw what it was, her cheeks flamed and she stuck it back in the bag. "Oh. Um, thanks. You shouldn't have."

"Every bride needs a pair of crotchless panties for her wedding night. You should start your marriage how you mean it to continue."

"Thanks, Mom. For the underwear and the advice." She tucked the bag aside and gave her mom a hug. Better not to mention she was going naked under the dress.

It was a beautiful dress, too. Long, white, and simple,

but she felt like a princess in it. She'd worn a simple dress
to City Hall, but it seemed like she should do it up for
the reception dinner, even though the invitation list was
small—her mom, her boss Johnny, a few people from
Berkeley, Francesca, and Gabe and Rhys, of course.
Despite Max's misgivings about them.

He'd come a long way, though. He wasn't nearly as antag-
onistic with Rhys. She and Gabe had even left them alone
once. Of course, when they returned, Max had a bloody lip
and Rhys had a cut along his arm, but it was progress.

She sighed, putting her hand on her stomach. She
wanted Gabe and Rhys in their lives—close in their
lives—especially during the next phase.

"How is he?" Mom asked.

"Who?"

She pointedly eyed her belly.

Carrie blinked in shock. "How did you guess?"

"I was there once, too." Her mom hugged her, squeez-
ing her firmly but not too tight. "I'm so happy for you,
honey. Max doesn't know, does he?"

She shook her head. "Not yet."

"I didn't think so. Otherwise he'd probably carry you
on his back everywhere, he's so protective. Which is
sweet." Smiling, she smoothed back Carrie's hair. "When
are you telling him?"

"Telling him what?" Max asked from the stairs.

They both jumped.

Her mom was the first to recover. "I better go put on
my party clothes. I want to make sure I look good, in case
I meet any eligible men in the course of the evening." She
patted Carrie's shoulder, gave Max a peck on the cheek,
and left them alone.

"Tell me what?" he asked as he zipped her dress the rest of the way. "You aren't still feeling the effects of the Book of Water, are you?"

"Not more than before." Some of it stayed with her. Every now and then, Max said he felt a bit of the sea in her touch, but she always told him any magic he felt was because of their love.

He turned her around by the shoulders and studied her, concern lining his forehead. "Then what is it?"

"It's a surprise. A sort of wedding gift." To distract him, she gestured to her slightly enlarged cleavage. "Does it look okay?"

"You look mouthwatering." His hands snaked around her waist. "I don't know how you can look innocent yet so sinful at the same time."

She laughed.

His cell phone beeped. Cursing under his breath, he pulled it out of his pocket, read the screen, and texted a quick reply before putting it back.

"Something important?" she asked, slipping on her shoes.

"Just Francesca with a question about the flowers."

She wrinkled her nose. She still didn't trust Max's assistant, but she felt bad for her, too. After all, Max asked her to leave right after the wedding to deliver the Book of Water to its rightful Guardian. It was like adding insult to injury, making Francesca watch them get married and then, in effect, banishing her from the only home she'd ever known.

But it wasn't like there was anyone else who could be trusted with the Book of Water. The Keeper hadn't been happy that an outsider was delivering it. It seemed that only close family could know about the scrolls without serious repercussions. Meaning death.

The Keeper also wasn't happy that Max, Rhys, and Gabe were in such close proximity. Carrie thought it was odd that after all these centuries the Guardians knew each other. Almost like they were being reunited.

He had been happy about her and Max, though. He told Max he knew by following her he would find his destiny. Carrie thought the Keeper was a pretty smart guy.

Max studied her with his searching gaze, so she smiled for him. "Maybe Francesca will find her own Guardian to love."

"No more thoughts of the scroll or Francesca." He tipped her head back. "Tell me about my surprise."

She laughed, placing her hand over his scar. "Our child is going to be so relentless. I hope you're ready for that."

His brow furrowed. She knew the second he'd realized what she'd said by the way he looked down at her stomach.

Taking his hand, she placed it right over their baby. "In six months."

She didn't need to ask what he thought. The way he smiled, slow and full, like the sun coming out from a long bout of night, was answer enough.

A Note from Kate

I took some liberties in writing CHOSEN BY DESIRE. Ahem.

For example, while there was really a Yongle Emperor, he didn't use mystic scrolls to bring twenty years of peace to China. I made all that up. Shocking, I know. He *is* believed to be the greatest Ming emperor, though. I picked him because his era name, *Yongle*, means "perpetual happiness." It seemed fitting.

The stuff from the scroll—also made up. Mostly. The passage stating, "Wood feeds Fire. Fire creates Earth..." is part of the Cycles of Balance from the Chinese doctrine of five phases. I'd go into more detail about the philosophy, but it's complicated. Wikipedia has a pretty good description, though.

Guanyin is a *bodhisattva*—an enlightened being (or immortal). Her name means "observing the cries of the world." She's basically a goddess of compassion and mercy. She's also kind of like the patron saint of the kung fu style I study, which is why I named my fictional monastery after her.

Also, I bent the tenure process at Cal (aka UC Berkeley) to fit my purposes. And I may have tweaked the topography in Santa Monica. Just a little.

And lastly, I'm pretty sure there isn't enough iron in blood to turn someone into a metal statue. That was, as we authors like to call it, dramatic license. Nate, however, calls it making shit up.

THE DISH

Where authors give you the inside scoop!

♥ ♥ ♥ ♥ ♥ ♥ ♥ ♥ ♥ ♥ ♥ ♥ ♥ ♥ ♥ ♥

From the desk of Shannon K. Butcher

Dear Reader,

For thirty days, I lurked inside the mind of a deranged serial killer. And let me tell you, it may be an interesting place to visit, but I'm glad I don't have to live there. Thirty days was long enough, and I spent every one of them looking over my shoulder, in the backseat of my car, and under my bed. Just in case.

Luckily, I had some professional help with the profile for the killer in LOVE YOU TO DEATH, but little did I know how much more it would creep me out when I realized I was creating this character from bits and pieces of *real* people and *real* crimes. In fact, it creeped me out so much that the security system and our dog were no longer enough. I went out, bought a gun, and learned how to use it, just in case someone like Gary decided to come calling.

Ridiculous? Probably. But my Sig Sauer, its magazines holding eighty bullets, and I all feel much better.

This book opened my eyes to a world that I'd never really thought about before. Sure, we see reports on the news about murder and abduction, but there's always a kind of distance to those stories. This project forced me to put myself inside the heads of both the victims and the killer, and after doing so, every story I've seen on the news has suddenly become real—a waking-up-with-nightmares, buying-a-gun kind of real.

Being able to write about two people who fall in love during such a difficult time was something I wasn't sure I could do, but I hope I pulled it off. Elise and Trent and their love for each other brighten up the darker parts of this book, and their relationship high-lights just how important it is to have someone to lean on when things become impossible.

I won't spoil the end of LOVE YOU TO DEATH, but I can confidently say that I've never felt more sat-isfied with the justice I've inflicted on my deserving characters than I did with Gary. I hope you agree. And if you do decide to crawl inside the mind of a serial killer by reading this book, I recommend doing so with the lights on and the doors locked.

Enjoy!

Shannon K Butcher

http://www.shannonkbutcher.com/

♥ ♥ ♥ ♥ ♥ ♥ ♥ ♥ ♥ ♥ ♥ ♥ ♥ ♥ ♥ ♥ ♥

From the desk of Kate Perry

Dear Readers,

Hot naked men!

An unorthodox beginning, I know, but you have to admit it caught your attention. Also, it's vastly more interesting to talk about hot naked men than it is to discuss, say, tutus. Not to mention that hot naked men and my Guardians of Destiny series go hand in hand. Tutus? Not so much.

For instance, in the first book, MARKED BY PASSION, we have Rhys, the British bad boy who's got it all—except the woman who sets him on fire. Rhys is hot on so many levels, and when he strips down...I'd suggest keeping an extinguisher on hand.

And then there's Max, the hero of CHOSEN BY DESIRE, the second Guardians of Destiny novel. A past bettayal has Max closed off—until he meets the right woman, who makes him want to bare it all. Naked, he's a sight to behold. Plus, he's got a big sword, and he knows how to use it.

Unclothed, finely chiseled men. Sassy heroines who tame them. Kick-ass kung fu scenes. Much more exciting than tutus, don't you think?

Happy Reading!

Kate Perry

www.kateperry.com

♥ ♥ ♥ ♥ ♥ ♥ ♥ ♥ ♥ ♥ ♥ ♥ ♥ ♥ ♥ ♥

From the desk of Sue Ellen Welfonder

Dear Reader,

Sometimes people ask me why I set my books in Scotland. My reaction is always bafflement. I'm amazed that anyone would wonder. Aside from my own ancestral ties—I was born loving Scotland—I can't imagine a place better suited to inspire romance.

Rich in legend and lore, steeped in history, and blessed with incredible natural beauty, Scotland offers everything a romantic heart could desire. Mist-hung hills, castle ruins, and dark glens abound, recalling the great days of the clans and a time when heroism, loyalty, and honor meant everything. In A HIGHLANDER'S TEMPTATION, Darroc MacConacher and Arabella MacKenzie live by these values—until they are swept into a tempestuous passion that is not only irresistible but forbidden, and acknowledging their love could destroy everything they hold dear.

In writing their tale, I knew I needed something very special—and powerful—to help them push past the long-simmering feud that could so easily rip them apart. With such fierce clan history between them, I wanted something imbued with Highland magic that would lend a dash of Celtic whimsy and lightness to the story.

Fortunately, I didn't have to look far.

One of my favorite haunts in Scotland had just the special something I needed.

It was the Thunder Stone, an innocuous-looking stone displayed on the soot-stained wall of a very atmospheric drovers' inn on the northwestern shore of Loch Lomond. Said to possess magical powers I won't describe, the stone is often borrowed by local clansmen. I've eyed the stone each time I've stopped at the inn and always thought to someday include it in a book. A HIGHLANDER'S TEMPTATION gave me that opportunity.

Changed into a prized clan heirloom and called the Thunder Rod in A HIGHLANDER'S TEMPTATION, the relic provided just the bit of intrigue and lore I love weaving into my stories. I hope you'll enjoy discovering if its magic worked. *Hint*: Darroc and Arabella do have a happy ending!

With all good wishes,

Sue-Ellen Welfonder

www.welfonder.com

Want to know more about romances at Grand Central Publishing and Forever? Get the scoop online!

GRAND CENTRAL PUBLISHING'S ROMANCE HOMEPAGE

Visit us at www.hachettebookgroup.com/romance for all the latest news, reviews, and chapter excerpts!

NEW AND UPCOMING TITLES

Each month we feature our new titles and reader favorites.

CONTESTS AND GIVEAWAYS

We give away galleys, autographed copies, and all kinds of fun stuff.

AUTHOR INFO

You'll find bios, articles, and links to personal websites for all your favorite authors—and so much more!

THE BUZZ

Sign up for our monthly romance newsletter, and be the first to read all about it!